PANDEMIC IN PROGRESS

Pandemic in Progress

JK Lincoln

"If this is a virus, it will mutate. That's what viruses do. It's their job."
Dr. Stanley Patel

Prologue

Tight loops of razor wire topped the twelve-foot high cement block walls. They fascinated me in an obscene sort of way—obscene because of which side of the wall I was on.

I had stopped wondering how I got here, or rather how I could let this happen. It was obvious there had been machinations going on without my knowledge. Would Marcus actually get me out of this place? No, that was magical thinking. Everything pointed to him taking me out—out of existence, that is. Unless someone else had stepped in. Could Marcus be in one of the detention centers, also? What were the chances? He wasn't in this one, though, that was for sure. I had searched every face for a familiar one and found no one that I knew.

Marcus said I'd only be at the detention center a few days—or a week or two at most—because it would *look good*. The days were mounting, and I was still here.

Detention center. What a euphemism that was. It was a prison plain and simple. I, Dan Indigo, was in prison.

The early part of the first day wasn't so bad. It was novel—like the virus that kept me here. I had special freedoms, which I appreciated. Inside the Quonset hut where the prison's office was located, I made a video to send to my wife, Eden; and they told me I could email her twice a day. Then I had a video conference with Marcus, who filled me in on everything that was happening. Kind of.

1

But toward the end of the first day, everything changed. While on video, Marcus suddenly got a funny look on his face, the chat abruptly ended, and the screen went dead. I had tried to get him back to no avail. Then on the second day, when I wanted to send my second email of the day to Eden, they told me my email privileges had been cut to once a day.

Imagine that! Did they know who I was? Yes, they did, and apparently it didn't matter. Except for the two men at my side, I was like any other poor slob locked up in this makeshift prison.

After that, I could only email once a day. And I expected them to censor any email going out or coming in. That went without saying. It didn't take a genius to figure that one out. Marcus never answered any of my emails, though I had tried sending more daily. But my solace was Eden's emails. I wasn't allowed to print them, so I had to memorize them. Lucky for my photographic memory. Later, I'd go over them again and again in my head. They gave me much comfort.

The morning of the second day had been the worst. I rubbed my sore ear that served as a bitter reminder. It was that day they lined me up, along with the two men beside me and all the rest of the men and women in the prison. One by one, they punched a hole in the lobe of our right ear. I rubbed my finger over the hole, almost a quarter of an inch in diameter. It still angered me that they *marked me* like that with little explanation. Then again, I didn't get an explanation for much these days, only what I could discern from Eden's emails. And she hadn't heard anything about the earmarks.

Since then, each hour was as unremarkable as the next. I walked around the prison grounds as best I could in the mud. And there was almost always mud. It was fifteen acres, with two small concrete shower buildings and the metal Quonset hut. All the other shelters were large heavy canvas tents, except the barn that was a metal-sided structure.

Originally, they had guards in quads who drove around the grounds keeping order. That was my private little joke. Keeping order on the fifteen hundred shell-shocked people who were almost as surprised as me as to how they ended up here. They were quiet, they were peaceful, they were scared. There was no need to keep order here. But when the quads kept getting stuck in the mud, they had to replace them with horses. And the horses helped me keep my sanity.

Glancing at the two men beside me, I shook my head in disgust. Straight-backed, rigid, and humorless, they were there as my protectors. That's what I'd heard, anyway. I felt more like they were my preventers. Preventing me from what, I wasn't sure. But there had been no need for protection in all this time. Just the sight of the two men intimidated anyone who might come up to annoy me—or befriend me. And they would have had to protect with their fists, because no guns were allowed in the whole compound.

These two were Ted Kenyon and Vincent Boyd. There was a third one named Bob Haines. None of them spoke except to make rude comments or shove me around. It was almost like characters from a silent movie escorting me everywhere. The three of them took turns sleeping, so there were always two of them by my side.

I hated that. I put up with them following me into the shower on the first day. On the second day, I grabbed an extra towel on the way in, soaked it in water, threw it at the men and shouted, "I need some privacy here!" They had stepped out then and hadn't returned. A heavy canvas curtain, set into the floor and ceiling with bolts, separated *my* shower from the showers of the general population. So there was no danger of me mingling with the others—or escaping.

The privacy I received in the showers had made me crave more. So when I traipsed through the mud to visit the horses, I insisted the two men wait outside for me. They searched the place first—for what, I didn't know—and limited my time inside, but still, the horses helped me cope with my circumstances.

As I walked the perimeter of the prison, I looked again at the coils of razor wire at the top. Razor wire was far more treacherous than barbed wire. No one was getting out of here. And that was the plan, wasn't it? I glanced up as a shadow appeared on the ground in front of me. It was a large red-tail hawk gliding by. It delighted me so much—its beauty, its freedom—that I exclaimed, "Look at that!" to the two men beside me. Since I never got any response from them when I talked to them, I had stopped speaking to them. So my words caught them off-guard, and they looked up at the bird.

Out of nowhere, a hand tapped me on the shoulder. As I turned, a smiling man grabbed my hand in both of his and shook it vigorously. Before Ted and Vince could shoo the man away, he said, "So nice to meet you, Mr. President!"

CHAPTER ONE

President Dan Indigo

Ninety days earlier.

After I finished my morning workout and shower, I picked up my two Executive Protective Services agents—Secret Service—as I walked to the Oval Office. These two were Eric Costa and Justin Kirkpatrick.

"Morning, Eric, Justin."

"Morning, Mr. President, sir," they said in unison.

"How was your workout this morning, Mr. President?" asked Justin.

I lifted my head and beat my fists on my chest like an ape in the jungle. "Great! I feel strong and ready to take on the world." The two men beside me chuckled. "How are those two kids of yours, Justin? Are they looking forward to Christmas?"

"Oh, yeah. They're both on their best behavior and can't wait for Santa."

"Eric, how's your youngest son? Is he enjoying college life?"

"He loves it, although he says it's difficult to turn down all the parties he's invited to!"

"That makes sense," I said. "But it sounds like he's handling it well. Good for him."

Although they were making small talk, the two agents' eyes were always moving as they walked toward the Oval Office, even at this early hour when the place was almost empty. They were always on high alert, no matter the time, no matter the place. That was their job.

When Eric and Justin deemed everything safe and secure, I settled behind the big Resolute Desk in the Oval Office. I loved the holiday season at the White House. Since it was still dark outside, the lights inside were still on, flashing red, green, blue, yellow, purple. I was like a kid with Christmas—I loved every light, every Christmas tree, and every clichéd Christmas song, especially the old standards.

Minutes ticked by and light started coming in through the set of windows behind me. I had gone over everything that needed going over and felt ready to start the day. The sound of familiar voices drifted in through the closed windows. Then a door opened and continued conversation sounded in the office next door. A large dog bounded into the room, wagging his tail and yipping his delight.

"Bear!" I said, as I wrapped my arms around the big dog and rubbed my face into the fluffy neck. After Bear licked my face over and over, he put his paws on my lap. "Oh, Bear, you know that's not very *presidential* if I let you do that to me," I whispered into the dog's ear as I moved him back to the ground.

Bear was a large, red and black German Shepherd imported directly from Germany. Directly, because Eden and I had gone there to pick him up. That was a side trip, though. Our main reason for the trip to Germany had been an official meeting with Angela Merkel. The meeting had gone well, except Angela had fawned over the puppy for so long that Eden and I had to stay another day. Angela's fear of dogs was well known, so I was leary of bringing Bear into the meeting. But he was so small and so friendly, Angela couldn't help herself but fall in love with the round ball of fluff. For a while, Eden and I feared we would have to leave the puppy with Angela. Rumor had it that the experience with Bear helped her overcome her fear of dogs.

I stood up, wiped stray dog hairs off my suit—or tried—and proceeded to the outside office. Standing in the doorway, I watched the two women who hadn't spotted me yet. These were the two most important women in my life. Well, there was my daughter Zoey, too, but she had moved to Pennsylvania with her husband, and although we talked often, I didn't see her much any more. But I saw these two every day. They were best friends.

Jannika White, middle-aged, black and beautiful as the saying goes, had been my private secretary for decades. It hadn't started out great, but now she was a loyal supporter and one of my greatest assets. She liked to joke that her last name was as close as she was ever going to get to being white.

And the woman standing to her right, dressed in a black skirt and the silk turquoise blouse that I had given her, was my beloved wife, Eden. She was as beautiful as the day we had met. And she still made me feel like I had just fallen in love. We had never spent a night apart until my presidency. And even now, it was seldom and only when I couldn't arrange it any other way. Even to the President of the United States, some things were out of my control.

Bear bounded next to me, sat down, and wagged his tail, hitting it against the wall. It drew both women's attention.

"Hello, Mr. President," said Jann, batting her eyelashes at me in a mock display of flirting that she had seen Eden do to me a hundred times.

Eden smiled and walked slowly toward me. She wrapped her arms around me and kissed me, while reaching behind me and squeezing my butt with her hand.

"Hey!" I said, surprised, and stepped back.

Then we all laughed. Bear wagged his tail some more and nuzzled both of our hands. "If the press ever gets a picture of that, they'll have a field day. Especially if they take it from behind and can't tell that it's you! I can just see the headlines now. 'Mystery woman squeezes President's butt.' And the subheading would be, 'Eden, the First Lady, said no comment.'"

7

"That's exactly what she would do!" chortled Jann, doubling over with laughter.

Footsteps sounded coming down the hallway toward them. Eden held her head aloft, listening, then gave Dan a quick kiss on the lips. "See ya later, darlin'. See ya, Jann," and she walked out the back door.

Vice-President Marcus Lowry stepped into view with his usual politician's smile that was his trademark. "Hi, Dan. I thought I heard Eden's voice."

I would prefer if Marcus would call me Mr. President when other people were around, but he probably didn't because we had been best friends since high school. It was probably hard to remember.

"You just missed her, Marcus."

"Just like always, I guess," said Marcus, as he headed inside the Oval Office, carrying his usual offering of donuts and hot cocoa.

I started to follow and didn't notice Jann sneak up behind me. She gave a quick squeeze to my butt and hid behind the door so Marcus couldn't see her.

"Oh!" I said as I jumped forward.

Marcus turned toward me. "What happened?"

"Oh, nothing," I said. "Bear just goosed me. That's all." Turning around, I gave Jann a dirty look, but she was giggling behind her hand. I closed the door, not to keep anything from Jann—I'd trust her with my life—but other people were filtering into the office, and they didn't need to know all that went on in this room.

To quiet the rumbling in Bear's throat, I put my hand on the big dog's back. Then I sat at my desk, and Bear lay down beside me.

"Why do you keep that woman around?" asked Marcus.

I didn't have to hear the name to know who Marcus was talking about.

"There are plenty of professionals you could get who would do a better job for you than *her*."

"Marcus, we've had this conversation before. Jann *is* a professional. And she does a great job for me—and has done a great job for me for *decades*."

"Yes, but that's when you were a lawyer and *just* a senator. Now that you're the President, you need someone—I don't know—more *presidential* than she is."

"Marcus," I warned.

"Come on, Dan. You know she is a thief! How could you have someone like that in a vulnerable position like this?"

"She is not a thief, Marcus. That was a long time ago, and she has been an exemplary trusted employee since. Now, not a word more."

Before Marcus said another word, which I knew he would, the phone gave a quick buzz and a knock sounded at the door. "Come in!" I knew that would be the President's Daily Briefing.

Bear sat up to look as the tall man in the dark suit came through the door with envelopes in his hand. "Hello, Alan."

"Mr. President, sir." Alan handed me the envelope and then an identical one to Marcus.

"Thank you," I said.

Alan nodded and left the room. Bear lay back down by my feet, his job done.

Both envelopes were torn open. "Let's see," said Marcus. "Is there anything of interest here?"

Each of us scanned our daily intel report. "Most of it looks like updates," I said. "Except this little item here that mentions a pneumonia of unclear cause in Wuhan, China." I did not realize then how that *little item* would change my life forever.

CHAPTER TWO

Jannika White

After Alan dropped off the intel reports and left her alone in her office, Jannika White thought about Marcus Lowry and frowned. She wasn't sure what it was about him that made her dislike him so much, but there was definitely something. Part of it, she was so sure, was his smile. Dan called it a politician's smile, but she thought of it more as a smarmy cat-who-swallowed-the-canary grin.

One thing was certain. The way he always walked right past her desk without acknowledging her made her feel the way she used to feel growing up in the projects in Boston. Inferior. Her mind drifted back to those sorrowful days.

Her father had abandoned the family after she was born, and her mother worked two jobs to support her two children. Jann's older brother got killed in gang violence when he was fourteen. Somehow Jann maintained an A average in high school—until she got pregnant and had to quit.

She and her new baby lived with her mother for several years, where they barely had enough money to survive. Jann worked nights and her mother worked days. And when a drunk hit-and-run driver killed her mother, she and the child were on their own. It wasn't long before she was out of money, out of food, and out of hope. Jann took the only action she could. She left her four-year-old son, Ricky, with a neighbor, and went out to find a way to feed her family.

With the last few cents she had, she took a bus away from the poor side of town and toward the rich side of town. *Toward* instead of *to*, because she didn't have enough money to get all the way there and had to walk the last few miles. Jann remembered thinking that she was like Robin Hood, stealing from the rich and giving to the poor. And that made her feel better about it, because her mother had always taught her that above all else, it was important to be honest. Still, she had a few twinges of guilt because the *poor* that she would give it to, was herself. But she knew what she had to do to feed her son, and she would do it.

She arrived at the exclusive neighborhood with upscale department stores, but the long walk had tired her, so she sat down on a bench to rest. She hadn't rested long enough when the perfect target exited the store and started walking in the opposite direction. Jann knew she had to act fast or miss her chance. The woman was pregnant, and Jann felt bad about that, but she had never done this before and needed an easy target. Standing up quickly, she ran the few steps to the woman, grabbed her purse, and took off in the other direction. Although she expected the purse to slip off the woman's arm, it didn't. Jann tugged harder, thinking it might pull the woman over and then the purse would come loose.

That's not what happened. The woman not only remained standing, but she turned around and grabbed the strap back from Jann. It surprised her so much to lose her trophy that she sank to the ground and burst into tears.

Eden Wakefield, the woman who helped her up and guided her to the bench, turned out to be the perfect target after all. It was because of her that Jann was in the White House now. Eden had driven Jann back to the projects where they picked up her son. Then she had driven them to her home, given her and the boy a hot meal, and tucked them both away into the guest room.

What followed was like a fairy tale, including Eden, who Jann still considered her fairy godmother. Jann had acquired new clothes, a new job, and a college degree. None of it would have been possible without Eden and her husband, Dan Indigo. Dan needed a new secretary at his law firm, and Jann got the job. She attended night school while Dan and Eden cared for Ricky, and now, many decades later, she was personal secretary to the most powerful man in the free world: Dan Indigo, President of these United States.

Sure there had been problems. Despite going to the best schools, her son, Ricky, had gotten himself into trouble. But at least he didn't get involved with gang violence. Jann was grateful for that. He had turned himself around, and now he had a good job and lived in Arizona. She missed him, but he was doing well.

The door to the Oval Office opened and Marcus Lowry walked out. As he walked past her, Jann said in a voice dripping with sarcasm, "Goodbye, Mr. *Lowry*." He said nothing, but he gave a stutter step and walked on. She smiled to herself, because she knew every time she said that to him, it would remind him of the time she said, "Goodbye, Mr. *Lucky*."

Jann wanted him to remember that she knew something about him that he didn't want her to know. How valuable it was, she didn't know, but she realized that was what prompted him to keep trying to talk Dan into firing her. Eden had confided to her about that. Marcus knew she had something on him. Although she had something on the woman, too, she never planned to use that against her. She thought the woman deserved the job she had—despite the way she had gotten it. What Jann had on Marcus, though, she just might use at some point. When the time was right.

Jann gave a quick glance inside the Oval Office to see if Dan had heard her, but he was on the phone. Although he normally frowned on her harassing Marcus, the only time he had gotten angry was when she had used her best "mammy" voice. So she had never done that again. Dan had been too kind to her through the years for her to chance making him angry. But he knew how Marcus treated her, so although Dan didn't like her mocking the guy, he understood it.

She thought again of her *humble* beginnings and realized how lucky she was to be here. If Eden was her fairy godmother, then Dan was her fairy godfather. Sometimes she considered writing a book about her life called *Lucky Me: From the Projects to the Whitehouse* by Jannika White. If nothing else, it would give people hope.

Jann smiled at the thought of someday writing a book, and at how lucky she had been, and how wonderful her life was. Sometimes she thought she was living in Wonderland.

And then her phone rang.

CHAPTER THREE
Wuhan, China

On the second floor of the Wuhan Memorial Hospital, Dr. Kung Longwei, with his head hanging, walked down the hallway toward his office. On the last rounds of his shift, he had visited his four new patients—an elderly husband and wife, a young female college student, and a man who worked at the Wuhan Seafood Market—and none of them were doing well. Earlier that day, they had arrived separately at Emergency in the early hours of the morning. They all presented with flu-like symptoms, and yet they did not have the flu. They also tested negative for pneumonia, although their coughs and fevers suggested it. The x-rays displayed multiple blurry shadows scattered in the lungs. It was an unusual chest infection, but he had no idea what kind.

Now, many hours later, none of the patients had improved despite his best efforts. They seemed resistant to the usual methods of treatment. Two of them, the elderly woman and the female college student, had such severe shortness of breath, they were put on ventilators, which did nothing to improve their conditions. A nasal cannula helped the elderly husband to remain stable. The middle-aged man from the Seafood Market also had a nasal cannula, but his painful headache, intense coughing, and high fever made him the sickest of the bunch.

Their symptoms felt somehow *familiar,* and yet he did not want to even consider that possibility. Now he awaited the results of their latest tests. As he plodded past the nurse's station, someone called out, "Doctor, those results you've waited for are on your desk."

"Thank you, Nurse!" His stride lengthened and his pace quickened.

Dr. Kung turned into his office and slid into his chair. He closed his eyes and prepared himself to open the report. He hoped to find a reasonable explanation for the symptoms and lack of response from his patients. His rational mind told him that twenty years of practicing medicine wasn't *that* long, and there were conditions he had never seen. This could be one of them. But was it his rational mind or his mind rationalizing? Dr. Kung feared with a deadly certainty what he would find. Taking a deep breath, he opened the report.

Later, when he recalled his first glimpse, he couldn't remember which came first—the cold sweat or the feeling of dread in his gut.

CHAPTER FOUR

President

Maintenance had removed all vestiges of Christmas and my beautiful Christmas lights; New Year's Day had come and gone; and now it was time to settle in to business. In the Oval Office, I knelt by the fire waiting for the kindling to catch. No one could start a fire as well as I could, and after having to endure, too many times, the damn thing smoking for half the morning, I always started it myself. Besides, I enjoyed doing it. Although I had been starting fires for years wherever I lived, it felt *different* here somehow.

I wouldn't admit this to anyone but Eden, but when I started a fire in the Oval Office fireplace, it made me feel like Abraham Lincoln—you know, the log cabin and all. I realized it was a stupid thought, because this room wasn't even here when Lincoln was president. He worked in a different room. Still, that was how I felt.

Those feelings did not have to be realistic. That's what Eden told me, and I believed her. So when the kindling caught, and I added the first log of the day, it satisfied a secret part of me. After putting up the screen, I inhaled deeply the pleasing scent of burning log, and then, smiling, I sat at the desk. The Resolute Desk. It wasn't here when Lincoln was here, either. Gazing at the dancing flames and listening to the crackling sound of the fire relaxed me. Closing my eyes briefly to enjoy the moment, I opened them and got to work.

The Daily Brief of the past few days had contained no more information about the new kind of pneumonia—just that it was there. Chatter continued, but with no explanation. It made me uncomfortable, and after a brief discussion with my two *unofficial* advisors, Eden and Jann, I had called a cabinet meeting to discuss the potential risks involved. Isa, my Chief of Staff, had scheduled the meeting for later that morning.

With the latest brief in front of me, I read it over again—which I didn't need to because I remembered every word. It mentioned the strange, new pneumonia, but no further information was available. I didn't know why, but the whole subject had an ominous feel to it.

I didn't know how long I sat there pondering the lack of information, but the sound of my cell phone ringing brought me back from my thoughts. "Hello!"

"Dad? Good morning!"

"Zoey! Good morning to you, too! How are you? Aaron? The children?" My daughter Zoey was the light of my life. I didn't get to talk to her as often as I liked, but when I did, I cherished every moment.

"Everyone is great, Dad. Aaron has to go to Italy for at least two weeks for business. Neither of us is looking forward to that, but it is what it is. Rose and Sage are doing great. Hey, is Mom around? She's not answering her cell."

"She might be on her way here, or maybe she's still in the shower at the residence. Anything I can help you with?"

"I wanted to tell her a funny story about the kids. Want to hear it? I know you're busy."

I felt a stab of regret and forced it to go away. Since my presidency, I didn't have as much time as I would like for my children and grandchildren. I couldn't even remember the last time I talked to my son, Douglas. "Yes, Zoey! Of course I have time!

Please tell me." Inadvertently, I glanced at the grandfather clock to my right, but I had plenty of time before the meeting.

"Remember I sent you the pics of the kids from Halloween? They were a ballerina and a pirate? Well, today they told me they wanted to get dressed in their costumes again, so I said fine. A few minutes later, they come out with Sage dressed in the ballerina outfit, and Rose in the pirate garb. But Sage had his cowboy gun belt on, and Rose had taken an ace bandage and wrapped her leg so it looked like Captain Hook's peg leg. Sage was shooting his guns and Rose was running around saying 'Aargh!' It was the cutest thing!"

"That does sound cute, Zoe. Do you have pics?" As I talked, I had turned my head around looking out at the Rose Garden and I saw Eden and Jann walk by. "Ah, here's your mother now."

"Yes, I have the pics. I'll send 'em. Can you give Mom your phone?"

"Sure thing," I said as I walked to the door. "Morning, Jann, Eden." I smiled at them. "Eden, Zoey's on the phone." And into the phone I said, "Love you, Zoe. Talk to you later. Here's your mom." I handed the phone to Eden, kissed Jann on the cheek in greeting, and stepped back into my office.

Bear had followed me to the other room to say hello to Eden and to get a thorough petting from Jann. As I sat at my desk, Bear strode into the office, with his tail wagging, and a big smile on his face. He approached me for a quick nuzzle and then lay down by the side of the desk.

I heard footsteps approaching, and Marcus walked into the office. He placed the donuts and hot cocoa on the desk. "Hey, Dan."

"Marcus," I had asked him so many times not to bring me donuts, but since he never listened, I finally stopped asking.

As Marcus opened the package to grab a donut, I noticed that the fire could use another log. "Marcus, do me a favor and put another log on the fire. Just set it in the middle there."

Marcus walked over to the fire, took away the screen, and gingerly picked up a log before shrieking and dropping it on the floor. "Ew! A spider!" He stomped his foot with a look of disgust on his face.

Bear growled and I jumped up. "You didn't kill it, did you? I catch and release spiders! You know that!" I walked over to see the poor spider squished on the floor and I shook my head. Then I picked up the piece of wood, placed it into the fire, and replaced the screen.

"No, how would I know that?"

From the other room, Jann called, "Because you were at last year's Christmas party when Dan was half drunk and made a big showing of releasing the spider that he caught."

"I'm supposed to remember that?" asked Marcus, as he gave Jann a dirty look.

I wiped up the spider with a piece of tissue, examined it to see if I could still determine what kind it was, and threw the tissue into the trash.

More footsteps sounded. Marcus, who had a better vantage point than I, whispered under his breath. "Here comes caterpillar eyes."

Jonathan Sharpe appeared in the doorway with his usual tight smile. Bear stood up and growled. With a furtive glance at the big dog, Jon nodded toward me and then Marcus. "Mr. President, Mr. Vice President." Then he asked, "I thought there was a meeting this morning?"

"Ten o'clock, not nine," I said. Jonathan Sharpe was tall, slender, with thick short hair, a constant five-o'clock shadow, and very heavy eyebrows—which is why Marcus gave him that nickname. He had come highly recommended and was previously the Administrator of the Transportation Security Administration, and the National Security Advisor to my predecessor.

"Oh, so I'm early. Sorry. See you in an hour." And he walked off.

When the footsteps faded, Marcus looked at me and said, "Why does *he* have to attend the meeting?"

"Marcus, he's the head of Homeland Security. Of course he has to come!"

"I don't like him or trust him," said Marcus.

"I don't really like him, either, but it is what it is."

"I don't like him, either," chimed in Jann from the doorway.

"That's weird," said Marcus. "Why don't any of us trust him?"

Three pair of eyes went to Bear, who was standing by the desk, his hackles still raised, his gaze in the direction of the disappearing sound of footsteps. Only one person said a word. Jannika. "Duh!"

CHAPTER FIVE

Jann

After Marcus left the premises, and Jann's irritation of him began to fade, she thought back to when she, Dan, and Marcus all looked at Bear as he stood growling as Jon Sharpe left the room. What did it mean? She had heard that dogs were a good judge of people, and if she trusted anyone, it would be Bear.

On the other hand, Bear *always* growled at Marcus. Marcus claimed that it was because he had accidentally stepped on Bear's foot when he was a puppy and Bear never forgot it. But Jann didn't believe that.

As Marcus told the story, it was at Eden's birthday celebration. Jann was at that celebration, and nothing like that ever happened. She remembered because she was so enamored with the new puppy that she carried him around all day, took him out to do his business, and when she had to do *her* business, the puppy came into the bathroom with her. Bear was never out of her sight once for the entire day. Marcus never came near the pup, never even tried to pet him. Now that's suspicious. Never trust a man who doesn't like dogs, and never trust the person whom a dog growls at. Besides, if you're going to lie about an event, at least make it general so no one can pin you down.

Marcus was an idiot, anyway. She thought that about him even before she had caught him in that scandalous position. He and Isa Zimmerman coming out of his office late at night, he zipping up his zipper, and her buttoning her blouse. They both pretended not to see her, but she saw them all right. Jann was close enough that she could see the whites of their eyes. Who said that, anyway? Oh, yes, it was some guy named *Prescott* who was a colonel in the Revolutionary War. She remembered that odd fact, because her son, Ricky, was living in *Prescott*, Arizona. For now.

Jann felt a rush of exhilaration and overwhelming love at the thought. It was "for now" because Ricky, his girlfriend, and her four-year-old son were all moving to Oceanview, Maryland, where she lived now. It was a dream come true for Jann. When Jann had received Ricky's call the other day that they had decided to move here, it had filled her with joy. And she hadn't yet had a chance to tell her best friend, Eden, about it. Joy shared is joy doubled. She couldn't wait to tell her.

As if by magic, Jann heard a sound behind her, and in walked Eden from the Rose Garden. They had that kind of connection, her and Eden. Jann had it with Dan, too, if truth be told. It was like that from the beginning. Jann needed one of them, and they appeared. And Jann hoped that she could be that way for them, too, someday. It hadn't happened yet.

Jann jumped up and hugged her. "Eden, you won't believe what happened! Ricky called, and guess what? He's moving back here! My Ricky's coming home!" She pulled away from Eden, but when her eyes filled with tears, she embraced her again.

"There, there, Jann," Eden said softly, as she stroked her back. "Tell me."

After a few sniffles, Jann nodded and pulled away. "He called me. I haven't had a chance to tell you! Ricky called me! He got a job at the airport! So he and Keesha and Jace are all moving back here! He asked if I could find him a place to live while they get settled. Then he's going to buy a house! He's going to stay!" She broke into tears again, but instead of grabbing back hold of Eden, she sank into her chair and cried into her hands.

Eden stepped forward and began rubbing her shoulders. "That's so wonderful, Jann. I'm so happy for you. When are they coming?"

"Soon. Ricky starts his new job in a month. They're packing now and will drive out here in a week or two after they finish." She looked up at Eden with watery, still-teary eyes. "I can't tell you how happy I am. I can't believe this is happening. My dream has finally come true. Ricky's coming home."

"Oh, Jann." Eden leaned down and hugged her.

"Hey!" barked Dan from the Oval Office. "What's going on in there?"

Eden raised her eyebrows at Jann. "I better go in and calm the beast." They both quietly giggled as Eden walked into the other room.

Jann could hear them talking and heard Dan say, "Yeah? So what? What's the big deal?" She knew that he didn't really mean that. His uncharacteristic barking and hard demeanor was a disguise for his hurt feelings about Ricky.

Dan and Ricky were like father and son. In many ways, Jann thought Dan was closer to Ricky than he was to his own son, Douglas. By the time Doug was old enough to appreciate playing ball with his father, Dan had become so involved in politics that he didn't have the time for him like he had for Ricky. And when Ricky got into trouble and made no effort to talk to Dan—because he was so ashamed—Dan took it very hard. He had stopped asking about Ricky's welfare years ago, and whenever Ricky's name came up, he buried his face in a book or quietly left the room.

What a homecoming they'd have. She had no idea.

CHAPTER SIX

Keith Enright

"Breaker one-nine, this is The Snake Doctor in the blue Bull Dog with the reefer. I'm heading south on 95 from the Silly Circle. Is it clear up ahead?"

"Hello, Snake Doctor. This is Tree Top in that big Anteater comin' at you. You're clear for a while, but check again after a few miles. There was a bear heading south, and he might have turned around by now."

"Thanks, Tree Top. Keep the shiny side up!" Keith Enright was glad to leave Washington D.C. The congestion drove him crazy. He preferred the open road.

Keith adjusted the volume on the CB radio and turned the satellite radio up. It was a song by the Stones. He sang along for a few lines before turning it off. The lines of the song went through his mind. You *can* get what you want, and he was proof of that. His new *big rig* was proof of that. And it was all his and all that he ever wanted. It wasn't really new, just new to him. But it was *perfect*.

Keith pondered his life and how he had come to possess this incredible machine. It was one of those philosophical ideas—that the person you are today is the integration of everything you have been in the past—everything good, everything bad.

24

Keith regretted what happened to him and regretted what he did, but he didn't regret what came about because of it. Still, he always kept that idea in mind. Who he was today wouldn't be the same—and not nearly as good—if those things hadn't happened.

Too much to drink, and drunk enough to think he and his friends could get away with stealing a car. They had planned a quick joy ride, but Keith was driving and ran into another car. Although the other driver wasn't injured, he ended up having a heart attack. He lived, thankfully. Keith's friends got community service, but since Keith was driving, he got sentenced to six months in a juvenile detention center.

It wasn't an easy six months, but if the ends justified the means, then it was worth every minute. And there were some tough minutes. More than once, he had to use his fists to protect himself—or to protect someone else who couldn't fend for himself. And that simple act of kindness had broad and beneficial implications for him.

His conditions of release, when the time came, were for him to see a counselor and to join Alcoholics Anonymous. Keith was not an alcoholic. He told them that over and over in all the discussions he had while he was in the juvenile detention center.

Although that was in the days prior to marijuana being medically acceptable, and though the authorities still considered it a dangerous drug, he admitted that he preferred marijuana to alcohol. He had seen what alcohol had done to his father and wanted no part of it. The drunken night that had cost him his freedom was a birthday celebration: his seventeenth birthday. Keith remembered the night. Happy Birthday to me.

Whether they believed him or not about the alcohol, he never knew. The official statement was that because his father was an alcoholic, he was at risk. So the condition held.

After he joined AA, he was assigned a sponsor. That sponsor had agreed to report on his progress and report if he missed any meetings. That sponsor, Glen Makowski, changed Keith's life.

Glen was a forty-something truck driver and recovering alcoholic. He had lost his wife and the respect of his children before he managed to quit drinking, and he credited AA with his new life. Unfortunately, his new life did not include his wife or children. Sometimes there's just too much water under the bridge, Glen used to say.

Keith had matured while in the detention center, and upon his release, he knew one thing for certain: he never wanted to return to a place like that. So he followed the conditions of his release, as instructed, and with a good attitude, because he was so happy that he was free again. When he attended his first AA meeting and met Glen, the two had bonded instantly. With Glen's sons refusing to speak to him, and with Keith's father a sloppy drunk who didn't care about anything except his next drink, Keith and Glen became father and son. That's how they felt about each other and that's how they acted.

Glen got Keith into the trucking business, and Keith thrived there. He had been saving up for years to buy a rig of his own, and was almost there when Glen died suddenly of a heart attack. He left his beautiful rig—Mack truck and refrigerated trailer—to Keith. Upon hearing what was in the will, Keith immediately contacted the two sons to see if they wanted the rig. Keith thought it only fair to ask them.

But he got a surprise. Even after all the time Glen had been sober, the two sons still resented their father's actions when they were young. So they told Keith they were glad he called. Because they wanted to give him the house their father had left to them. They wanted nothing to do with it or anything else of their father's.

Although the house needed fixing up, it was bigger than Keith's and much more suitable for a family. Keith sold his house and moved into Glen's, enjoying every moment of fixing it up. He felt Glen there with him, cheering him on, as he had always done. And when he asked his girlfriend, Jeni, to marry him, and she said yes, Keith thought his life couldn't get much better.

But he had no idea what was in store for him.

CHAPTER SEVEN

President

I walked through the door to the Cabinet Room expecting to see Jon Sharpe already sitting there. And when he wasn't there, I felt relieved. I stroked Bear's coat, and said, "I wish you could tell me why you act like that toward him, Bear." The dog looked up, wagged his tail, and gave me a doggy grin.

The fireplace already had a fire going when I walked up to check on it. Whoever had done it, had done a good job. All right, all right, maybe other people *could* do it as well as I could. But I *enjoyed* lighting the fire. I warmed my hands and returned to the center of the oval mahogany table where my seat was.

Traditionally, the president occupied a spot at the east side of the table with his or her back to the Rose Garden. But the first time I came into this room several years before, it had been snowing, and I had wanted to watch the snow. I remembered dragging my chair to the other side. Marcus came in, asked what I was doing, and then said, "Just leave it there. All the chairs are the same."

Ah, Marcus. He was a good and trusted friend and had been for decades, so I always forgave him his shortcomings. The chairs weren't the same. The president's chair was two inches taller than the rest of the chairs in the room. And my chair said

"The President" on an engraved brass nameplate on the back of the chair, like all the other chairs had nameplates for the person who sat in each of them. That was right after I was sworn in, so Marcus was still feeling badly about not being president himself. He was over that now.

I turned at the sound of someone entering the room. Corrie Corrigan, the Press Secretary, stepped into the room and looked around. She was 28 years old, had vast experience for someone her age, and was a tremendous asset to the White House. We were lucky to get her.

"Hello, Mr. Pres!" Corrie bounced up to me and gave me a kiss on the cheek. She was short with dark brown curls framing her face. Everything about Corrie was bouncy, from her personality to her looks. Corrie reminded me of the character Tigger in one of my favorite childhood books. I'd never tell her that, of course. But if I did, I felt certain that she would take it well. If I ever saw her without a smile on her face, I would know the world was in trouble.

"Hello, Corrie!"

"So what's up for today's meeting?"

"Nothing for you, I'm afraid. It's a preliminary meeting that I hope never goes any further than that."

"You've got that right, Mr. President," said an accented voice that belonged to Dr. Stanley Patel. Dr. Patel was an epidemiologist and the Surgeon General. He was born in the United States, raised in India, and then returned to the states for his formal education.

I had asked him to attend this meeting. I would have liked to have talked to him alone, but the rest of the cabinet had started filing into the room. Murmurs of "Mr. President" were heard as they walked by me to find their seats.

Marcus sat across the table from me—the traditional seat for the vice-president. Eden, Jannika, and Corrie Corrigan sat together on the chairs against the wall.

Everyone was there, and it was time to start. "Ladies and gentlemen, this will be a very brief meeting for some of you, but

I wanted everyone to get a heads up just in case things turn out badly. In my daily brief for the last few days—I know some of you have seen it, too—there has been mention of a pneumonia of unclear cause in Wuhan, China. Vic, can you speak of this, please?"

Victor Galloway was the Director of National Intelligence, and Alan Laing was the Deputy Director and the one who delivered the reports. But because they were both in attendance, the nod went to Victor.

"I'm sorry, Mr. President, but the one line is literally all we know about it. China is being tight-lipped as usual. But when we find out any additional information, I can guarantee that you'll be the first to know."

"Thank you, Vic. All right, everybody, so now you know what this is all about. There are many of you in here that regardless of what happens, it won't affect you. So, if you feel you are one of those, please stand up and excuse yourselves."

"Excuse me, Mr. President," said Dr. Patel. "Excuse me for interrupting, but if this thing goes south, then it could affect a lot more of you than it would seem at the outset."

"What are the chances of it going south?" I asked.

"There is no way to know. It could just blow over and affect no one but the people in Wuhan. Or, worst-case scenario, it could become a global pandemic and potentially affect everyone on the planet. We don't know yet if there is successful human-to-human transmission. But if there is—" He shook his head and frowned. "And if this is a virus, it will mutate. That's what viruses do. It's their job. So if it's not dangerous now, it could be later."

"With that grim picture of the possibilities, all who think their department won't be affected *at this time* may leave."

Half the room stood up and filed out the door. As they went, I ticked off who I thought would have to return if this turned bad: Secretary of Transportation, Secretary of Education, and Secretary of the Treasury, among others. I just hoped it wouldn't come to that.

Of those left in the room besides Marcus and Dr. Patel, were Isa Zimmermann, the Chief of Staff, Victor Galloway and Alan Laing, Jonathan Sharpe, Dana Ogham, the Secretary of State, Dominic Tibble, the Secretary of Health and Human Services, Harlan McDonald, the Secretary of Defense, and General Bryce Skora, Chairman of the Joint Chiefs of Staff. I didn't know what the last two were doing here. If they were going to fight this thing—if it needed to be fought—it wouldn't be with the military.

"Thank you all for staying. There is nothing more we can do at this point until we have more information. But when we do, we will inform you right away. You can be certain of that."

The rest of the cabinet and assorted others filed out, saying, "Thank you, Mr. President," as they went. Corrie left and said, "Goodbye, Mr. President." She was always formal when anyone else was around and only chummy when we were alone or with Eden and Jann.

"I'll see you later, Dan," said Marcus as he left. I noticed he walked out with Jonathan Sharpe and had his arm around him. Marcus was the consummate politician, making up to people he didn't like and making everyone like him.

Now the only ones in the room besides me were Eden, Jann, and Dr. Patel. I nodded glumly to Jann and Eden and then turned to Dr. Patel, whom I addressed differently when we were alone. "Okay, Dr. Stan. Now tell me what you really think."

"I pretty much did, Mr. President. At this point, it could go either way." He stood up, walked closer, and leaned across the table to me. "But I can tell you this. If it starts spreading, get our people out of China immediately."

I didn't know at the time that recommendation would be the undoing of me: President Dan Indigo.

CHAPTER EIGHT

The man

Walking into his office with his rage building, it was all he could do to keep himself from slamming the door as hard as he could. But he didn't. Although his hands were shaking with the effort, he closed the door with a soft *thunk*. Then he sank into his chair behind his desk and balled his right hand into a fist, which he waved in the air. The tension centered in his gut, and he could feel his face getting redder and redder. It felt like he was about to explode.

Dammit dammit dammit! He *hated* that man! Every little thing about him, from his dog to his wife to his secretary. Dan Indigo had no business being president. The man was weak, indecisive, and stupid. He *hated* him.

He opened his bottom desk drawer with such force that it threatened to come out of the slot. Grabbing the catcher's mitt, he started pounding his fist into it as hard as he could. Even with all the padding, the pounding hurt, but his rage was winding down, anyway. Taking a deep breath trying to calm himself, he removed the mitt and placed it back into the drawer. Then he slammed the desk drawer closed. His attempt at calming hadn't worked yet; his heart felt like it was going to beat itself right out of his chest.

The Cabinet meeting was a stupid idea and a waste of his time and everyone else's time who attended. The same information could have been disseminated in a brief communication. His secret thought was that the president liked to be in that room to show how powerful he was. *I'm better than you. I'm more powerful than you. I can call stupid meetings with no positive outcome just because I can.* He hated that. And the stupid pneumonia would probably disappear all by itself. Other diseases had. So probably this one would as well. That's fine, though. It would make the president look like the stupid ass that he was. That was perfect.

Although, maybe this pneumonia would present an opportunity to *do something*. He had to *do something*; he knew that. This couldn't go on. His rage and his impotence to do anything were wearing him down. And he couldn't let that continue. In order to make something happen, he had to have all his senses, his perceptions, his shrewdness, and yes, his brilliance, honed to a fine edge. And with that edge, he would slice the president to ribbons.

CHAPTER NINE

Jann

Jann sat in her platform rocking chair in her living room with her cat, Sneezy, on her lap. As Sneezy purred, she kneaded Jann's thigh with her padded feet. Sneezy knew better than to have her claws out as she did that. Jann took a deep breath and petted the cat. There was nothing like a purring cat to make you relax. It was almost like a meditation. And she needed that after her long, almost completely frustrating day.

After checking the newspaper, the online newspaper, Craigslist, and calling local realtors, Jann had gone to see at least fifteen houses. She stopped counting after twelve, but she had seen at least three after that, probably five. And none of them fit Ricky's requirements. They were all in Oceanview—an upscale neighborhood—and some of them had a fenced yard and some didn't, a couple of them needed work, and the two possibilities she found did not allow dogs. Although Ricky, Keesha, and Jace didn't have a dog, Ricky had said that he had promised the boy one, and he didn't want to wait until they bought their own house. Jann had gotten home, exhausted and defeated, and was about to heat something in the microwave when the front doorbell rang.

It was her neighbor who wanted her to keep an ear open to anyone who needed a rental. And the rental was exactly what Ricky wanted, including allowing animals! The neighbor was a good friend; she took Jann to look at the place—a large mother-in-law cottage—and Jann immediately gave her a deposit. The place was perfect, and it was just down the street. She wasn't sure how Ricky would feel about that, but oh well, he did say Oceanview.

Jann felt so wonderful that she could finally do something for Ricky. He had been away all of his adult life and had kept her at arm's length for years. Ricky had *allowed* her to visit him once, several years prior, when he was still working in Phoenix, Arizona.

It was before he had met Keesha. He took Jann to some touristy places and then sent her on her way. She didn't understand it and felt very hurt by it. Jann knew she had done her best by him and couldn't imagine him blaming her for anything that had happened. Now she thought he couldn't face the embarrassment of what had happened to him.

When he was growing up with Dan Indigo as the father figure in his life, Jann considered herself very lucky that she didn't have to bring Ricky up in the projects where he most certainly would have ended up in trouble. But although Ricky attended the best schools and was influenced by the best people, he still ended up in trouble.

It was one of those weird situations where Ricky was in the wrong place at the wrong time. It started out innocent enough, just a high school graduation party. But of course there had to be alcohol and loud music, and then some of the more delinquent members of the high school crashed the party. They brought marijuana, and Ricky admitted he had smoked some and that it wasn't the first time. Everything still might have turned out all right, even after a neighbor called the police when the music got even louder. Sadly, one of the newcomers was a drug dealer. Thank goodness Ricky was still seventeen, or it could have been much worse.

Jann sighed when she remembered that she had told Ricky that Dan, a congressman at the time, had pull and could probably get him off. Ricky not only felt embarrassed to admit to Dan what had happened, he also didn't want to complicate Dan's life, as he was about to make a senate bid. So he got time in what Ricky called "juvie."

When he got out, he had turned eighteen, and he immediately joined the navy. She had missed him, but she knew he'd get valuable experience. And he did. The navy trained him in aviation electronics. When he got out, he had impressed his instructor so much with his abilities that he got him a job at the airport in Phoenix, Arizona. He had on-the-job training for the civilian side of things, and then he spent the next few years at the airport in Prescott as an Avionics Technician.

Ricky loved it. And he was good at it. The only problem had been that he was three thousand miles away. But now he was moving back, and Jann couldn't feel any happier.

When he was young, she always thought with all the benefits that she gave him, and the influence from Eden and Dan, that maybe her son, Ricky, would grow up to do something great. And then he got into trouble and shattered her dream. But he had come out of it all right, and now he was happy and successful. That's all that mattered. Maybe he was saving hundreds of lives by finding and fixing electronic issues that kept airplanes in the air instead of coming crashing down. She smiled as she thought that, but she never in a million years would ever imagine the role that Ricky would ultimately play in the world.

CHAPTER TEN

Wuhan, China

With a grimace, Dr. Kung Longwei closed his eyes, willing the offending words to go away. But when he opened them, the words were still there. *SARS-like coronavirus*. It was what he was most afraid of. He had been at this hospital when SARS, also known as Severe Acute Respiratory Syndrome, first appeared in 2002.

His young son, Jian, was an infant then. Every night when he got home, Dr. Kung would take off his shoes, walk inside, remove his clothing and take a shower before even greeting his wife and son. So afraid he would give it to the boy, he held his breath and wore a clean surgical mask as he held the boy. But like his name, Jian was strong and never caught the dreaded disease. Within two years, the disease was contained. It had disappeared for all these years. Until today.

And now, almost twenty years later, a SARS-like coronavirus had reappeared. Dr. Kung opened his top desk drawer and rummaged around inside until he found a red pen. He circled the words *SARS-like coronavirus*, then took a picture of the document with his phone. Signing into his 2Chat social media account, he sent the picture off to other doctors in the hospital, as well as one of his former classmates, Jin Huifang, who worked in another hospital. With the picture, Dr. Kung recommended they take precautions. After that, he alerted hospital authorities about the cases. Then, tired, discouraged, and scared, he went home.

Before going to work the next morning, Dr. Kung tapped on his phone to check his 2Chat account. Oh, no, he thought with alarm. The picture he had taken with his red circle around *SARS-like coronavirus* had been shared all over. He looked at it, shook his head, and thought that something bad would come of this. It wasn't enough that the virus scared him to his core. Now he had to contend with *this*.

When he arrived at the hospital and stopped by his office to check his email, he found that his fears were justified. There was an email from the hospital's Discipline Board. He clicked on it.

Dr. Kung:

It has come to our attention that you have been spreading rumors and harming the stability of the hospital's working environment. You will cease and desist immediately. Information about this mysterious disease should not be arbitrarily released. We must avoid causing widespread panic at all costs. If you continue doing this, you will be held ACCOUNTABLE. In addition, YOU WILL NOT DISCUSS THIS NEW DISEASE WITH ANYONE, including your wife. There will be consequences and they will be severe.

The Board

Following that email was a second email from the Board addressed to all the doctors in the hospital.

Doctors:

You are hereby forbidden from passing messages or images related to the new virus that has shown up in our hospital. You will not wear protective clothing or masks or give anyone a reason to panic. Treat it as you would any other disease.

The Board

Dr. Kung was furious, humiliated, and even more scared than before. A SARS-like virus and they weren't allowed to wear masks or protective clothing? He set his jaw, knowing what he must do. Walking to the supply room and opening the door, he removed a protective jacket from the rack. He slipped it on and put his doctor's lab coat on top. It barely showed. There was no way to hide the mask, but he put that on, too.

After visiting his patients, he would reveal to every doctor he came across how he was protecting himself and advise them to do the same. He would tell them they were at risk with the Board if they did, but they were at risk of their lives, if they didn't.

CHAPTER ELEVEN

President

The water from the hot shower beat down on my back in a luxurious fashion. I moved my head to focus the water on my sore neck. Too many long hours, which was the way it was for a president. Although I had finished washing and rinsing, I felt reluctant to leave the safety and comfort of the hot water. Then I heard a knock on the bathroom door.

"Hon, it's Alan Laing. He has information about the pneumonia in Wuhan," Eden said.

Alan Laing was the Deputy Director of National Intelligence. He always wore mirror-finish expensive shoes. I hoped he wouldn't get them wet.

"Send him in, Eden." This wasn't my first shower interruption in my years being president. That's why Eden and I installed an opaque shower door long ago. I turned off the water.

"Sorry for interrupting you, Mr. President. But you said you wanted news as soon as we received it."

"That's fine, Alan. Just hand me that towel, please." I opened the shower door a crack and accepted the towel from Alan. After giving myself a quick dry, I wrapped the towel around my waist and stepped out, trying not to splash any rogue water onto Alan's shoes. "What do you have?"

"Shall I read it to you, Mr. President? It's still not much, but it doesn't sound good."

"Yes, please, go ahead." I stood there, dripping onto the cotton terrycloth floor mat.

"According to information gleaned from 2Chat by a doctor who works in a hospital in China," Alan stopped reading from the paper in his hands and looked at me, "2Chat is China's version of Twitter." Then he continued reading, "medical personnel have discovered a Sars-like coronavirus in Wuhan. There is no indication that it can be transmitted from person to person, but there is also no evidence it can't be. That's all we have right now, sir."

"Dammit, I was hoping it would just go away and be a false alarm! Dammit all to hell!" I said, shaking my head.

"Mr. President?" Alan said, somewhat sheepishly.

"Oh, it's not the report, Alan, it's just the implications of what needs to be done now. There is enough going on without this shit." I was in the middle of negotiations on one of my campaign promises—the one that got me elected. I was trying to get Congress and the Senate to agree to term limits. It's not easy when both sides of the aisle are against you. But now a more urgent matter had cropped up. "Thank you for bringing it to my attention. I appreciate it. We will have a meeting in the Situation Room later today. You'll be notified. Thank you."

"Goodbye, sir," said Alan Laing, his mirror-finish shoes still intact.

I pulled the towel from my waist and began drying my hair. It was a full crop of graying and white hair and took some time to get it dry. "Eden!" I called out. Although I didn't know where she was in the residence, I knew that if I bellowed loud enough, she'd eventually hear me.

Eden appeared in the doorway. "Yes, dear?" As I wiped my hair, she stood there with a crooked smile on her face, appraising my naked body. "Still handsome after all these years," she said, taking a step forward.

"Not now, hon." I held out a hand to stop her from coming any closer. "Did you hear any of that?"

"No, I was putting on my makeup."

"The new pneumonia in China didn't disappear like I hoped. It turns out it's a Sars-like coronavirus."

She nodded. "I remember that from several years back. It was bad."

"Yes, and remember the last meeting? Dr. Stan advised that if it escalated at all, we should start evacuating people right away. But I'll check with him again today, now that we have more information. I'm going to arrange a meeting in the Situation Room. I'd like to have you there, if you can."

"Sorry, dear, I have meetings all morning and afternoon. Just have Jann email me her notes. I'll go over them."

Scowling, I put the towel down and grabbed my robe. "That will have to do. Thanks, darlin'."

"No problem, dear. You know I'm always at your beck and call." She batted her eyes at me and walked away.

Although she said it with a straight face, we both knew it wasn't true. When I first decided to run for the Senate, I begged her to take Indigo as her last name. She insisted she was keeping her own last name: Wakefield. I told her that I might run for President one day, and how would it look for the First Lady to have a different last name as the President. Her answer was that she would feel honored to have me change my last name to Wakefield. Then she added we could discuss it again when I decided to run for President. Of course we never did, and she was still Eden Wakefield, and I was still Dan Indigo. It worked out.

Two hours later, I sat at the head of the table in the Situation Room with Bear resting at my feet. Looking around the room, I checked all the faces to make sure that everyone who had agreed to attend the strange pneumonia meeting was here. Corrie Corrigan was also in attendance. I glanced at my Chief of Staff, Isa Zimmerman, who arranged the meeting, and she gave an almost imperceptible nod. So I began.

"Thank you all for joining me here today. We have some new information on the *strange pneumonia* that I reported last time. Victor?"

Vic shrugged. "We don't know much more than before, but I'll fill you in." He then read what Alan had read to me earlier.

Dr. Stan moved uncomfortably in his seat and shook his head. Before he could speak up, I said, "Spit it out, Dr. Patel. Tell us what you think."

"It's a SARS-like virus, Mr. President. That can be extremely dangerous. Just because the Chinese aren't admitting to person-to-person transmission doesn't mean it isn't happening."

"Wait a minute," interrupted Jann. "Sorry for the stupid question, but what is SARS?"

I smiled at Jann and winked at her. She knew exactly what SARS was, because we had discussed it that morning. And although I had noticed the blank looks on some of the faces in the room when Dr. Stan mentioned SARS, I chose to ignore it. But Jann always had the ability to ask "stupid" questions when other people didn't want to show their ignorance. Thank you, Jann!

"Oh, sorry. SARS stands for Severe Acute Respiratory Syndrome. That's why it was first identified as a strange pneumonia —it's a respiratory illness. Depending on how contagious it is, this could spread around the globe in no time. And I know what you're wondering, Mr. President. Yes, it is critical that we get our people home immediately. Until we know more details on the virus, sir, it's the safest action we can take."

"Wait a minute," said Dominic Tibble, the Secretary of Health and Human Services. "Isn't the common cold a coronavirus? I think we're overreacting here a bit."

"And didn't my dog have a vaccination for coronavirus?" asked Dana Ogham, the Secretary of State.

"Yes and yes," said Dr. Stan. "There are many kinds of coronaviruses. Some are innocuous like the common cold, and some are deadly like SARS. But this is a *novel* coronavirus. Brand new. Never been seen before. There's no way to tell what this one is like until we get more information about it. But I believe it is better to be safe than sorry."

"Better safe than sorry?" asked Isa. "Your proposal would cost us hundreds of thousands of dollars." She was formerly the Chief Financial Officer of a Fortune 500 company. Whenever she talked, she sounded bossy. I don't think she meant to sound that way, but that's how it often came out.

"And if we do the wrong thing here, it could cost us hundreds of thousands of lives," said Dr. Stan. "This is not overreacting. This is being proactive."

"All right, doctor," I said. "What exactly are the chances of that many deaths?"

"It's hard to know, of course, with this little information. It all depends on the R-naught number." He held up a hand to silence any questions. "I'll explain what that is. This is a very simple explanation of a very complex issue. Plus, it is only one factor in determining if a pathogen will cause an epidemic. R-naught is a pathogen's basic reproductive number that hints—only *hints*—if it could cause an epidemic or not. It estimates how contagious a disease is. If person A has it, how many other people will that person infect. The regular flu is one to two. Ebola is two. The SARS virus from 2003 was about two and a half. Measles has an R-naught number of fifteen! Many things go into the guesstimate of what the R-naught number is.

"The upshot of all this," Dr. Stan continued, "is that we don't know. But if we guess wrong, hundreds of thousands of people could die all across the United States. Maybe even millions."

"All right," I said, in a gruffer voice than I had intended. "I am not risking the lives of that many Americans. My final decision is that we bring them home now. Dominic, Dana, and I don't know who else needs to be involved. Maybe Harlan?" Harlan was the Secretary of Defense.

"The CDC should be involved, too, Mr. President," said Dr. Stan.

"Isa, you organize all this between the departments." She nodded and turned toward the people I mentioned. The others at the table started rising from their seats.

"Corrie? You and I need to talk." I stood up and walked out of the room with Bear at my heels and Corrie bouncing along behind. If I had only known then that the decision I made would change my life forever.

CHAPTER TWELVE

Corrie Corrigan/the flight

Corrie Corrigan, the White House Press Secretary, wearing a dark blue dress with a white belt, stood behind the podium ready to address the newspeople in the audience. She flashed her trademark smile, briefly, then sobered up for the announcement she was about to make.

"A SARS-like virus has emerged in Wuhan, China, and we will do everything in our power to keep it from spreading to the United States.

"Through a close collaboration between the State Department, Health and Human Services, the Center for Disease Control and Prevention, and the Department of Defense, we have arranged an evacuation flight from Wuhan. We have closed our consulate and ordered all United States diplomats to leave. Any seats left on this initial flight will be for business people and their families. That is all I have right now."

After several day's delay, both bureaucratic and logistical, the empty 737 landed in Wuhan. It stood fueled and ready while a long line of people waited for attendants to check their papers and medical personnel to check their temperatures. They had already been checked once when they first arrived for the flight. The second time would be before they enter the aircraft. With the diplomatic staff all accounted for, vulnerable individuals at higher risk from the virus would get next priority. That would include small children, senior citizens, and people with certain health conditions.

Some people were seen giving up their seats for the more vulnerable—or the more desperate. One person could not board because of a fever. A child could not board because her mother, in another city at the time of the evacuation, held her passport.

Aboard the plane and during the many-hour flight back to America, the passengers stayed separate from the crew. Three times during the long flight, everyone on board was checked for a fever, and everyone checked out normal.

When the flight arrived in Alaska for refueling, medical personnel escorted everyone off the aircraft and ushered them into a large room. After completing a health screening, they were served a full breakfast, and before boarding the plane, their temperatures were all checked again. Everyone still checked out normal. So far.

Although the flight was originally scheduled to land at the airport in Bakersfield, it was diverted to the Constitution Air Force Base in central California. Once off the plane, the passengers were once again given a health screening and given keys to their new living quarters, where they would be in quarantine for fourteen days. No one knew the incubation period of the virus or even how soon symptoms might show up, but fourteen days was a reasonable guess for clearance.

The medical personnel and other workers checking the passengers and getting them settled were in various states of dress. Some of them had eye and respiratory protection, gloves, and hazmat attire. And some of them had masks only or nothing at all. Several of the doctors wore business suits. One person found the difference in outfits so amusing that she took a video of the scene. She thought it might be funny on her Facebook page.

Sometimes the difference between the truth and a lie can be determined from a single frame on a single video. And thus it was.

CHAPTER THIRTEEN

Wuhan, China

It had been a week since Dr. Cheung Fan had received the communication from Dr. Kung Longwei about the SARS-like coronavirus, and since then her hospital had an explosion of new cases. She, herself, had at least four patients who had tested positive for the new virus. To curb the spread of the virus, Dr. Cheung had written her own 2Chat post warning about the outbreak of the disease and advising her colleagues to wear protective clothing, as she always did.

Within hours of her post, it had spread faster than the virus it mentioned, and her name had remained intact. When she realized it was out of her control, she thought she would be punished, but there was nothing she could do to prevent it. And having to make the choice over again—she had chosen to be a doctor to save lives—she would have made the same choice to warn her fellow doctors.

Look where it had gotten her. After hospital management admonished her, she thought that would be the end of it. And yet, here she sat at a dirty, pockmarked table in the Public Security Bureau. The table, a rectangle with several chairs set haphazardly around it, had spilled soft drinks and food crumbs all over it. It wouldn't surprise her at all if there were some coronavirus germs right on the sticky table top. How right she was.

On the table in front of her was a statement that said she admitted to the illegal behavior of making false comments, spreading rumors online, and severely disturbing the social order. The statement also contained a line about promising not to commit further unlawful acts. To say she was being coerced to sign was putting it mildly. They had insulted her and threatened her, but aside from one very hard slap on her face, they had not physically harmed her. But the threats would have sufficed. Dr. Cheung would sign anything if it meant continuing to practice medicine. Unfortunately, that was not to be.

She picked up the pen in front of her and signed her name. After she signed the document, they allowed her to leave and return to the hospital to finish her shift. Unbeknownst to her, earlier in the day, the chief at the bureau had asked an officer who was leaving work early due to sickness, to cough on the pen. He coughed on it several times while turning it around in his hand. Then he placed it on the interrogation table next to the document.

The Public Security Bureau announced it had detained several people for publishing and spreading rumors online and causing adverse impacts on society. They said there will be zero tolerance, and police would punish any other rumormongers to the full extent of the law.

Several days later, Dr. Cheung Fan developed a fever and a nasty cough. She was admitted to the hospital. When her condition deteriorated, they moved her to the intensive care unit with oxygen support. She later tested positive for coronavirus. Where she got it, from her own patients—or not—will never be known.

CHAPTER FOURTEEN

Jann

Jann arrived at her desk at 7:15 A.M. Dan was already in the Oval Office and the door was closed, which was unusual, but not unheard of. And Marcus wasn't in there with him. She knew that because there was no smell of hot cocoa and donuts in the air. Dan didn't want the donuts, and she had heard him tell that to Marcus on numerous occasions, but Marcus still brought them in every single day. It wouldn't surprise her if he did it deliberately to compromise Dan's health. And as far as the cocoa, Marcus was probably setting him up so he could poison him someday. Nothing would surprise her about that jerk.

She heard the phone ringing in the Oval Office, and it reminded her of her conversation the night before with her son.

"Mom? That you?" he had coughed into the phone. "Sorry."

"Ricky? Why are you calling so early? It must be what—five o'clock over there?"

"It's Rick, Mom. I'm a grown man now, remember? And yes," he coughed some more, a deep, hacking cough, and then had to catch his breath before he continued, "I know it's early, but I've been up most of the night, anyway, with this damn cough."

"Have you seen a doctor? It sounds really bad."

"It's just the flu—you know, fever, aching all over, sore throat, headache—but it's taking me forever to get over it. I got it from Jace, who picked it up at pre-school. His teacher said he got it from a classmate whose parents just returned from overseas. They probably caught it on the airplane home." He coughed and couldn't stop coughing. "Ouch. My chest hurts from so much coughing."

"I'm worried about you, Ricky, er Rick."

"Don't. I'm not calling to complain. I wanted to let you know we won't arrive there as planned. Keesha can't drive all that way by herself, and I'm too sick to drive." Ricky coughed into the phone again. "Sorry."

Jann held her breath while she asked, "You're still moving here, though, right?"

"Yes, Ma, still moving there. No worries. But I can't drive while I'm coughing like this. And Keesha doesn't want me leaving the house with a fever, anyway." More coughing. "We're all packed, so it's kind of hard to live this way, but we don't have a choice right now. Luckily, we gave more notice than we needed, so if it lasts a while, we won't be out on the street."

"Your little house here is waiting for you. But I'm worried. Are you sure you don't want to see a doctor? You know, because it's lasting so long."

"No, Ma. It's not getting any worse, and I'm tough! I'll be"— he stopped to cough another long, drawn out hacking cough —"fine." He laughed.

"Well, if you're laughing, Ricky, it can't be that bad. When do you think you'll be leaving Prescott, then?"

"Keesha says I have to be fever-free for twenty-four hours before she'll let me leave the house. Today's fever was less than yesterday's. So it could be any day now. She's taking good care of me, Mom."

"It sounds like it, honey. Well, I'm eager to see you and to meet Keesha and Jace. You take care of yourself. I love you."

51

Ricky coughed before he could answer. "I will, Mom. I will. And Mom? It's okay if you call me Ricky. Bye. I love you." He coughed into the phone as the call ended.

Jann had sighed when she hung up the phone, and she sighed again thinking about it. She hated that he was sick, but it sounded like Keesha was watching over him. Although they hadn't met yet, Jann liked her already. Since Jann didn't hear the door behind her open and close, the hand on her shoulder surprised her.

"What's up, Jann?" Eden asked.

"Oh! You scared me, Eden. I didn't hear you come in."

"What's wrong? You usually don't sigh like that."

Jann smiled at Eden. "You know me too well. It's Ricky. He's got a bad flu, so they're leaving Prescott later than they had expected. But he's still coming, so that's good."

Eden leaned down and hugged her. "Don't worry about it, Jann. He'll be fine, and you'll see him in no time." She sniffed the air.

Jannika chuckled. "That's exactly what I do! No, he isn't here yet. You're free to go in and see Dan without his obnoxious presence." Eden smiled at Jann, turned, knocked softly at the closed door, and walked into the Oval Office, leaving the door ajar.

Jann knew why Eden avoided Marcus at all costs. Marcus had once cornered Eden in the kitchen. Jann was the sole recipient of that story or confession or whatever you wanted to call it. Eden reminded Jann that just because Marcus was a jerk where relationships were concerned, it didn't mean he was a bad vice-president. That's one of the reasons Eden had never told her story to Dan. And that story was probably one of the reasons Jann disliked him so much.

Outside the Oval Office, Jann could hear Dan and Eden kissing and softly talking. She was sure they were hugging, too. She loved their relationship. Maybe she could have a relationship like theirs someday. Or maybe not. Jann didn't care. She was perfectly fine on her own. As she listened to their soft talking, she had no idea it would be one of the last times the President and First Lady would be together like that for a very long time.

CHAPTER FIFTEEN

President

Eden was in the Oval Office with me when Alan Laing came in to give me the Daily Briefing. I felt grateful she wasn't still sitting on my lap. That didn't embarrass me, but it didn't seem very fitting for a president to have a woman on his lap—wife or no.

"Hello, Mrs. First Lady. Hello, Mr. President," said Alan, his shoes still shiny enough to see myself.

"Hello, Alan," said Eden.

"Hey, Alan. Anything new today?"

"Afraid so, sir. You know the team that took care of the people coming in from China?" When I nodded, he continued. "There's a whistleblower. We're investigating the claims now."

"Good-by, gentlemen. I'll see you later, dear." Eden winked at me and left the room.

"What are the claims?" I started to ask and then reconsidered. "If it's all in the report, I don't need to waste any more of your time, Alan. Anything else?"

"Yes, sir. More cases of the virus in Wuhan. A lot."

I shook my head and stuck out my hand to receive the report. Alan nodded and walked out of the room without saying another word. Opening the report, I began with the whistleblower. That was closer to home than the virus in China.

It wasn't good. The whistleblower claimed that many people in the welcoming committee—who examined the people, took their temperature, and gave them their housing assignments—did not have proper equipment to protect them from this highly contagious virus. *And* that they didn't have proper training for the job.

Dominic Tibble, the Secretary of Health and Human Services who had orchestrated everything, said he didn't believe that had taken place and that safety protocols were always followed. So he denied the claims. That complicated matters.

"Damn it!" I threw the report on my desk.

"What's up, boss?" asked Jann from the other room.

"Oh, there's a whistleblower reporting problems with the evacuated people from Wuhan. And the virus is getting worse, but I haven't even read about that yet. I've got my hands full, as usual, Jann."

"I know you can handle it, boss."

"What can you handle, Dan?" asked Marcus, as he barged into the room bearing his usual donuts and hot chocolate.

"Have you read the Daily Brief yet?"

Marcus put the donuts and hot cocoa onto the desk and pulled the report from under his arm. "No, not yet, but I've got it right here."

"Take a look at the part about the whistleblower."

Before Marcus had finished reading it, I added, "Whistleblowers can kill you politically. I need to take care of this right away."

"Is it true?" asked Jann.

"Probably," I said. "It often is, but there usually isn't enough evidence either way. So it turns out to be a he said/she said situation, where nobody wins but everybody feels bad."

"Maybe you'll get lucky this time, Mr. President," said Jann.

I had my hand on the phone to call Isa, my Chief of Staff, to set up a meeting, when Marcus spoke up.

"Yes, this is not good at all, Dan. You need to do something about it right away."

"That's exactly what I was about to do." I tapped the number to reach Isa. "Isa? I need you to arrange another meeting with everyone who was at our last one. If you can't remember who was there, Jann can give you a list. It needs to be this morning, and if anyone can't make it, they *must*—and I stress *must*—be available by phone during the meeting, so we can get their input. No delay on this one, Isa! Do it now!" Before I hung up the phone, I added, "When you let everyone know, you can tell Harlan and Bryce their presence is not needed at this time."

"Yes, sir, Mr. President. Should I tell Harlan and Bryce not to come?"

"No, just give them an out. If they want to come, let them come." Harlan, Secretary of Defense and Bryce, Chairman of the Joint Chiefs of Staff, didn't need to be in on a whistleblower discussion.

"I'll let you know the time, Mr. President."

"Thank you." I hung up the phone. Although I wasn't usually that brusque, I always felt I needed to be if Marcus was in the room. It was like I had to prove to him I was capable of the job I had been elected to. Yes, it had been years, and I was doing a good job, but I still felt I needed to prove myself. At least to him.

That was my big secret. Well, I had discussed it with Eden, but no one else. From the very beginning, I always thought that Marcus would make a better president than me, and I thought he should have won the nomination instead of me. It all stemmed back to me thinking he was smarter than I am. That probably came from him telling me that for years, but I *believed* it. Eden told me I was nuts to think that, but the fear of my own inadequacy lingered. So when a situation like this developed, I felt defensive. That's stupid, isn't it? See, I knew Marcus was smarter than me.

"There will be a meeting this morning. We'll figure all of this out, and then we can focus on the virus. I haven't read that part yet, but Alan said there were a lot more cases."

"Yes," said Marcus. "It says here that one of their doctors has it." He shook his head. "Dangerous stuff."

I opened the Daily Brief again and searched for the section on the virus. Before I finished reading about it, my phone rang. Fewer than five minutes had passed, but Isa had already arranged the meeting. That's what made her so valuable. She did what needed to be done, and she did it quickly and efficiently. After hanging up the phone, I said to Marcus, "The meeting will be in an hour. Dr. Patel is driving in. If he doesn't make it in time, he will be on the phone so we can consult with him, if need be."

"This is about the whistleblower, not anybody's health. What do we need *him* for?" asked Marcus.

"Because it's about health care workers who handled the evacuees! Duh!" said Jann from the other room. "Shouldn't we know if protective gear was even required? That's why we need him! Duh!"

Marcus looked through the door, but from where he sat, he couldn't see Jann. His face got red, and he looked as if he was going to explode. But all he said was, "Yes, I guess so." Then he stood up and left the room.

Sometimes when I looked at Marcus, I got a cold chill. Bear just growled.

CHAPTER SIXTEEN
Keith Enright

Keith Enright's trucking route took him up and down Interstate 95 from Portland, Maine, down to Jacksonville, Florida. He used to drive all over the United States, but after Glen died, he had changed his route. Now that he and Jeni were getting married, he might limit his route again, but for now, up and down I-95 was his home turf.

His favorite truck stop of the whole trip was outside of Springfield, Virginia, which was a few miles west of D.C. It was always a relief to get out of D.C., and stopping there on his way into the city prepared him for the congestion to come. Eli's Truck and Save had everything a trucker could ever ask for and had it at reasonable prices, as well. He'd bought tires there, chains, serviced his truck, but mostly he stopped to eat. They had great food and pretty waitresses. One in particular, Valerie, was why he hadn't stopped there in more than six months.

Valerie was a nice girl. He liked her, and she liked him. He had spent many a happy night in her company. But she was just a nice girl, not a one-in-a-million girl like Jeni.

Once he met Jeni, he knew his time with Valerie was over. Yes, he should have told Val. It was easier to just not stop there any longer. What did they call that? Ghosting? Yes, that's what it was. Disappear from someone's life with no explanation. It was a terrible thing to do, and he regretted it, but he hadn't wanted to see her cry. She probably cried anyway when he didn't show up week after week after month, but at least he didn't have to see it. He knew it wasn't a kind thing to do, so maybe he was a coward. So be it. Keith never saw himself as a hero, anyway.

There was never any future for them, and he had never promised Val a future. He may be a coward, but he wasn't a liar. They had fun together, and that was the end of it. Keith never called her to set up anything. When he was passing by, he stopped at the truck stop and they got together. There were never any texts or calls between them. But to see her cry when he told her they were done was too much for him. Then again, maybe he had it all wrong. Maybe she wouldn't care at all. All this fretting and worry may be for nothing. He was on his way there to find out.

When he was one hundred miles out, his truck started slowing down. It happened again at fifty miles. Now, just ten miles from Eli's, and he was limping along in the slow lane, at barely the minimum speed. He didn't think his truck wanted to go there any more than he did. The idea made him laugh, but he remembered Glen used to talk about the truck as if it were a person.

Keith pulled into the truck stop and filled up with gas. Usually, he waited until he was on his way out, but he wanted to gas up on his arrival this time, in case he had to make a quick getaway. He had no idea what to expect, but he wanted to be prepared.

Walking into the bright lights, he glanced around, and then reluctantly sat at one of the seats at the long counter. It's where he always sat. There were three waitresses there, but none of them were Valerie. One of them he recognized as Marilyn, one of Valerie's friends. Oops.

Marilyn, a blue-eyed blonde, walked over and put a menu and a cup of coffee in front of him. She had a frown on her face.

Before she said anything, he turned his head in both directions as if looking for someone—although he had already checked. But it got the hoped for response—the answer he was looking for.

"If you're looking for Val, lover boy, she ain't here. She left last month to go back to Kansas and go to school. She got tired of waiting for you to turn up. So where ya been? Jail again?"

Keith inwardly flinched at that. He hoped it didn't show. Val knew about his past but had promised not to tell anyone. He supposed he couldn't blame her, though, after he never showed up.

"No, Marilyn, not jail. I'm getting married."

"What a jerk! You could have at least told her!" She turned to walk away and then faced him again. "What do you want? Don't worry, I won't spit in it, although I'd like to!"

"Cheeseburger and fries. With a vanilla coke."

She wrote it on her pad and walked away. Keith sipped his coffee and pushed the menu to the edge of the counter.

A big burly driver with what looked like prison tattoos on his hands asked, "Where were you in the slammer?"

Keith shrugged. "Just juvie."

He half expected the guy to move over like in that song, but instead, the guy said, "You gonna believe her about spitting?"

"Do you think I should?" asked Keith.

The guy laughed. "No!"

They were both still laughing when Marilyn put the plate in front of him and crossed her arms. "Take a bite," she said.

Keith looked at the cheeseburger and looked at her. He went to pick up the top bun, but she pushed his hand away.

"Take a bite I said!" She had a mean look on her face and kept her arms crossed.

As his eyes moved up to meet hers, he thought about the consequences of his next action. He could walk out and not have to worry about spit on his hamburger. But if he did that, he knew he could never return. She said she wouldn't spit in it, but she could have asked someone else to spit in it. Oh, hell, it was only spit. She wouldn't poison him. Would she?

Without taking his eyes off hers, he picked up the cheeseburger and took a bite. A big one. It tasted fine.

Marilyn's blue eyes danced with laughter. "I told you I wouldn't spit in it! And nobody else did, either." Her laughter abruptly ended. "That doesn't mean you don't deserve it! Because you do! Val wouldn't have wanted me to, so in her honor, I didn't." Then she walked away in a huff.

Keith put the cheeseburger back down on his plate and gingerly opened both ends. It looked as fine as it tasted. She had done nothing to it. He sighed and finished his meal. When he got up to leave, he left the money on the table with a huge tip. The guy next to him was still eating, so he patted him on the back and said, "See ya, bro."

He walked out to his truck, sat there a minute, and sighed in relief. Jeni knew about Valerie—he didn't have any secrets from her. Now he'd have to tell her the rest of the story. She wasn't the jealous kind, but he thought it would make her happy that Valerie was gone.

As he pulled out into traffic, he felt good that not only was that over, but now he could return here. It was the best truck stop on the East Coast. What he didn't know was that at one of his next stops at this place, it would change his life forever.

CHAPTER SEVENTEEN
Wuhan, China

Chui Junjie had been a news anchor for a large state television station. The 47-year-old man had an illustrious career, but had decided to quit his job to report from Wuhan. He described his reason as needing something new and exciting in his life. He got it.

Chui posted more than one hundred videos of interviews to his 2Chat account. He spoke to students at college campuses, employees of funeral homes, and since no doctors would talk to him, he spoke to several nurses.

One nurse, after a promise of anonymity, told him that doctors had known all along there was human-to-human transmission, but their supervisors warned them to keep it quiet. So nobody warned the people.

It was when he was returning from a visit to the Wuhan Institute of Virology that the inevitable happened. A public-security vehicle chased him at high speed. He videoed the whole thing, including himself shouting, "They're chasing me! Please help! I need help!"

Chui arrived back at his apartment, still upset. He wasn't home long when the knock came on the door. The video showed his face looking terrified. Looking through the peephole, he reported two big men outside, both wearing black masks and black clothes. He opened the door, and the video ended.

Chui was never heard from again.

Tiong Weimin was a young 23-year-old man who worked part time in a clothing store and spent the rest of his time as a citizen journalist adding more and more horror stories and frightening videos to his blog each day.

One of his videos showed an overwhelmed medical clinic. Another video that showed fifteen body bags loaded into the back of a van went viral five minutes after uploading it, reaching over one million views. Another very sad video showed a hysterical woman calling her family with a dead relative next to her, slumped over in a wheelchair.

After a prolonged interview, the police confiscated his laptop and ordered him to stop posting rumors that would spread panic online. When he continued posting videos and accounts of dead bodies, police demanded that he leave his apartment. When he refused, they surrounded his home, blocking off any escape routes. Firefighters breaking down his door was the last video he ever posted.

Tiong Weimin was never seen again.

Social media in China reported that after authorities detained Dr. Kung Longwei, he disappeared, whereabouts unknown.

Dr. Cheung Fan, still in intensive care and not doing well, granted one last interview. She said that a healthy society shouldn't have just one voice. And she added that if officials had been honest and disclosed the fact that the new disease was spread person-to-person, it would have been a lot better. She said there should be more openness and transparency.

And then, a victim of the new disease herself, she died quietly in the night.

CHAPTER EIGHTEEN

President

The meeting was about to begin. Everyone was in attendance, including Harlan and Bryce; and Dr. Stan walked in just as I noticed him missing. Bear sat at my feet with his head on my lap.

"All right, everybody. Thank you for coming. There has been a whistleblower incident at Constitution Air Force Base. The first thing we have to determine is if it's true. Dominic, did those people expose themselves to a possibly lethal virus? And were they trained to handle such a situation?"

Dominic Tibble narrowed his eyes, cleared his throat, raised his voice an octave, and said in an authoritarian voice, "Sir, we did everything by the book. Everyone was fully trained and dressed properly in protective gear. The allegations are completely false."

"Excuse me for interrupting, but we have come into possession of some new evidence." Jonathan Sharpe held up some photos. "They're not from the whistleblower, but somebody else came through with a video. We extracted these photos from it."

He handed them across the table to me. Bear didn't move or growl at all. I glanced through the first couple of pictures and they showed some people wearing protective dress with surgical masks and others in full hazmat suits. Shrugging, it looked like Dominic was correct, so I looked up at Jonathan, but he just nodded at the rest of the photos. When I got to the third photo, I gasped. There were two doctors in the frame and possibly a third partially in the frame, wearing business suits and taking people's temperatures. The next picture showed more of the same. Doctors and nurses dressed like a day at the office. "Oh, my God. You better see these, Dominic, because these people are dressed anything but *properly.*"

I handed him the pictures. He tightened his lips, shook his head, and then passed the pictures on to the next person. "Maybe, but they were trained!"

And in his best politically ingratiating look, Marcus said, "Yes, but Dom, if they were properly trained, they wouldn't have dressed like that, would they?" He put the picture with the doctors in business suits in front of him and tapped it with his index finger.

"I have to say," said Dr. Stan, in his usual quiet voice, "whether they were trained or not, people in the medical profession should have known better. Evacuating people from a foreign country is unprecedented. Wouldn't you have thought they would make an effort to protect themselves?"

"Let's get back on track," said Isa. "None of that matters anymore. What matters is this is now a political issue. What are we going to do about it? We need to mitigate the damage that's already been done."

General Bryce Skora, Chairman of the Joint Chiefs of Staff, who I didn't think even needed to be at the meeting, said, "We can downplay the virus, like it didn't matter that they didn't dress properly."

Jonathan Sharpe said, "No, that's not a good idea. A doctor in Wuhan has already died."

"And what happens if hundreds of thousands of people die from it? Or millions? Then where would that put us? No, I agree with Jonathan. We cannot downplay this virus. We don't know enough about it." Dr. Stan kept shaking his head no, even after he finished speaking.

"How about," Marcus said slowly, "if we *imply* that it didn't matter that they weren't dressed, but we don't actually say it?"

"How would we spin that?" asked Jonathan.

"Easy," said Marcus, putting both hands in front of him on the table. "The President goes to California to soothe everybody's hurt feelings. It would show that he isn't afraid of the virus, and they shouldn't be either. It wouldn't hurt if he shook a few hands while he was out there."

I was so happy that he used the term "President" instead of addressing me by name that I must have missed the gist of what he was saying.

"Makes sense," said Jonathan. "But I don't know how safe that would be."

"Not safe at all," said Dr. Stan. "It's out of the question."

"Wait a minute," said Marcus. "Stan, didn't you tell us there was no evidence of human-to-human contact? If not, then there is nothing to worry about."

"Mr. Vice President, lack of evidence is not evidence of lack. This virus is dangerous enough that we need to err on the side of caution—especially for the President of the United States!"

"I'm sorry, Stan, but without knowing if it's even *contagious* or not, I think this is the only answer that I see that would smooth things over *politically*. If he," Marcus nodded toward me, "wants a second term, then he has to do something to make the people believe in him." He picked his hands up off the table and put them down again with a thump. "You want to be reelected, right?" Marcus glared at me, making me feel cornered. Bear looked around and growled.

"Yes, but—" I began.

"It's the only solution," said Marcus. "It's settled. He'll do it. Now who will take care of gathering all the medical people and other personnel who were at the Air Force base?"

Jann stood up and slapped her hand on the table. "No! He can't do that! It's not safe and you know it!" She scowled at Marcus.

Marcus looked at her, the smile fading from his face. "Jannika, *sit down*! This is not your conversation. It has nothing to do with you! Sit down!"

As Jann slowly took her seat, Dr. Stan spoke up. "I agree with Jann. It's not safe. People have already died from this disease. We can't risk the President's life like this."

I felt disembodied at that moment. The conversation swirled around me as they talked about me as if I wasn't there. And I didn't feel like I was there. It was like I was an observer, not a participant.

"Oh, don't make such a big deal about it, Stan. Not one person on that plane tested positive. Right? Yes, of course I'm right. So, in reality, none of those health care workers were at any real risk, and Dan won't be, either."

I noticed that Marcus called me Dan, but at that moment, it didn't matter. My head was spinning, and my heart was beating hard inside my chest.

"*Marcus,*" Dr. Stan said, "the people evacuated from China are not out of quarantine yet. Since we don't know how long the incubation period is on this very new disease, they could very possibly be infected, which means the health care workers *are* very much at risk. If you insist on sending the President to California, you could be signing his death warrant." He spoke with more authority and power than I had ever heard him before. Usually, he was very low key.

Dr. Stan had emphasized *Marcus*, because in all good White House etiquette, he should call him Mr. Vice President. Yay, Dr. Stan.

"And if he doesn't go to California, he would be signing his *political* death warrant. One is a possibility, the other is a certainty." Marcus looked around the room. "We all like working under this administration, right? Well, if we do, then you all must agree with me that Dan must go to California. It's the only choice to patch things up with the whistleblower."

I had remained quiet during this tête-à-tête because it felt like it was out of my hands. The people in this room would make plans for my future, and I would listen and do nothing to intervene. Perhaps if I would have said something, then everything would have turned out differently. But at the time, my thought was, is it a good idea for me to risk getting sick or is it more of a risk not doing anything? Politically, it made sense. A first-term president always worries about reelection.

Nobody said anything, so Marcus continued, "Now let's set this thing up. Dominic, you will be in charge of getting all the workers together at the Air Force Base. Isa, you make travel arrangements for the President." His voice droned on, but I didn't hear the rest until Dr. Stan spoke again.

"Let the record show," he nodded toward Jann, "that I am totally against this, but if you're going to do it, make sure that it's done outside. There is less risk that way."

"How much of this is for public consumption?" asked Corrie Corrigan.

Marcus didn't even wait for me to answer. "Not much of it. Just say that the President will be traveling to California to personally thank all the medical personnel who participated in the Wuhan airlift."

"What about the whistleblower allegations? That will get out if it hasn't already. That kind of thing always does," said Corrie.

Marcus nodded. "Say that a whistleblower has come forward, and the President will personally investigate the charges."

The conversation went on, but I couldn't focus. Even strong, decisive men have their weak moments. That was one of mine. I stood up and said, "You all arrange this. I'm going back to my office." Jann stood up to accompany me until she realized she needed to stay until the end of the meeting, so she sat back down. I had a photographic memory for everything I saw with my eyes, but conversations—anything I only heard with my ears

—didn't last very long. That's why Jann was so valuable. She wrote down every word. I should have paid more attention.

CHAPTER NINETEEN
The man

He walked down the hallway toward his office, barely able to contain his excitement. Stepping inside, he closed the door softly behind him. A huge smile erupted on his face, and he began clapping his hands together so no one could hear the sound but him. He jumped up and tried to click his heels together, but he wasn't as nimble as he used to be.

Sitting at his desk, he opened the bottom drawer and pulled out the catcher's mitt. He threw it into the air and caught it again and again, whistling the entire time.

What a stroke of luck this was! Who knew a whistleblower could step in and help him in his quest to *do something*? Dr. Patel had said that it was important for the meeting to be outside to minimize the risk of exposure to the disease. And he was sure that bitch, Isa, would follow Patel's recommendations to the letter. No matter. He was not without power himself. He could do a thing or two to push things in the right direction. No doubt about that.

Mr. Big Shot, Mr. President Dan Indigo, sat there like the ignorant fool he was while the rest of us discussed the situation. Patel didn't want him to go and had argued against it, but in the end, the idiot was going. Oh, what a relief it was! Finally, the president might get what was coming to him. And it wasn't something he had to plan. It happened like it was supposed to happen. That proved to him he was moving in the right direction. He was *doing something,* and that was everything.

Inspired, he tapped out the number on his phone. "Honey, don't bother cooking tonight. We're going out to celebrate! I'm about to change the world!"

CHAPTER TWENTY

Jann

Jann was horrified. It was all arranged. Dan would travel to California and meet with all those people who had probably been exposed to the deadly virus. She wondered why he didn't stand up for himself in there. Although she had looked at him at one point, and he looked as if he was about to either get sick right there at the table or else faint. Politically, she understood he needed to do something in defense from the whistleblower. But to put himself in harm's way? It was too much.

When she got back to her office, she wanted to talk to him, but his office door was closed. He was talking, but not in his normal voice. He was probably telling Eden about it, and she would be none too happy. If he exposed himself to the disease, he exposed her as well. And if she couldn't talk him out of it, no one could, so Jann knew there was no reason to even try.

As she pondered this, the door in back opened, and Eden walked in with her cell phone to her ear. She looked at Jann and said, "Could you take care of Bear for two or three days?"

"Sure! Of course!"

Then Eden walked into the Oval Office without even bothering to knock. That had never happened before, but it only took a minute for Jann to figure out why. The person on the phone with

Eden was Dan, and now their conversation had gone up a few decibels. If Jann could make it out correctly, Eden insisted she would go with him. If he was going to risk his life—and hers if he caught it—then she was going to be right there by his side. It was not easy talking Eden out of something once she had her mind made up, so Jann was pretty sure Eden would win this argument.

A few minutes later, Eden walked out of the office, swaying her hips and smiling. She left the door open behind her, walked up to Jann, and whispered in her ear, "I'm going, and I'm sure you'll know when before I do, so that's when we need you to take care of Bear."

"No problem, Mrs. First Lady!"

Eden sashayed back out the door from whence she came, and Dan came storming in. "That blasted woman insists on going with me! She won't take no for an answer!"

"You knew she was that kind of woman when you married her, Mr. President."

"Dammit, Jann! That's *why* I married her! But you don't have to remind me!"

That's when Isa walked in, all six feet and two hundred pounds of her. She was one tough broad.

"Mr. President. I have everything arranged," she said in her gruff, manly voice. "You will meet the people *outside* on the broad front lawn. Dr. Patel said it was much less risky that way, so I insisted that it be outside." She smiled at him. "Don't worry, I look out for you, Mr. President."

"You're going to have to look out for the First Lady, too. She insists on going," grumbled Dan.

"I can arrange that. Will she be meeting all the medical professionals too?"

"I'd like to say no, Isa, but if I know Eden, she will insist on it!"

"I'll take care of it, sir," she said and treaded heavily out of the room.

"She's good, Mr. President," said Jann. "That's one thing Marcus did right."

"What do you mean *Marcus*? *I* chose her! Marcus tried to talk me out of it!"

Before Jann could let that sink in, the phone rang, and when she answered it, her face lit up.

"Mom?"

"Ricky! I've been so worried about you. Thank you for calling. I didn't want to call and wake you in case you were sleeping."

"I wanted to let you know how much better I am. I'm still coughing, but not as much. And my fever is down. Keesha still won't let me go out yet. But we'll now be there sooner than expected. We're flying out as soon as my fever is normal for 24 hours. The new job wants me to start as soon as, so we're flying instead of driving." Cough, cough, cough. "That's the first time I've coughed in an hour! Anyway, we're shipping our cars out and hopefully will fly out in a day or two."

"Ricky, I'm so glad you're feeling better. You sounded awful yesterday."

"I felt awful yesterday. But I rested all day, drank fluids, did what Keesha told me to do," Ricky chuckled into the phone, "and I'm much better today."

"What a relief! Do you need me to pick you up at the airport?"

"No, I'll need a car to get to work, but Keesha will need a ride during the day to get groceries or do errands. If you could help out there, it would be wonderful."

"Of course. No problem. She can borrow the car whenever she needs it. I'm so excited that you're moving here! And I'm totally looking forward to meeting Keesha and Jace."

"Keesha is nervous about it, and Jace doesn't know what to think."

"Tell Keesha not to worry. I'm not the Wicked Witch of the West or anything." Jann hesitated and then quietly asked, "You didn't portray me as the wicked witch, did you?"

"Of course not, Mom! Why would you even think that? It's just *first time meeting the family* jitters. That's all. You'll get along great. And Jace is a pleasure to be around. He's a great kid."

Jann sighed, and Ricky continued.

"Anyway, I just wanted to let you know. I'll keep you posted. Gotta run now. Love you, Ma."

"Bye, Ricky. I love you, too."

After hanging up the phone, Jann wondered why Ricky would even ask why she would think that. He hadn't returned to the East Coast once since leaving for the service, and he would only let her visit him every few years and for a brief time. She never understood that. The last time she had visited was before he met Keesha, and that was more than two years ago.

She thought maybe she owed Keesha—not just for taking good care of Ricky, but for convincing him to move back here. Yes, it was Keesha who had absolved him of the guilt he felt from so many long years ago. She was certain of that.

Jann thought he was a good man—he had a good job, and all indications were that he treated Keesha and Jace well. But the truth was that she had no idea.

What a surprise it would be for her—and Ricky—when he turned out to be a hero.

CHAPTER TWENTY-ONE
President

Two days later, the morning of the day Eden and I were to leave for California, I sat at my desk still pondering my actions—or lack thereof—at the meeting the other day. It wasn't very presidential of me to sit there and have everyone talk about me like I wasn't even there. But the people around me were bright people who looked out for me. I trusted them.

The entire episode felt confusing to me. Should I go to California and risk getting this disease? Was it even a risk? The disease wasn't in the country yet, and perhaps never would be. Nobody evacuated from China had it, and therefore the workers who helped them with re-entry into the country shouldn't have it, either. But Dr. Stan said that since they don't know how long the incubation period is, there is still a risk. And the people from China *were* still under quarantine.

Then there was the other side of the equation that confused me even more. The whistleblower. If that wasn't dealt with correctly, it could affect my re-election. If I handled correctly, then it could be a boon to my re-election.

That is why I essentially stood aside and let the best minds in the country decide for me. The chance of risking my life by catching the disease could alter my judgment. Maybe it wasn't a risk at all. Maybe it was. At this point, there was no way to know. So it was best to allow the people on that committee decide for me. Would I catch the disease? Would it even be an issue? Time would tell.

I pounded my fist on the desk and punched in Dr. Stan's number. "Dr. Stan? Listen. We can't go on calling this thing 'the disease' or 'the weird pneumonia.' I need a name!"

"Well, technically, it's a coronavirus, but so is the common cold, so let's not refer to it as that. The latest thing I've learned is that they think it came from bats and mutated its way into human beings. We have swine flu and bird flu. The World Health Organization calls it bat flu. I think we should, too. What do you think?"

"That's perfect! I like it! Thank you!"

"Listen, Mr. President, I'm glad you called before you left. Please remember to only see those people outside. That is of utmost importance. Absolutely do not go inside a building with any of them, even for a minute. We don't know the scope of this disease yet, and I couldn't think of anything worse than the President of the United States being the first one to come down with bat flu. *Just don't go inside* with those people."

"No worries, Dr. Stan. Isa has it all arranged that we're meeting on the lawn or something. There are no plans for me to go inside with anyone. Don't worry about it."

"All right. Have a safe trip. Let me examine you when you get back, and be sure not to touch your face as you're shaking their hands, and to wash your hands thoroughly when you finish with them."

"I'll be fine. I'll see you when I get back." We said our goodbyes, and I hung up the phone.

Before I figured out what task to complete before we had to leave, I noticed Eden at the door, holding Jann's hand and pulling her into the room. Jann closed the door as they stepped through.

"Dan," Eden said, standing at the side of my desk, "I'm sorry but I can't go to California with you."

"Eden, I didn't want you to go, anyway! So what's the big deal?" That's when I noticed that all the color had drained from her face. "Eden, what's wrong?"

She broke down then and wrapped her arms around me as I rose to accept her into mine. "What's wrong, sweetie? What's wrong?"

"It's Zoey, Dan. It's Zoey."

I put her at arm's length so I could look at her face, still colorless. "What's happened? An accident? Is she okay?"

"No. Zoey has breast cancer." Eden pulled me back to her and started sobbing uncontrollably. "She starts chemo tomorrow, and I'm going to be there with her. Aaron is still in England with his work and can't return for another week or two. I need to be with her."

Jann had come over and was hugging Eden from the side and rubbing her back. Tears were streaming down her face, too. She had known Zoey since before she was born. "Oh, Eden, I'm so sorry. Poor Zoey. But she'll be fine. I know it."

A mix of emotions washed over me. I felt grateful Eden wasn't going with me to California to be possibly exposed to who knows what. But breast cancer scared me. My daughter had breast cancer. My oldest child. My sweet girl, Zoey. "When are you leaving, Eden?"

She had calmed down some and pulled away from me. Jann kept rubbing her back. "As soon as I pack. I came here to tell you first. I'm leaving now."

This was a situation that I didn't know how to handle. "Should I call her?"

"No, Dan, don't. Zoey said she didn't want to talk about it. She doesn't even know that I'm coming. But I need to be there with her. I can't let her go through this alone. And I know it's really hard on a person, so I'll be there to take care of Rose and Sage."

Eden hesitated and then continued. "Dan, I know you don't approve that Zoey declined Secret Service protection. But you know for a trial attorney it makes sense."

"She made that decision ages ago. Why bring it up now?"

"Because I don't want any agents with me while I take care of her."

"Eden!" I said in my sternest husband voice.

"I'm sorry, Dan. I've decided. I'm leaving now."

Settling down some, I said, "You'll let me know about Zoey, then?"

"Yes, of course." Eden hugged me again and walked out of the room with Jann's arm around her.

When she left, I just kept staring after her. Would my daughter be okay? Could she survive the big C? And would I survive my trip to California?

CHAPTER TWENTY-TWO

Jann

Jann sat in her rocking chair with Sneezy in the place of honor on her lap. Bear lay at her feet. She had seen Eden off, both of them hugging and crying. And later in the day she had seen Dan off, him acting stoically nonchalant and her begging him to be careful. Besides Ricky, those two were the most important people in the world to her. Worrying about them—and Zoey—kept her busy while she was waiting for Ricky, Keesha, and Jace to arrive. They had missed a connecting flight and were a couple of hours late.

She jumped when the knock came at the door and Bear barked. "Bear, quiet. Stay!" So involved in her worries about Dan and Zoey, the time had flown by.

Opening the door, Ricky rushed into her arms, picked her up, and swung her around. "Mom! I've missed you!"

When he put her down, she looked up at him—she was five feet two inches, and he was well over six feet. "Oh, Ricky, how I've missed you!" She threw her arms around him and hugged him again.

Then she took a long look at her son, whom she hadn't seen in so long. Even in this cold, he had bare arms covered with colorful tattoos. His hair hung in long dreadlocks down his chest.

And he had an earring in one ear. Grabbing hold of one of his dreads, she said, "And what's this?"

Keesha looked up at Jann's son with love in her eyes. "They're wonderful, aren't they?"

If it was good for them, then she was okay with it. "Oh! Where are my manners? Please come in."

When Keesha stepped through the door with little Jace by the hand, Jann put her arms around the woman and whispered, "Welcome to my home. It is very nice to meet you." Then she bent down and looked eye to eye with Jace—he was the cutest little boy she had seen since Ricky was a boy. Opening her arms, she said, "Do you think you could give this old lady a hug?"

Jace put his arms around her neck and said, "Yes, but you're not old."

Jann laughed and said, "I'm keeping this one!" She held out her arm. "Come in and make yourself at home."

Keesha looked at her before walking any further. "We heard a dog. Is it safe to come in?"

Ricky put his arm around her and tried to lead her through the entryway. "Come on, Keesh. My mom wouldn't have a dog that was dangerous." Then he looked at his mom. "Would you, Mom? I didn't even know you had a dog."

"Bear isn't my dog, he's Dan's and Eden's."

Ricky held his hands up in the air and rolled his eyes in mock amazement. "Ohhhh, the president's dog. Is it still okay if we touch him?"

Jann knew it was mock because she remembered how close they were before Ricky got into trouble. And she knew from tidbits that Ricky slipped out with now and then that Ricky missed the connection.

"Oh, Ricky," she gave him a gentle push, "I know you don't mean that."

"You mean the President of the New-nited states?" asked Jace.

"Yes, Jace, the very same. Would you like to meet his dog?"

Keesha had a worried look on her face. "Are you sure it's all right?"

Ricky took a step back and put his arm around her. "My Keesha is afraid of dogs. She got bitten when she was a kid, and now she won't let us have a dog. Right, Jace?"

"Right!" said Jace and high-fived Ricky. "And we want a dog!"

Keesha pulled away from Ricky and looked up at him. She was taller than Jann but shorter than Ricky. "It's the *only* thing I'm afraid of!"

Ricky laughed and hugged her. "She's right. This is one tough cookie I have here."

Jann liked the way they were together. Comfortable. Intimate yet respectful. And Jace was a doll. "No worries about Bear. He'll be fine. If you're uncomfortable, I'll call him off. Bear! Come!"

The big dog lumbered in, smiling his toothy grin. Ricky knelt down so his face was at the same level as Bear's. "Bear? Friends?" Bear leaped over and started licking Ricky's face. Ricky put his hands into the thick fur around the dog's neck, while Bear continued to cover him with wet kisses. "Jace? You want some of this?"

"Yeah!" Jace came over, and Bear started licking him in the face. Giggling, Jace tumbled to the floor, with Ricky following suit. Soon the three of them were rolling around on the floor, with Bear making sounds that were somewhere between growling and howling. But there was nothing angry or mean in the sound. Anyone could tell—even Keesha, who was deathly afraid of dogs—recognized that sound as pure joy.

Jann could see it on her face, but asked anyway, "That doesn't scare you, does it?"

Keesha inhaled deeply and shook her head from side to side. "No, I can feel joy from all three of them. I, um, I'd like to join in, but I don't want to interrupt."

Jann took Keesha's hand, knelt down and pulled Keesha with her. "Bear and gentlemen?" The big dog hesitated and looked up. Jace was on his back, giggling. Ricky was out of breath from being so recently sick. "Can we join in, please?"

Ricky leaned up from the floor and pulled Keesha down beside him. Bear immediately began licking her face. Jann stood up and felt immense happiness watching them. Her family. Ricky and Keesha may be just boyfriend and girlfriend, but it felt much deeper than that. She liked the girl and hoped that Ricky would someday come to his senses and get serious.

Retreating to her rocking chair, she watched until the four of them lay on the floor, exhausted. Even Bear lay with his head on his forepaws and his tongue lolling out of his mouth. He probably hadn't had that much playtime in a long time.

Finally, Ricky sat up and pulled Keesha up. "See? I told you she was fearless. Just like that, and she's over her fear!" Then he bent back over and picked Jace up and carried him to the couch. The little boy had a long day with the flights and all the traveling. Ricky lay him down on the couch, and then he and Keesha cuddled up on the other end.

"Well," he said, "Keesha and I have something to tell you."

"Wait," said Keesha. "Mrs. White, I just want to thank you for bringing that dog in here. I've never had an experience like that in my life. I've always been so afraid to get near dogs—especially big dogs. But Bear is wonderful!" Bear looked in her direction at the mention of his name and thumped his tail on the floor. "I want to get a dog now!"

Jann and Ricky laughed, and Jace slept through the news. "That's great, Keesha. But I can't take the credit. I'm just babysitting. Dan is in California and Eden is in Pennsylvania. Oh, Ricky, it's Zoey. She has breast cancer." Ricky was six when Zoey was born, and he had always considered her his little sister.

"Oh, no. I hope she's okay."

"We're all praying and keeping our fingers crossed," said Jann. "Now what about your news?"

"Keesha and I are getting married. And I'm going to adopt Jace."

"Ricky, that's wonderful! Congratulations! I'm so happy to have you in the family, Keesha. And please call me Mom, not

Mrs. White." She clapped her hands. "And now I have a grand-son, and he is so cute! I just love him!"

Ricky stood up and pulled a sleeping Jace into his arms. "Well, Mom, now that we've told you the big news, it's time for us to leave. It's been a long day for all of us, and I need to get this guy into bed. No need to show us where the place is. I checked it out on Google maps and know that it's just a few doors down."

Jann stood up and followed them to the door. She tapped a sleepy-eyed Jace and said, "What do you think of your new gramma?"

"I have a gramma?" he asked and then his head slumped over again, asleep. Keesha was so touched by the interaction that Jann saw tears come to her eyes.

Then, for the first time, she looked at her son's back. When he was playing with Bear, he was mostly on his back, and other than that, he had been facing her. But now she saw that he wore a denim vest with a picture of a motorcycle on the back. Over-laid onto the motorcycle were the letters RPC.

She started putting it together—the earring, the tattoos, the denim vest with the motorcycle on it. She knew he had a motor-cycle—but this—this was something altogether different.

A shudder went through Jann's whole body. Fear crept up-ward until it lodged in her throat, making her question almost a croak. "Ricky, are you in a motorcycle gang?"

CHAPTER TWENTY-THREE

President

I woke up early, even though the interaction with the medical group wasn't for several more hours. Constitution Air Force Base was full service. They cleared out the fitness center for my benefit, and I did a shortened version of my regular morning routine with my secret service agents standing by. The reason I shortened it was because the men at the base are serving their country, and I've always thought that being kind was better than being selfish. After coming back to my suite and taking a shower, I relaxed on the bed and called Eden. I wanted to know how everything was going with Zoey.

After the hellos and I love yous and miss yous were out of the way, I asked her about Zoey. Her answer stunned me. Eden reminded me of several months back when little Rose had an infection on her knee. She had skinned her knee, and no one— not even Rose—had noticed that it had gotten red and inflamed. But their dog, Tika, a solid black, female German Shepherd, started pushing her nose on little Rose's knee through her jeans. When Zoey looked, she saw the infection and started treating it right away. Luckily, they didn't have to see the doctor.

A week ago, Tika started pushing her nose right at the edge of Zoey's breast, and she wouldn't stop. Zoey couldn't feel a thing beneath where the dog was pushing, but after the experience with Rose's knee, Zoey paid attention and made an appointment to see her doctor.

The doctor didn't believe her, of course, but Zoey kept insisting. So he scheduled a new mammogram and ultrasound. When they both came up negative, the doctor felt certain he was right, and it was nothing. But Zoey wouldn't let it go. So the doctor told her to go home and make a mark on her breast *exactly* where the dog was pushing. Tika again pushed and pushed, and Zoey found a dry spot where one of Tika's nostrils had been. She marked it and returned to the doctor the next day.

He inserted a scalpel into the exact spot and sent off the liquid results to be biopsied, while reassuring Zoey again that he was right, and it was nothing. The doctor was wrong. It turned out to be a severe, aggressive form of breast cancer that, left untreated, could have been deadly. And ironically, if the doctor had been more careful and incised *around* the place instead of *directly on* the place that Tika had indicated, Zoey might not have needed chemo at all. But the doctor never believed the dog had actually found anything, so he wasn't careful. He had only done the procedure to appease her.

"So anyway," said Eden, "she goes in for her first chemo today. The chemo itself will be between one and two hours, but there is time before and time after that she has to be there for various procedures, so we will be most of the afternoon."

"Call me when she finishes? I should be on my way home. The event shouldn't take long at all, and I should be home sometime this evening. Out of danger. I'm still glad you're not here with me, but I'm not glad about the reason."

"I know, dear, but I'm with Zoey now, and she'll be fine."

"All right. I love you and miss you and will talk to you later."

"Love you, dear, bye."

I hung up the phone and thought about how grateful I was that Tika was such a great dog and that Zoey was smart enough to follow up on it. She would be fine. Of that, I was sure.

While I waited for the event, I sat down to read a book. That's how I thought of it: an event. A politically motivated event. I just had to get through it and get home. It wouldn't be long now.

A knock on the door startled me.

"They're ready for you, Mr. President," said Derek Moran, one of the Secret Service agents who accompanied me.

"Be right there, Derek." I was ready; I just needed to take a deep breath and get on with it.

The ride over in the car was brief, but long enough for me to feel nervous. When we stopped, I took a deep breath to calm my nerves and stepped out of the car.

Twenty-two people had lined up on a broad expanse of lawn. Men and women who were doctors, nurses, and other medical personnel. I thought I recognized one or two who were in the pictures. Smiling my best smile, I walked up to the woman on the end of the line and shook her hand. After she gave me her name, I said, "Thank you for your service. We appreciate it."

Somewhere in the middle of the pack, when I shook the man's hand, he said, "I'm Dr. Edgar Croft." Out of all the people I had already talked to, he was the only one who addressed himself as doctor, and I knew for certain that he wasn't the only doctor here. At least two women that I saw had name tags on that said *Dr.* The man took me so off guard that I replied, "I'm President Dan Indigo. I appreciate your service." He smiled, and I moved on. But I remembered Dr. Edgar Croft very well from the pictures. He was one of the doctors wearing a business suit and no protective gear at all. I restrained myself from wiping my hand on my pants before I shook the next person's hand. Just a few more handshakes, and I could wash up and go home.

But that's not what happened.

CHAPTER TWENTY-FOUR

Jann

Jannika White sat at her desk in the White House with a smile on her face and Bear at her feet. Gone was the fear that wracked her body last night. In its place was a quiet, warm glow of pride in her son.

When she had asked the question the night before, Ricky had turned around, looked at Keesha, and said, "This is going to take a while. Do you mind, Keesh?"

With her hand on his arm, she looked up at him. "No, of course not."

So Ricky walked back into the living room and put a sleeping Jace across his lap with his head on Keesha's lap. "It's a national organization, Mom. I've been involved in it for a few years now, and they have a chapter here, too. I've already transferred my membership."

"Why would you have to transfer?" asked Jann.

"It's a big deal to become a member. They had me fingerprinted and everything."

"I don't understand, Ricky. I've never heard of being fingerprinted for a motorcycle gang."

"Mom," he said patiently, "it's not a gang. Let me just finish, okay?" When Jann nodded, he continued. "It's an organization that protects children. We work with state and local officials. RPC stands for 'Riders Protecting Children.'

"You know how sometimes one parent gets a restraining order against the other parent after he or she discovers child abuse? And you know how many times the *bad parent* ignores those restraining orders? That's where we come in. The bad parent comes to call and instead of accosting a scared spouse and child, they have *us* to deal with.

"And you know how when the case comes to trial, often an abused child feels too scared to speak, because the bad parent is there glaring at them and reminding them again how they threatened them not to speak." Ricky eased Jace from his lap and stood up. He placed his arms across his chest and glared at her. "So if I'm in court with the kid, it's like magic—the bad parent doesn't dare try the glaring routine." Then Ricky smiled at her lovingly. "And when I look at the kid like this and flex my muscle," Ricky did it, "the kid isn't afraid anymore. Because the kid knows that before the perpetrator can get to him or her, the perp has to come through *me* first."

Jann had wanted to cry as he told the story. When she was growing up in the projects, there was a family where the father would get drunk and beat up the wife and kid. She still remembered signing the kid's cast and not knowing what to say besides *get well soon*. For someone—her son—to stick up for these kids touched her more than she could say.

Ricky sat on the edge of the couch and leaned forward. Keesha stroked Jace's head, who still slept. "It's such a great program. You can't imagine the light in a kid's eyes when he or she goes through the welcome ceremony and becomes part of our 'family.' Two of us are assigned to each kid, and we do what has to be done." He shook his head. "I wouldn't have moved back here if RPC hadn't had a chapter. It means too much to me. I feel like I'm doing important work."

Jann, tears running down her cheeks, stood up and rushed across the room to put her arms around her son. "You *are* doing important work, Ricky. And I can't tell you how proud I am of

89

you." Jann stood up. "Now go. Get out of here. I know you're all tired. I love you all."

Jann sighed at her desk and allowed a tear to run down her cheek at her thoughts. Bear stood up and licked it away. She buried her head in the dog's fluff. "Thank you, Bear."

"What's *he* doing here?" Marcus's sharp voice pulled Jann out of her reverie

"I'm taking care of him while the President is out of town." Bear raised his hackles, growled softly, and showed his teeth.

"A vicious dog like that has no place in the West Wing."

Jann stood up to make her point. "He has as much right to be here as you do. More. And he's not vicious except toward *you*."

Jonathan Sharpe walked into the office. Bear looked at him and growled, but didn't stand up like he often did when Jon entered the room.

"Yeah, right," said Marcus, pointing to the dog and looking at Jon. He tried the handle of the door to the Oval Office. "Why isn't this open? I need to go in."

Jann frowned, closed her eyes, and said, "Duhhhh. He's not here." She knew it was unprofessional, but she also knew Marcus. If she showed any sign of weakness, he would pounce on her like a cat on a mouse.

"You have the key. Let me in."

Although she wanted to scream out, "Hell no, I won't let you in!" instead, she said with all the professionalism she could muster, "No, *Mr. Vice President*. It's not your office."

"I left something in there! I need it!" said Marcus.

"Then have the president call or text me. And I'll open it then."

"He's too busy. He's doing the ceremony today and—" Abruptly he shut up. Then, "You won't open it?"

"No, I'm sorry. It's not my place."

Marcus snorted and stomped off down the hall.

Jon and Jann looked after him, then Jon asked, "When will the President be back?"

"Supposed to be later tonight," said Jann.

"Don't count on it," said Marcus from down the hallway. "Oh, and Jon, I need to talk to you. Can you call me or see me later?"

To Marcus, he said, "Yes, Mr. Vice President, I need to talk to you as well." Then to Jann, "I'll talk to him tomorrow then." Jon followed Marcus down the hallway.

Minutes later, Jann heard voices in the Oval Office. She recognized them. Although the door from her office to the Oval Office was locked, there were three other doors. So Marcus found his way inside, despite her protests.

And Jonathan Sharpe? What was he doing in there with Marcus? Were they in cahoots? Cahoots for what, she didn't know. But she knew she didn't like it. And whose idea was it? Marcus had initiated entry, but it looked like Jon followed like a little lamb. Which came first? The chicken or the egg?

CHAPTER TWENTY-FIVE

President

After getting to the end of the line, all the handshaking and politicking finished, I had an enormous smile on my face, because I knew my exposure to the unknown was over, and I could go home. Derek Moran was right beside me, ready to escort me back to my official vehicle.

The man dressed in military attire, who had led us out to the main lawn, came and shook my hand. I thought that was the final goodbye, but he cleared his throat, turned toward the twenty-two people and announced, "Ladies and gentlemen, please join me in thanking the President for coming out here to see us." He began clapping and everyone else followed suit. When the clapping died down, he continued, "And I want to tell you the exciting news! I just received a call from the White House, and President Dan Indigo will join us for lunch in the James Madison Officer's Club!" Everyone starting cheering and clapping again.

It was all I could do to keep from falling over. Instead of being almost over, it was just beginning. Dr. Stan's words kept swimming around in my brain—"Just don't go inside"—making me feel seasick. Unless the Officer's Club had outside seating, I was in for it. Looking at my watch, I saw it was almost one o'clock. Would I have time to call Eden?

"Lunch will be served at thirteen hundred hours! See you there!" Then the military guy turned to me. "Shall we go, Mr. President?" He pointed to a building not far from where we stood. "It's right over there. We can walk."

I looked at Derek and nodded. He nodded back. With Derek at one side and the military man—what was his name again? He had introduced himself earlier. That's right. Arthur. Major Arthur something. Gavin Dennison walked behind me.

The officer's club was in a nondescript beige building that needed painting. A sign over the door announced *James Madison Officer's Club*. James Madison, although considered the father of the constitution, was one of many men who created it, and the document itself was composed of several documents blended together. Thinking about that took my mind off what I was about to do. Risk my life for the sake of politics. There was still a chance they had outside seating, but it looked doubtful. Maybe if the lunch was in a large conference room with a lot of air circulation, it would be almost as good as outside.

The major held the door open for me. Derek walked in first and looked around before he nodded his head that it was safe for me to enter. I walked in with Gavin following close behind.

Looking around, I saw my worst fears realized. The narrow room accommodated several narrow tables. I had hoped that I would be seated at the head of the table, which would have limited my exposure somewhat. But the table, with chairs on either side of it, stood between the bar and the outside wall. The narrowness of the table precluded a "head of the table." A place card in the middle of the table had my name on it. Shit. Arrangements couldn't have been much worse if someone had set me up.

To the right of the narrow table sat another narrow table with several people seated and eating their lunch. At the bar, two men sat there nursing beers and watching the silent television monitor above. The scene was getting worse and worse. I had half expected them to close the club for the hour we'd be there for lunch. But again, no luck.

Various airplane parts and sports memorabilia hung on the walls as decorations. The bar had bright green, albeit fading, padding and all the chairs in the room matched. I took the one opposite my name plate and sat down. What little room there was behind me, Derek and Gavin stood on guard. But in these close quarters with these medical people, I didn't think there was a chance of catching a bullet. The real danger here was catching the dreaded disease—the one called bat flu.

People were trickling in and sitting at the table. I smiled at everyone, but when Dr. Edgar Croft plopped himself down in front of me, I had to restrain every bone in my body from getting up and leaving the area. A hint of a frown might have escaped my lips. "Dr. Croft," I said, trying to conceal my horror at this even worse turn of events.

"President Indigo. So nice to see you again. You're welcome to call me Ed."

He coughed in his hand, but he had made his hand into a loose fist with a hole at the end that was facing me. Uh-oh. The entire scene was a nightmare. Who was it who had arranged this lunch, anyway? My time in California was supposed to be a quick meet and greet, and that's all. How did this happen?

Those questions eluded me as I made conversation with Ed and the other doctors and medical personnel. Gavin exited to the kitchen while the cooks prepared my meal, and when it arrived, it tasted surprisingly good. There were more than a few coughs at the table, lots of laughing, and since it was a bar, plenty of drinking went on, too. I admit that I imbibed more than I should have. But I felt so overwhelmed at the circumstances, I had to do something to hide my anxiety.

By the time I walked out of there hours later, with Gavin and Derek by my side, there were more than a couple of times they had to help me stay on my feet as we made our way to the presidential vehicle. That was the least of my problems.

CHAPTER TWENTY-SIX

The man

It was dark. Everyone had left, even Jannika and the damn dog. Even so, he locked the door of his office as he walked in. Then he sat in his chair and put his feet up on the desk. That wasn't something he normally did—it wasn't professional. But he could do it now. He could do just about anything now.

But it wasn't time to celebrate. Although there was a good chance that the Damn Dan Indigo was exposed during his oh-so-well-planned lunch—the man stopped a moment to pat himself on the back—that wasn't necessarily the end of it. The disease didn't kill everyone. So he had to make a plan to make sure that the transition of power would be smooth and flawless. He had to *do something* to make sure Dan Indigo was out of the White House for good.

Putting his feet back on the floor, he leaned back in his chair and began poking at his cuticles. Then he put a finger into his nose and pulled out a booger. He held it up in front of him and for a second considered eating it. Just because he could. But he hadn't done that since he was a kid, so he rolled it between his fingers and flicked it away. The time was coming that he could do any damn thing he wanted.

An idea flitted by in his mind. Sitting up straighter, he grabbed it and ran it through, dissecting every piece of it. A slight smile pricked at his lips. Then it broadened. Depending on how the disease progressed in the United States, it might work. And it was a brilliant plan, even if he did have to say so himself.

After taking a deep breath, he settled back into his chair again. He didn't want to get ahead of himself, and if he pushed the idea before its time, then he could ruin everything. Now was a time for patience. Slow and steady wins the race. The plan was solid, and if God was truly on his side, it would work. Dan Indigo would fall into the trap willingly, and if he didn't, then he could simply be pushed. And that would feel so good! He imagined the feeling so thoroughly, and it pleased him so much that he giggled. Dan fucking Indigo was done, one way or the other. Done.

CHAPTER TWENTY-SEVEN

President

I slept during the long plane ride home on Air Force One. Between the anxiety of the day and all the liquor I had consumed, I needed a nap. Once at the White House, I would have fallen asleep in my clothes, but Eden called on the house phone. I had turned off my cell phone before lunch and had forgotten to turn it back on. If there was a national emergency, one of my secret service agents would notify me.

"Dan, are you all right? You sound strange."

"Hello, Eden. I was almost asleep. It's been a tough day. I drank myself almost silly at the Air Force base."

"Drank? I don't understand. I thought it was a quick meet and greet and then you'd fly home."

"Oh, dear, Eden. I don't even want to tell you. Someone arranged for me to have lunch with all those people. So I had to stay."

"What imbecile would do that!" It wasn't a question, and Eden's voice got that high pitch to it, like when she's upset. "Didn't you tell me that Dr. Stan said make sure you don't go inside with them?"

"Yes, he said that. I wasn't happy about it myself, but after the Major announced it to all the people, I couldn't very well back out. He said someone from the White House had arranged it."

"Yeah, I'll bet," said Eden, clearly controlling her rage. "Now what? We sit around and wait for you to get this thing?"

"At this point, Eden, there is nothing I can do about it. How's Zoey?"

"She's been sick on and off since we got home. Her nausea started while she was getting the IV infusion. You know how sensitive her stomach's always been."

"Oh, poor thing. I'm so glad you're there for her."

"It was an ordeal. It took a long time and a lot of paperwork before they even gave her chemo. Since they have her scheduled for several infusions, the next time she comes in they will put in a port so the whole thing will be easier."

"What's a port?"

"It's a little tube that's attached to the vein. Then they don't have to stick her with a needle each time."

"It sounds gross. The whole situation sounds horrible, and I feel so badly that my baby has to go through this."

"At least I'm here with her. I'm going to sleep now, Dan. I've been trying to call you for hours. Did you turn off your phone?"

"Yup. When I went to lunch."

"Oh, okay." She yawned into the phone. "G'night. I love you."

"Love you, too, honey, and tell Zoey that I love her, too."

After changing into my pajamas, I fell asleep and didn't wake up until the phone rang again while it was still dark. "Eden? Is everything okay?"

"Mr. President, it's Stan. I apologize for calling you at home, but I need to talk to you."

I sat up in bed and tried to clear my head. It was still dark. This time of year, I always got up in the dark to work out. Still, it was disconcerting. "Yes, Dr. Stan. What can I help you with *this early*?"

"China has confirmed human to human transmission."

"Oh my God!"

"The World Health Organization called an Emergency Committee to ascertain whether they should announce an international public health emergency. We need to do something."

"I'll call a meeting of our bat flu members."

"No, Mr. President. This is more serious than that. We need to do something the whole cabinet will need to approve."

"Oh, for crying out loud, Dr. Stan, is that really necessary?"

"More information is coming in all the time, Mr. President. And none of it is good."

"All right. I'll get Isa to arrange it. I assume you want it done today?"

"The sooner the better, Mr. President."

"I'll take care of it and see you later. Goodbye." I hung up the phone harder than I should have. But drinking so much the day before had shrunk my tolerance level. That's my excuse, anyway. Instead of waiting until after my workout, I called Isa and told her what we needed and that we needed it right away.

Three hours later, I was in the Cabinet Room ready to start the meeting. Bear was at my feet, and Jann was in her seat by the window. Isa had also called in Corrie Corrigan to be present. The only people not in attendance were Harlan McDonald, the Secretary of Defense and Victor Galloway, Director of National Intelligence.

"All right, I'm calling this meeting to order." The soft hum of voices in the room subsided. "And I'll turn the meeting over to Dr. Patel, who phoned me at dark-thirty this morning with some bad news about bat flu. Dr. Patel?"

Dr. Stan stood up and told them what he told me that morning. Then he said, "And I've been studying the Pandemic Playbook that the previous administration was kind enough to create."

That made me think of my friend, Susanna Pollard, who, although she was a one-term president, was one of the best. I didn't want to interrupt Dr. Stan, though, with praise for her.

"Wait a minute," said General Bryce Skora, the Chairman of the Joint Chiefs of Staff. "You said this disease came from China?

They're causing us all these problems? Maybe we should talk about a preemptive strike!"

"Um, I don't think so, General. Not at this time," I replied, horrified. Maybe he wasn't serious, but the General being the General, I think he was.

Dr. Stan turned toward me. "And, Mr. President, there is more news that I just received. Bad news. Three of the medical people whom you saw at Constitution Air Force Base have come down with bat flu. And there could be more. I hope to God that you followed my advice and stayed outside to greet them."

I cleared my throat, ready to confess, when Marcus spoke up.

"Some idiot," he looked around the room and glared at the people there, with his gaze resting on Jonathan Sharpe, "arranged for him to have lunch at the officer's club. I understand it is a pretty small room."

With an open palm, Dr. Stan hit himself on his forehead. "Oh, Mr. President, this is not good. You have definitely been exposed then."

Sighing, I said, "And I bet I know who one of them was: Dr. Edgar Croft, the doctor in the business suit in the pictures, and the man who sat across from me—at a very narrow table—during lunch."

Dr. Stan checked his notes. "No, he isn't. Dr. Geneen Byrnes, a nurse named Charles Idle, and Toby England, no designation. Do any of those names sound familiar? Did you meet them?"

"I met everyone who was there. And Geneen sat to my right. The other two names I don't recognize."

"All right," Dr. Stan said, shaking his head. "Since you've been exposed, you'll have to be quarantined." Everyone in the room moved their chairs back until Dr. Stan added, "He wouldn't have it yet, so none of you are in danger right now.

"But back to the playbook, we have moved past Phase 1, because bat flu is definitely a credible threat. And we are now enmeshed in the first part of Phase 2 because the medical personnel most certainly acquired the virus from the Wuhan evacuees." Dr. Stan looked at Dominic Tibble, the Secretary of Health and

Human Services. "Are your people following up on all the evacuees and making sure that all of them, *all of them*, are in quarantine?"

"Yes, sir," said Dominic. "Seven of the 199 are currently sick with bat flu. Two of the seven have been hospitalized."

"It's worse than I thought," said Dr. Stan. He looked again at Tibble. "We need to talk about declaring a Public Health Emergency."

And with that, the entire room erupted in conversation, most voices raised, making it impossible for Dr. Stan to continue. I pounded my hand on the table. No one heard it until I pounded again, and Bear stood up and barked. "Please, everybody. Please let Dr. Patel finish what he has to say."

"I feel strongly," said Dr. Stan, "that we are at the point for Dominic to make the declaration. And I don't think it will be too much longer before the President will have to declare a *national* emergency. Bat flu seems extremely contagious. If it continues on its current trajectory, we will have a pandemic on our hands."

"What's this going to do to the country?" asked Marcus. "The economy and everything?"

"It could save our country, Mr. Vice President. If this virus spreads exponentially, then we are all in trouble."

"I agree with Dr. Patel," I said. "Dominic, I think you should do it." After nodding toward Dominic, I scanned the rest of the faces. They started nodding their assent. It's not always easy getting these people to agree, so I felt lucky for the moment.

"One other thing I would recommend," said Dr. Stan, "is that when you make the announcement, suggest that people wear some kind of mask or face covering when they are around other people. That might have to become mandatory, so we might as well ease the public into it now. It should stop the spread of the virus to some extent."

Dominic nodded his head in agreement, and Dr. Stan continued. "All right, now that's settled, on to item number two." He turned his gaze to Jonathan Sharpe. "Jon, as secretary of Homeland Security, this is under your purview. We should close our borders."

The slow rumble of voices started again, but I held up my hand. Bear, feeling my movement, stood up and put his head on the table. All eyes were on him. "Let him finish." They quieted then, but I wasn't sure if it was from my plea or Bear's big head.

"At least no one from China enters the country except Americans. And we need to quarantine those Americans returning from there for two weeks. I honestly think it would be beneficial for us to give every single person—American or not—a fever check before admitting them into the United States. Americans with a fever get quarantined. We don't allow the others in. It's the least we can do right now, but if it gets any worse, and I think it will, we have to get stricter with our border and port of entry controls."

"I agree with this and don't think it's too much to ask.

Corrie leaned forward in her chair and spoke up. "All right, how much of this can I announce?"

"I would say wait for Dominic and Jon to make their announcements. We don't want it to look like you knew before them," I said.

"And be sure to mention masks, Corrie," said Dr. Stan. "The more they hear it, the more likely it is they'll comply."

"Good idea," I said.

"Mr. President, what about you?"

"What?" I asked, not understanding what she meant.

Dr. Stan spoke up. "Since we announced the President was going to California to meet the medical personnel, I think it would be reasonable to say that the President is currently in quarantine after being exposed during his trip to California." He looked at me, and I nodded in agreement.

"Out of those twenty-two people whom I met with, three of them got it! That is scary!" I said.

"Especially since you were exposed, Mr. President," said Dr. Stan.

"Yes, that, too. Isa, can you call the Constitution Air Force Base and advise them that everyone in the officer's club that night has been exposed to a potentially fatal virus? There were other people there besides the medical contingent."

"Yes, of course, Mr. President," replied Isa.

And that's when it hit me. A potentially fatal virus. And I was exposed to it. Shit.

CHAPTER TWENTY-EIGHT

The man

He walked into his office, closed the door, reached behind and patted himself on the back. "That could not have gone any better," he said to himself.

Sinking into his chair, he gloated. His face could barely contain his smile. With his hands on his belly, he thought he might have to eat more donuts, because it would be more satisfying if he had more of a belly to rest his hands on. But maybe that wouldn't be a good idea, because his last doctor's visit showed he had pre-diabetes. His doctor warned him to be careful, but he could do what he wanted. *No one* told him what to do.

It could not have worked out any better with Dan fucking Indigo sitting in that small restaurant with three, count 'em, three infectious people in close proximity. And one sitting right next to him! The man couldn't have lucked out any more if he had arranged the seating himself. Now he just had to keep his fingers crossed that Dan caught it. How could he not? If it was that infectious and he was sitting with those people for several hours? It was a done deal. It had to be.

The man sat up, put his hands on his desk, and steepled his fingers. He thought about how Dan was in for a big shock. Dan didn't know how many friends or allies the man had on his side.

There were a lot. And every friend of his was an enemy of Dan fucking Indigo.

With a big smile on his face, he threw both arms straight up in the air. "Yay!" he announced. "Touchdown!"

CHAPTER TWENTY-NINE
Corrie Corrigan

Corrie Corrigan stood at the podium wearing a teal dress. She lacked her trademark smile.

"The SARS-like virus, now called bat flu, has already spread across our country. In light of this, Dominic Tibble, the Secretary of Health and Human Services, has declared a Public Health Emergency. Jonathan Sharpe, Secretary of Homeland Security, has now closed our borders to anyone coming from China except Americans. And all Americans coming from China will have to go through a two-week quarantine." Her breath caught in her throat before she continued.

"President Dan Indigo has been exposed to several of the emergency personnel who had subsequently come down with the virus, and he is now in quarantine, as well.

"All Americans are advised to wear a mask or some kind of face covering to stop the spread of the virus. It is also advisable not to gather in large groups.

"That is all I have at this time."

CHAPTER THIRTY

Jann

Jann was already sitting at her desk when Dan walked back from the meeting. She looked at him and furrowed her eyebrows. No one else was around, so she said, "Dan, are you scared? Because I'm scared for you."

He looked at her with compassion and love on his face. "Not to worry, Janny, I'll be fine." Since he never called her Janny, she knew he was worried, too. But it was just like Dan Indigo to try to put her mind at rest. That's why he was such a good president. He put the people's needs before his own.

Dan smiled at her then, a sad smile, and retreated into his office with Bear at his heels. She got up and stood at his door. "Marcus looked at Jon when he announced that someone arranged the lunch for you. Do you think Jon did that?"

"Thank you!" said Dan. "You reminded me. I want to know that as well. Call him in here for me, will you? Hopefully, he hasn't left the White House."

Jann raised her eyebrows. "Really? You're just going to come right out and ask him?"

"That's the best way to find out, don't you think?"

"I'll call him now." She took the few steps to her desk, called him, and told him the President wanted to see him. He said he'd be right there.

As she waited for him to arrive, she wondered about Dan's idea to ask him straight out. Wouldn't it be better to talk around the topic and try to get him to confess, accidentally? Probably not. As long as Jon told the truth, then Dan's way was best. Sometimes being diplomatic about a situation wasn't the correct way to go. Dan had a knack for knowing when to be diplomatic and when to get straight to the point.

Jon walked by her and smiled a friendly smile. He had no idea what was about to happen. She hoped he wouldn't shut the door behind him, and he didn't. She wanted to hear every word.

But she didn't have to worry about that. With Bear by Dan's desk, Jon barely stepped inside the door. "Yes, Mr. President. What can I help you with, sir?"

"I'd like to ask you something, Jon, and I would like you to be honest with me."

"Of course, sir."

"Did you or did you not arrange for me to have lunch at the Air Force base?"

"Yes, sir, I did, but—"

"I don't want to hear your excuses, man! Get out of my office right now! I don't want to see you again any time soon!"

"But—" Jon began.

"Out!" roared Dan.

Jon backed out of the office with a confused look on his face. If he hadn't done such a heinous thing, she would have felt sorry for him. He looked at her. "I—"

"I think you'd better leave, Jon," Jann said.

The door to the Oval Office slammed shut, and she heard sounds of yelling within.

After waiting a beat or two while the two of them gazed at the closed door, Jann said, "I'd suggest you leave the White House as soon as you can. No telling what he might do when he's in a mood like this." She wanted to add, "After what you did, you'd deserve anything he decides to do to you," but she didn't. Jon looked abashed and still had that look of confusion on his face, which she didn't understand at all.

He took a few steps, looked back at her, looked at the closed door, shook his head, and walked away.

As the President raged on, Jann sat there a few minutes thinking. She didn't think he was talking to anyone, just angry at the world for what had happened to him. And what still *might* happen to him. With Eden in Pennsylvania with Zoey, who would look after Dan? Men were notorious for ignoring when they're sick.

The more she thought about it, the more she was certain of what she must do. After looking up the number, Jann tapped it into the phone and called Dr. Patel. Then she told him what she wanted and why she wanted it. He agreed and said he would have the documents copied and sent over by messenger.

In less than an hour, she had the documents spread all over her desk, and was re-stacking them in the order she wanted to read them. When she had them organized the way she wanted, she took a drink from her now cold coffee and picked up the first document. *Currently Known Symptoms of the Novel Coronavirus.*

And that's how she knew.

CHAPTER THIRTY-ONE

President

Days went by and nothing much happened. Per Dr. Stan's advice, I stayed in the Oval Office and anyone coming to visit either stood at the door, or if the door had to be closed, we both wore masks and stayed several feet apart. My big Resolute Desk made that part easy. While going to and from the Oval Office, both me and the two Secret Service agents, Eric and Justin or Gavin and Derek, all wore masks.

I lay in bed thinking how lucky I was not to have caught the bat flu. I had woken up a little stiff and sore, but I had a hard workout the previous morning. And I didn't feel much like working out, but I thought I would, anyway. Although I wanted some coffee or cocoa, the thought of donuts made me feel nauseous. I gave a little cough and sniffled. It was probably nothing, maybe a cold. I'd often get one within a few days of a long trip. Reaching down under the blankets, I scratched my burning and itching toes. They felt a little swollen. Maybe I had athlete's foot again, although I didn't know how I could have gotten it; after a bad bout with it several years ago, I had been super careful.

Not really feeling up to working out, I took my shower instead. Afterward, when I went to dry my feet, I noticed my toes. They were still burning and itching, and had red and purple blotches on them. They looked awful. But it wasn't fatal, thank God. I got dressed, and my shoes felt a little tight because of the swelling. Putting on my mask, I stepped out the door to meet my Secret Service guys.

Eric and Justin walked me to the Oval Office. Jann surprised me by already being at her desk. Bear went over to her and she put her face in the fluff of his big neck.

"Morning, Jann. How are you today?"

"More importantly, Mr. President, how are *you*?"

She answered my question with a question. I hate when people do that! "Doing fine. My shoes feel a little tight, but that's all."

I turned to go into my office, but Jann asked, "New shoes?" without even looking up.

"No, my toes are blotchy and swollen. No big deal. I'm fine." I took two steps into my office when Jann called out.

"Wait, Dan! Wait! Let me see them! Quick! Let me see them!"

I thought she was kidding, so I chuckled and continued to my desk. But she had put her mask on and followed me into the Oval Office.

"Dan, I'm serious. Let me see. This is important."

Jann rarely called me Dan in public—usually only when she was at the residence or Eden and I were at her house for dinner. So I sat down, took off my sock, smiled, and, after giving them a good scratch because they were still burning and itching, wiggled my blotchy toes at her. "See? They're fine!"

But Jann didn't think they were fine. Jann started backing out of my office. "You've got it, Dan."

"Got what? Blotchy toes?" I asked and held up my right hand like I was under oath. "I confess. I do! I have blotchy toes!"

"No, Dan, no. You've got bat flu. You've got it."

"What? You're making that determination from my toes?" I reached down and gave them another scratch before putting my sock back on. "Oh, come on! Not funny. Really, Jann. Not appropriate." Her joking about a thing this serious pissed me off.

111

"Dan, I'm serious! It's called corona toes, and it's one of the more unusual symptoms of bat flu. Not everyone gets it, but it *is* a symptom. If you don't believe me, call Dr. Patel. Call him now!"

My slight anger melted into anxiety. "You're not kidding, Jann?"

She backed out of the office until she was in the doorway. "Call Dr. Patel." Then she went into the rest room and washed her hands. I knew it was just hand washing, because she was out in an instant.

When I called Dr. Stan, he was on another line, so I left a brief message telling him about my itchy toes. Thirty minutes later, he walked into my office with a mask on. He moved to the side of the Resolute Desk and pointed down beside me. "Take your shoes off. Let me see."

"So she's right?" I asked as I swung my legs around after putting my mask on. "Move, Bear." The big dog moved to the other side of my desk after giving Dr. Stan a couple of quick sniffs and half a wag.

"Yes, unfortunately, she is right. But let's look to be sure. Do you have any other symptoms? Nausea, fatigue, congestion, coughing?"

I pulled my sock off and showed him my toes. Although I wanted to wiggle my toes to him like I did to Jann, it didn't seem appropriate. "Well, I didn't think I had any symptoms, but I felt too tired to work out this morning, the thought of donuts made me feel nauseous, I have been sniffling, and I've had a cough or two."

Dr. Stan didn't even have to take a good look. He took a brief glance at the red and purple blotches and shook his head. "You've got it, Mr. President. You've got it. We still need to get you tested to be certain, but I'm pretty sure you've got it."

"Shit!" I tied my shoe. "Now I have to call Eden to tell her I'm not fine. This morning, I told her I was."

"You're definitely not fine. And there is something you need to do before you call Eden. You've got it, several more of the evacuees have it, and two more of the medical personnel have gotten sick. It's even more contagious than I feared." He backed away before continuing. "The World Health Organization has now declared it a pandemic. It's time for us to declare a National Emergency, Mr. President. There really isn't an option. It needs to be done now. Are you up to it?"

I thought about the days since our last meeting. The Public Health Emergency had been announced, the closing of the borders to anyone coming from China except Americans, wearing of masks was encouraged, and me being in quarantine was mentioned. Corrie had done a great job of disseminating the information and none of it was taken badly. Maybe it was that more and more people around the country were showing up with symptoms. Hospital emergency rooms and critical care were already getting pushed to their limits despite the fact the pandemic had barely started.

"Yes, I'll make sure it gets done this morning," I said.

"What gets done?" asked Marcus as he put the hot cocoa and donuts on my desk.

The donuts smelled sickly sweet to me. "Oh, Marcus! Get these out of here now!"

"What? What's wrong with them?"

Dr. Stan turned toward Marcus. "You should have your mask on, Mr. Vice-President. He's got bat flu. The donuts are making him nauseous." Then he looked at me. "You've still got your sense of smell. That's a good sign. Hopefully you'll just have a light case."

Marcus grabbed the donuts off the desk and looked at me. "You've got it? Really? Are you okay?"

"He will be, God willing," said Dr. Stan. "He's going to declare a National Emergency."

"Is it really necessary? Isn't a Public Health Emergency enough?" asked Marcus.

"No, it isn't. Cases are skyrocketing. It's a pandemic, Marcus."

"What about him?" Marcus addressed Dr. Stan and motioned toward me as if I wasn't even there.

113

"I'm not dead yet, Marcus. Don't talk about me in third person like that! I'm sitting right here." Then I addressed Dr. Stan. "What about me, Dr. Stan? I can just hole up in the residence, right? Maybe get a nurse or something?"

"A nurse is a good idea. The disease has shown that it gets worse as it goes along. You might have a bad time of it in a few more days. Plus, a nurse will be there to determine if you need critical care—if you have shortness of breath or anything like that."

"I don't think the residence is a good plan," said Marcus. "That means all the people that come in and out of the residence are at risk. I think he should go somewhere else where it's just him and the nurse."

"That sounds better," said Dr. Stan.

"I'll go home," I said.

"No, Mr. President. I agree with Marcus. The residence is not a good idea."

"I didn't mean that home. Home! My ranch! I'll go to my home in Oceanview. A nurse can go there, too."

"I think that's perfect, Mr. President. I'll arrange for a nurse to accompany you."

Marcus looked at me, kind of shrugged, and smiled his politician smile. "Now don't take this personally, Dan." He turned to Dr. Stan. "Stan, is it time to utilize the twenty-fifth amendment?"

"Absolutely not!" I shouted. Eden had prudently *warned* me about Marcus in the past, but I always thought it was because of their nasty breakup before she and I started dating. I figured she still blamed him. Now I thought maybe I should have taken her warnings more seriously.

Dr. Stan looked at me and smiled. "Are you kidding me? Look at all that spunk he's got! No, seriously, he will not be under any kind of sedation or medication that affects his thinking. There is no reason for that right now. Depending on how the disease progresses, we can make a different determination in the future."

"All right," I grumbled. "It would be a good idea if everyone thought I was still in the residence. No need for anyone to know that I'm not there."

"Agreed," said Marcus. "It might make you look incapacitated or vulnerable. That wouldn't be good."

"No one has to know," said Dr. Stan. "Just get the National Emergency document signed before you go."

"That, and I'll have to let Corrie know of the recent developments. She'll handle it well. She always does." I took a sip of the hot cocoa that Marcus had left on my desk and almost gagged on it. "I guess I'm not up to hot cocoa, either."

"Mr. President, I'll be going now. I'll take care of arranging the nurse. Top security clearance, and she'll be available to you today."

"Thanks, Dr. Stan."

"Don't worry, Dan," said Marcus. "I'll take care of everything while you're recovering."

"I'd like an update several times a day."

"Are you sure you're up to it?"

"Yes, Marcus!" I screamed. "Stop treating me as if I was an invalid. I may have bat flu, but I'm still functioning fine!" His politician's smile was looking more and more like a crocodile's grin. And I didn't like it.

Marcus held up his hands. "All right, all right. No worries. I'll keep you up to date on everything." He strode out of the room, with the donuts in his hand, like he had just done something important.

As I sat at my desk, I tried to absorb the gravity of the situation. I couldn't. It was enormous. Bat flu was too new. Would I die or would I come out unscathed? There was no way to tell at this early juncture.

First thing I had to do was call Eden and let her know the unsettling news. No, I wouldn't. I'd call her once I got settled into our ranch. For now, I'd let Jann break the news to her. "Jann, I need a couple of things."

She came to the door with her mask on. Considering the circumstances, I hadn't taken mine off. "I need you to put together a National Emergency document for me. Get with Isa or whoever you need to put it together and then messenger it to me at the residence."

"I thought you were going *home*."

"Yes, I am, but I have some things to finish up here first, and then I have to pack."

"All right, got it. And was there something else?"

"Yes, I'd like you to call Eden and explain to her I'm not fine and that I'm infected. But don't tell her I'm still here."

Jann put her hands on her hips. "You want me to lie to your wife, Mr. President?"

"No, Jann, no. Just don't volunteer the information." I had never lied to Eden once during our entire relationship.

"What if she asks where you are?"

"Then tell her, but I can't talk right now. I've got to get out of here."

"Fine. I'll take care of both." She turned away and then turned back. "Dan, take care of yourself, will you?"

I shrugged. "I'll do my best. And Jann, thank you for noticing my corona toes. I appreciate you looking out for me."

She tightened her mouth, nodded, said, "Always, Mr. President," and walked to her desk. Picking up a pen, I began making two lists. The first was what I had to do before leaving. The second was what to pack.

Although it tired me out, I finished quickly. I stood up with Bear at my heels, turned to look at the Oval Office one last time, and walked out. Little did I know that would be the last time I saw the Oval Office for much longer than I had ever expected.

CHAPTER THIRTY-TWO

Jann

When Dan walked out of his office a little while later, Jann had already arranged to meet with Isa to prepare the National Emergency document. He had handed her a list and several papers to go with them. Now she dialed Eden, who was still in Pennsylvania. She knew why Dan didn't want to make the call—Eden would have a fit when she found out. She would be worried about him, but it would come out as anger. Jann knew it was better if she made the call. Eden wouldn't react the same way to the news from her.

"Eden? It's Jann. Dan wanted me to call you."

Eden laughed. "What's he gotten himself into now?"

"Eden, it's serious. He's got bat flu."

"No! He told me this morning he was fine!"

"He thought he was." Then Jann told her the entire story, including about the corona toes and that Dan would go to their ranch in secret.

"Oh, I wish I could be there with him. But I need to stay with Zoey right now."

"It's really contagious, Eden. It's good that you're not here."

"I guess so, but I hate him going through this alone. Regardless, I told Zoey that I'd stay with her for her first and second chemo treatment; and I will."

"When's the second one?"

"Next week."

"Well, Dan still won't be over it by then, so Dr. Patel might recommend that you stay away from him."

"We'll see what develops," said Eden.

"I love you," said Jann. "I've got to go work on the National Emergency document so it's ready before Dan leaves."

"Love you, too," said Eden. "Bye."

Next on her list was placing a call to Dr. Patel. She needed him to give her the correct wording for the National Emergency. Then she and Isa could do the rest. Jann had just gotten everything ready when Isa came stomping in. Isa Zimmerman was strong and powerful and much too big to ignore.

"You ready, Jannika? Because I've got a lot to do with the President sick."

Isa wasn't treating Jann like an underling. Jann knew Isa treated just about everyone that way, so it didn't offend her. But she had also learned the best way to handle it was to give it right back. "Isa, you said it. With the President sick—and look at this list of things he gave me to do—I'm swamped. So let's get this done!"

Isa nodded, pulled up a chair, and they got to work. They were taking care of the last details on the document when Marcus strode in.

"Where is he?" he demanded.

"Duh," said Jann. "Memory that short, Marcus? He's sick. Where do you think he is? He's in the residence."

He frowned and glared at Jann, then looked at Isa. "And what are you doing here with *her*?"

"We're finishing the National Emergency document, Mr. Vice President. Almost done." She was soft and easy with him—not her usual blustery self.

Marcus stormed out and Jann said to Isa, "He's a total asshole. Why are you so nice to him?"

Isa shrugged. "I kind of *owe* him. He got me this job."

Jann moved her chair away so she could look Isa in the eyes. "No, he did not. Dan wanted you as Chief of Staff and the asshole tried to talk him out of it. You don't owe him a damn thing!"

"I think you're wrong, Jann. He and I had made an, um, agreement." She inhaled deeply and shrugged again.

Jann laughed. "If you mean your *rendezvous* in his office down there, believe me, it didn't mean a thing. I heard it from the man himself,"—she nodded toward the Oval Office—"he wanted you to be Chief of Staff and Marcus tried to talk him out of it. Believe me, sister, you don't owe that bastard a thing!"

Isa had her mouth open in shock, but Jann could tell she still didn't quite believe it, so she raised her right hand. "I swear it's true."

She snapped her mouth closed and hissed, "That son of a bitch!" Then she stood up with her fists balled at her sides and took two steps toward Marcus's office.

"Where are you going?"

Isa turned around waving one near-ham-sized fist, "I'm going to—"

"You can't! You're the Chief of Staff in the White House!"

Isa winked at Jann and sat back down beside her. "You're right. I can't beat the shit out of him. But I'd like to!"

Jann realized it was all for show, which surprised her because she didn't think Isa had a sense of humor. "Well, he deserves it for that as well as other things." She frowned.

"Yes, I've seen the way he treats you. Can't you get President Indigo to do anything about that? I know you have his ear."

The statement didn't bother Jann, because it was well known about the relationship she shared with both Dan and Eden. "No, I'm just grateful that Dan doesn't fire me, which is what Marcus keeps telling him to do. He doesn't even bother to lower his voice when he talks about it.

"Why does he hate you like that?"

"I would say it's from when I saw you two come out of his office together, and I called him on it. But I think it goes further back than that. I don't know when it started, but it intensified after that happened."

"Do you think it would help or hurt if he saw the two of us together being friends?" asked Isa.

Jann grimaced. "I'm not sure if it would hurt or help, but I know exactly what he would do. He would spread the rumor that I'm gay, too." She looked at Isa and shrugged. "No offense. It's just that, you know, I'm not."

"No offense taken. I'm not exactly out of the closet, but I'm not so far in the closet that I've got hangers coming out of my mouth like some people I know."

Jann looked at Isa and tilted her head. "You know, Isa, it's been nice talking to you."

Isa smiled. "Nice talking to you, too, Jannika. I'll see ya later."

"Thanks for the help."

As Isa walked away, Jann thought she was one person who was good to have on her side. She didn't know why, but she thought it might be important to keep in mind.

CHAPTER THIRTY-THREE

President

I wasn't at the residence too long before there was a knock at the door. When I opened it, a woman stood there wearing a mask and white scrubs.

"Hi. I'm the nurse Dr. Patel sent over to give you a virus test."

"All right," I grumbled. "Come on in."

She walked in and began taking something out of plastic wrap. "This will feel weird but shouldn't hurt, Mr. President."

"What are you going to do to me?"

She held up what looked like an extra long Q-Tip. "I'm going to stick this far into your nose."

"Ouch," I said, before she even began.

"Pull your mask down, please."

I complied, and she stuck the thing up my nose, moved it around, pulled it back out, and stuck it into a plastic specimen bag. Then she stuck another one up the other side of my nose and did the same thing. After that, she put it into a second specimen bag.

"That's all, Mr. President. Dr. Patel will give you the results."

"Thanks." She opened the front door herself and left. My nose felt like something bubbly had gone up there and tears dribbled down my eyes. It felt weird but not painful. I was glad it was over, though.

As the day progressed, I felt tired and more miserable. Trouble was, it was still morning. As I lay spread-eagled on the floor of the President's Dining Room, trying to get up enough energy to continue, I wiggled my toes inside my shoes. They still felt swollen. Bear lay beside me with his big head on my chest.

I struggled to sit up and took a drink of water from the bottle I had brought with me. Then, on hands and knees, I crawled into the pantry and into the storage room behind it. Nobody went into this room. It was dark. There had been a light in there, but it had been removed and a lock put on the door. There was a box on the floor labeled "junk." It wasn't junk.

During the transition from her presidency to mine, President Susanna Pollard had invited me and Eden to the residence for dinner. After we ate, Eden and Susanna's husband were yukking it up over something that their two dogs, a mastiff and a chihuahua had done. So Susanna led me to the Dining Room, opened the door to the pantry and the store room behind it, and showed me this box packed away at the back of the store room. And I hadn't seen it since then. Honestly, I didn't think I'd ever need it. But I also didn't expect to be leaving the White House for any length of time during my presidency. Who could anticipate a pandemic? Who could anticipate getting infected with a novel virus?

I pulled the flaps of the box open and looked inside. There was a stack of shoe boxes. The top box contained four cell phones Susanna had called "burner" phones. A burner phone, for my application, was a pre-paid phone used for privacy. Therefore, I could keep all conversations or communications on that phone private. I pulled the box out. One of them had a broken screen. I didn't know how that happened, but it didn't matter, anyway.

In ordinary circumstances—but these were anything but ordinary—I would have given a phone to myself, Eden, Jann, and Marcus. But after Marcus had suggested moving forward with the twenty-fifth amendment, I had second thoughts. The broken phone would have been for Marcus. It must have been a sign from above that he shouldn't have one.

Susanna told me the phones were all prepaid for years, so I didn't have to worry about that. Just charge them up, she had said, and they were ready to go. If anyone was trying to bug my regular cell phone, this is the one I would use to prevent that. All four—now three—phones had each other on speed dial. I set the phones and their chargers aside and reached into the box.

The next shoe box contained two "bug detectors" nestled in a bed of soft cotton. They were hand-held devices with an antenna and a wand. I needed to remember to charge them before attempting to use them. I pulled up the cotton and found two instruction booklets underneath. When Susanna showed me all the equipment, besides having had a drink or two, I never in a thousand years thought I would need anything like it. With the state of affairs the way they were, it looked like I should have paid more attention.

Underneath the bug detectors was a boot-sized shoebox containing the surveillance equipment. Susanna told me she had them specially made to her specifications. The three small individual components all transmitted their information, via cell phone technology, to a central unit.

The central unit had three modes: "live," record, or both. Since there were three individual components, they each had their own "channel" on the central unit. So two could be recording while you listened to the third one live. Each of the components also used GPS technology, in case you wanted to track where someone was as you were listening to their conversations.

I replaced everything in the big box, put the flaps over the top, and struggled to stand up with it. Although it wasn't heavy, my fatigue was getting worse.

There were still a few items to take care of before I could leave for the ranch. The first on the agenda was to pack. Then I had to write at least two notes. And I still had to sign the National

Emergency document. While I packed, I plugged in one of the burner cell phones by my bed.

As I packed, I looked at the box in the corner, which I had intended to give to Jann to take care of. It wouldn't look right carrying that big box around. So I rummaged through the closet until I found a small carry-on and gently packed everything inside. It was perfect

At the time, I had no idea that the equipment—that I had once told Eden was silly—would end up saving the life of someone I loved.

CHAPTER THIRTY-FOUR

Jann

When the phone rang, Jann never expected it to be Dan. She had sent the document to him well over an hour ago, and she thought he'd be long gone by now. "Yes, Mr. President. Why aren't you home already? You need to take it easy and get well!"

"Jann, I appreciate your concern, but there is one more thing I have to do before I leave. Now, please listen carefully. I don't know who might be in the room with you now or who is listening. So do not ask any questions. Just listen."

"I'm listening, Mr. President."

"You need to pick something up here at the residence. Come alone and wear a mask. I will give you a small carry-on. Inside are the instructions on what to do with it. Do not let anyone else —*anyone*—near it. And if anyone asks what it is, make up something innocuous that will satisfy their curiosity but not prompt them to want to look inside. You must not show it to anyone. It is for you and you alone."

"You've got me curious, now, Mr. President."

"Your curiosity will be satisfied when you get it home. Only at home—while you are alone. You must not leave it alone in the office for even a minute. So go home early. Do you understand?"

"Perfectly. Should I come over right now?"

"Yes, please. I'll see you in a few. Goodbye, Jann."

"Bye, Dan."

Heavy footsteps approached. "So what's got you curious, huh?" Marcus said with his lips in a curl.

Jann stood and put her hands on her hips. "Are you always in the habit of eavesdropping on other people's conversations?"

A smile spread across his lips and he tapped himself on his chest. "I'm in charge now, and *every single thing* that goes on in this office, I need to know. Now tell me, what's got you curious? You were talking to Dan, right?"

Jann narrowed her eyes and gritted her teeth. She hoped Dan would get better soon, so she didn't have to endure this buffoon any longer than necessary. "Dan said he knew what he was going to do while he was at his ranch, but he wouldn't tell me what it was. That got me curious. I'm thinking it's probably riding his horse, which he absolutely should not do."

Jann walked toward the bathroom. "Now, I'm going in here. Would you like to know what I'm going to do? Number one!" She opened the door, about to step inside, when his voice boomed out behind her.

"Wait! You will never speak to me that way again! You, you," his face screwed up in disgust, "you poor white trash!"

Marcus was so volatile that Jann suspected if she came back with any witty repartee that Marcus could haul off and hit her. He wouldn't do that if Dan was here, but Dan wasn't there, and that put Jann in danger. So with her voice as even as she could manage, she said, "I guess you haven't noticed today that I'm black."

"Listen, bitch!" Spittle flew from his mouth, and he pointed a finger at her. "You will do every single thing I say with no guff! Do you understand? If I say 'jump,' you jump. If I say 'suck my dick,' then you'll open your fuckin' mouth. Get it?"

She kept her hand on the bathroom door—because she thought she could get in there and lock it quickly if necessary—and glared at him. "Good luck with that, Marcus! I bite!" She chomped her teeth together, stepped into the bathroom, slammed the door, and locked it behind her before he could get across the room.

With her hand on the sink to steady herself after the upsetting exchange, she took several deep breaths with the other hand on her heart, which was beating wildly. She didn't know how long bat flu lasted, but she hoped she would survive Dan's absence. If only Eden was here to protect her from Marcus. Then Jann corrected herself. No, Eden did not do very well protecting herself from Marcus, so that wouldn't have worked, anyway.

After calming herself down and doing her business, she washed her hands, and then put her ear to the door. Had he walked away? Or was he out there right now, rubbing his hands together and getting ready to pounce on her as she left the restroom? Jann knew she couldn't stay in there forever, and Dan was waiting for her, anyway. She stood up straight—to her full five-foot-two inch height—put her shoulders back and stepped out to an empty room.

Hurrying as fast and quiet as she could, she grabbed her purse and jacket, locked her desk, and slipped out through the Cabinet Room hoping that he hadn't anticipated her move and was waiting for her in there.

CHAPTER THIRTY-FIVE

President

After I finished packing, I brought my suitcase, for my extended stay at our ranch, and the carry-on for Jann, to the front door. Then I lay down on the couch to wait. My coughing was minimal, but my fatigue was intense. That was a good thing, though, because if I wasn't so tired, I would probably be consumed by the itching of my toes.

When I heard the knock, I struggled to my feet and made my way toward the front door. Grabbing my mask out of my pocket and slipping it on my face, I adjusted it before opening the door. My finger was already to my lips, so Jann wouldn't say anything in front of my two secret service agents. Although I trusted them explicitly, they didn't need to know about this. At least not yet.

"Ah, glad your mask is on, Jann. Please come in. It will only take a minute."

Bear had stepped out the door to greet Jann. "Bear! Get in here." I closed the door and handed Jann the carry-on bag. "You need to take this straight home. There are instructions inside that I wrote and instructions for the equipment." Jann started to ask a question, but I held up my hand. "Not now, Jann, I can't. But the letter will explain everything. I know you will think it's overkill, but please, trust my judgment and just do it." Forcing my face into a smile—not because I didn't want to smile at Jann—but because I barely had the energy, I said, "Leave now and go straight home. Understand?"

Jann grimaced. "Yes, Dan, but there is a slight problem. Marcus has been, shall we say, 'shoving me around.' I'm afraid he might try to follow me to my car or intercept me on the way there."

"That son of a bitch! I'll call and make sure he's in his office and then keep him on the phone to give you time to get to your car." I shook my head. "Man, I don't need this shit today."

Jann stepped back. "I'm sorry, Dan."

"No, no, Jann, not you. Him. I'll call right now. Don't worry."

"Dan, before you call him, let me ask you one question. You want me to take Bear?"

He sat by my side, and I patted his head. "No, he'll be fine with me. Let me call Marcus now."

"Um, I think I'll wait and make sure you have him on the phone before I go, if you don't mind."

"Yes, I just need to sit down first." Walking over to the couch, I plopped down and took a deep breath. I pulled out my cell phone and called Marcus at his office. He answered, and I nodded my head to Jann. She patted Bear and then slipped out the door.

"Marcus, hey."

"Dan? You home yet?"

"No, still in the residence. Not quite done packing yet."

"You shouldn't be there that long, Dan. Don't be a woman about this!"

"Thanks for your support, Marcus. Listen, while I'm gone, please use your own secretary. I've got Jannika working on some stuff for me and for Isa."

"What kind of stuff, Dan? Shouldn't I know about it since you won't be here?"

"Marcus, seriously, I'm not feeling well and I don't have time for your ego right now. You have enough on your plate filling in for me, so just listen to what I need you to do.

"If anything comes up, call me immediately. Even if nothing comes up, please check in at least two times a day, maybe three.

"If it's anything about bat flu or the pandemic, Dr. Patel will tell me, so no worries there." I kept up with miscellaneous blather for a few more minutes to make sure Jann got to her car safely. Then I finished with, "And Marcus, I apologize for making the comment about your ego. I'm tired and not feeling well."

"Yes, Dan," he said, which made me suspicious. I expected him to come back at me with some infuriating comment, although his ingratiating attitude was more in keeping with his politician's smile.

"All right, Marcus. That's all for now. Give me time to get to the ranch and get settled, then check in later this afternoon. Goodbye and thank you for all your help." After pressing the end button, I felt concerned about his reticence. That wasn't like Marcus. And it bothered me. But I was too sick to worry about it now.

Three hours later, I was snug in my bed on the ranch. Or rather, on my bed. And all of my clothes still on, because I had been too tired to take them off. Since I didn't yet have the strength to get up, I went over my morning following my blasted diagnosis and my subsequent packing.

After getting off the phone with Marcus, I had called Dr. Stan. Jann's question about taking Bear had me worried. Could I give it to my dog? Did they even know yet? Dr. Patel told me that although a tiger in some zoo had gotten it, and of course a few primates, there had been no indication that dogs could get it. So Bear would be safe with me.

Someone took my suitcase away while I was on the phone with Dr. Stan, and even through my hazy thinking, I remembered to bring my cell phone *and* the burner phone before I left the residence.

My two secret service agents for the day, Jeff Egan and Clive Holmes, had escorted me and Bear secretly through the bowels of the White House and out to the underground parking garage and to Jeff's car, a late model Lexus sedan. Clive said he was driving his wife's Prius, which would have never worked for what we did. We pulled a Bill Clinton: instead of driving to my ranch in what we called 'the Beast'—that huge cross between a Cadillac and a tank—we decided to sneak me out in the backseat of the Lexus. While Bill went to a hotel for his clandestine meetings, we went to my ranch in Oceanview, about an hour from the White House. And nobody was the wiser. I knew I'd be safe and secure there.

Of course, the occurrence that ultimately happened there was precipitated not by a stranger but by someone I had once considered a friend.

CHAPTER THIRTY-SIX

Corrie Corrigan/Keith Enright

Corrie Corrigan walked up to the podium and looked out. Instead of wearing her usual smile, the corners of her mouth drooped. She felt sick inside with what she was about to share with her eager audience. The fact that President Dan had the bat flu scared her. She loved and respected the man, and hated to see anything bad happen to him.

Clearing her throat, she began. "I have two items today. First, the World Health Organization has now characterized the outbreak of bat flu to be a pandemic. The rates of infection have continued to go up in every state in the United States. So President Dan Indigo has now declared a National Emergency. A copy of this document is available right here,"—she held up a stack of copies—"but I'd like to present you with the most important provision that will affect us all.

"The spread of bat flu jeopardizes our hospitals and health care systems. They are now remanded to discontinue all voluntary procedures and non-essential services, and to prepare for an escalation of bat flu patients." She paused, swallowed, and blinked a few times to keep her tears at bay.

"And with a heavy heart, I'll advise you of the second item. Today, Dr. Stanley Patel has confirmed that President Dan Indigo has tested positive for the bat flu. After careful consideration, Dr. Patel has decided the President will remain in the residence with a nurse on call during his convalescence. Dr. Patel will check in with him daily to see how the disease is progressing."

One reporter raised his hand and asked, "Is there any indication whether the twenty-fifth amendment will be invoked?"

"No. At this time, that is unnecessary. President Indigo is well enough to take phone calls and handle anything urgent right from the residence."

She handed the papers to an assistant and ambled away from the podium without answering any more questions.

Keith felt miserable. It had started out feeling like a bad cold, and he didn't worry about it at all. But when the headache and body aches came on him, and he got a fever, Jeni suggested he go to one of the drive-up clinics in town and get tested. So he had sat inside his old pickup truck for forty-five minutes feeling miserable until it was his turn. It turned out that yes, he had it.

At first, Jeni tried to cook him a soft-boiled egg. The smell of it made him feel nauseous. When a few hours later, he had lost his sense of smell, he thought it might alleviate the nausea and vomiting, but it didn't. Aspirin barely managed the headache and muscle aches, but he didn't want anything stronger. Keith had heard too many stories about how easy it was to get addicted to the drugs doctors prescribed.

The worst part was the coughing, because that made him retch even more. On the third day, when the symptoms felt unbearable to handle, Jeni took time off work to take care of him. Most of the time, he stayed in bed, where she catered to his every wish. If he hadn't already decided to marry her, he certainly would have then. Jeni's research into the virus said it would probably last two weeks. He counted the hours and hoped that he didn't die in the meantime.

Little did he know how having the bat flu would change his life and change him as a man.

CHAPTER THIRTY-SEVEN

Jann

Jann couldn't remember Dan ever being so serious before. Yes, there had been a number of crises at the White House, and he always acted appropriately, but this seemed different—almost personal. She could attribute it to the virus, but she didn't think that was fair. Keeping all of that in mind, she took what he said to heart. She drove straight home.

There were several times her anxiety got the best of her, and she thought she was being followed, but they all turned out to be false alarms. When she pulled into her garage and pushed the button for the door to close, she felt very relieved. Home safe.

Jann opened the door between the house and garage, and with her purse and the carry-on in tow, she stepped through. Another deep breath, as if she had just accomplished some huge feat that took more courage than she thought she had. In a way, it was true. She had no idea what was in the carry-on, but it was important to Dan, no, not Dan, to the President of the United States. And if it was important to him, it was important to her.

She set her purse in the kitchen and brought the carry-on into her bedroom. Where to put it for safekeeping? Although she had needed to stop at the grocery store, she didn't dare stop on the way home. Now she needed a safe place to keep the precious cargo until she returned. Jann had always considered her home safe, but this felt like it needed more circumspect handling.

She stuffed it under her bed with her spread almost reaching the floor and covering any evidence of it, but she wasn't satisfied. Opening her closet, she knelt down, moving boxes out of the farthest corner. Then she stuffed it in there and put the assortment of boxes in front of it. Unless someone knew it was there, it would go unnoticed. Practically hidden in plain sight. Perfect.

While driving home from the grocery store, she considered driving by the President's country house. It was right here in Oceanview and only a few miles away. But she thought he still had things to do at the White House, so he probably wasn't even there yet. She hoped he would take his illness seriously and slow down, but she doubted if he would. That wasn't like him, and that scared her.

Back home, she put her groceries away as quick as she could, because by this time, her curiosity was getting the best of her. What was in the carry-on? Why did Dan think it so important that he instructed her to drive straight home?

There was only one way to find out. She dragged it out of the closet, set it on the coffee table in front of the couch, and unzipped it. Sticking in her hand, she pulled out three cell phones labeled #2, #3, and #4. #3 had a broken screen. Cell phones? Jann already had a cell phone, and these were cheap flip phones. What the hell? Then she stuck her hand in again and pulled out the letter Dan had written to her. The first two lines were, "Jann, this is of the utmost importance to me and to your country. Please follow these instructions exactly."

Jann shook her head, put the letter down on the coffee table without reading any more of it, and retreated to the kitchen to make some tea. She reached into her cabinet and pulled out her standard fare of peppermint tea, then returned it and pulled out her seldom used box of Chai tea. The Chai tea should give her the little punch she needed for this job. It might give her a little courage, as well. Dan wasn't the type for melodrama or hyperbole, so for him to say the words "utmost importance" scared her.

The work she had done for him while he was an attorney was important work, as was the work she did for him when he was a senator. And, of course, her work in the Oval Office was important. But the first line in Dan's letter creeped her out. It was more like fifty per cent creeped her out and fifty per cent terrified her. She didn't know what cheap cell phones had to do with anything, but there were more objects still in the bag. Now she was almost afraid to put her hand in there to find out. She felt like the responsibility for the whole world rested on her shoulders. It wouldn't be too long before she would discover that she was right.

CHAPTER THIRTY-EIGHT

President

I woke up later, lying on my bed fully dressed. That was by design. It was just a nap. There was no way I was going to get under the covers. Someone who is under the covers is really sick. You have to set a limit somewhere. I also had a raging headache, and the aches in my legs seemed to have intensified. Putting on my slippers, I padded into the bathroom and opened the medicine chest. The bottle of aspirin in there was several years expired. Why even bother?

Shuffling out of the bedroom, I wondered if the nurse had arrived yet. Secret service would have let her in, and as bad as I felt, I wouldn't have had any trouble sleeping through her entrance. I had meant to run the bug detector through the house before her arrival, but I didn't have the energy. Now, if I found one, I wouldn't know if it was here already, or if *she* had brought it in.

"Hello? Hello? Anybody home?" There were some provocative smells coming from the kitchen, and Bear, who walked beside me, sniffed the air.

"Just us chickens," said a voice.

Bear and I walked into the kitchen, and there, drying her hands, stood a woman in blue nurse's scrubs. She was taller than

Jann and shorter than Eden, which would make her about five feet five. Bear stood by my side, not growling or showing his teeth, so I figured she was harmless.

"Hello, Mr. President," the nurse said, making a deep bow.

I chuckled, but it made me cough. "I'm not the king, for chrissakes! And I don't have an ego that requires all that pomp and circumstance. While we're here at my house, please call me Dan. At the White House, 'Mr. President' would be appropriate. What shall I call you?"

"Nurse!" she said, while putting a surgical mask over her pretty face. Then she laughed. "Just kidding, Dan. You can call me Joyce."

"I can tell you're going to be a lot of fun, Joyce, but I don't think I'm well enough to appreciate you just yet." Pulling out a chair from the kitchen table, I sat down with a thump.

"Oh, introductions are not quite complete. Joyce, this is Bear, and Bear, this is Joyce." At mention of his name, Bear's tail swished across the floor.

Joyce walked up to him and stuck out her hand. "Nice meeting you, Bear." Bear put his paw into her hand and wagged his tail.

"All right, if either of you gentlemen needs anything, just let me know."

"Listen, Joyce, I'm not feeling horrible, but I have a throbbing headache and body aches. Any chance I can get a couple of aspirin?"

"Yes, of course Mr., er, Dan, or if you want, Dr. Patel has authorized the use of more effective pain killers."

"No! No opioids! I can just see the headlines now—*US president caught taking opioids while the world is in a pandemic crisis!* Aspirin will be just fine. I can handle it."

"Well, you've still got grit!" Joyce was kneeling over her medical kit that she had put on the floor in the corner. With the bottle in one hand, she filled a glass of water with the other and set both of them on the table before me. "You must not be feeling too terrible."

JK Lincoln

"Not terrible, but I'm not used to being sick at all. And since I am President of the United States, this is terribly inconvenient."

Joyce pulled something else out of her medical kit and slipped a piece of plastic over my finger. "This will just take a minute. I want to see how your blood oxygen is doing." She nodded, slipped it off my finger and put it back in her kit. She took out a forehead thermometer and took my temperature. "No temperature, that's good." She took a step away and put her hands on her hips. "I understand that it's inconvenient, Dan, but this disease is nothing to be cavalier about."

Joyce walked to the sink, washed her hands for a long time, and without turning toward me said, "Many people have died, Dan." Although I couldn't see her face, her shoulders moved up and down like she might be crying.

Trying to lighten things up, I said, "What are you making, anyway?"

"Dr. Patel wanted to make sure that I keep you well fed and well hydrated, but not to force you to eat if you don't feel like it. Are you hungry?"

"No, but I think I will be later. This morning I felt nauseous, but I'm not feeling that way now. Whatever you're making smells delicious."

"Thank you." Joyce took a pitcher from the counter, filled it up with water, and set it on the table. "You need to drink this much liquid today. I'll bring a glass to your bedroom for you—which is where you should be right now. Rest is important, Dan. Do you need me to help you back in there? I noticed you barely made it into that chair."

"No, thanks, I'll take it slow and easy. And yes, the bed sounds good about now." I stood up. "Nice meeting you, Joyce."

"Nice meeting you, too, Dan. I'll have dinner ready whenever you're ready. And if you need anything, just call out."

"It will be a while before I'm ready for dinner. I have to call Eden, and another nap wouldn't hurt." I shuffled back to the bedroom and only had to use the wall for balance twice. And Bear walked at my other side in case I tilted that way.

I lay down on the bed and took a couple of deep breaths. Feeling the bed beneath my body was an unexpected pleasure. I had left my cell on the bedside table, and I picked it up and tapped the Eden icon.

"Dan!" Eden answered without any preamble. "How are you? I've been worried sick, but didn't want to call and wake you up in case you were sleeping."

"I'm okay, or as okay as can be expected. I'm very fatigued, have a bad headache, and body aches. But I can still breathe, and I think that's the most important thing."

"All right," Eden took a deep breath that I could clearly hear, "then in that case, I'm going to yell at you, and I might cry while I'm at it!"

She's going to yell at me and maybe cry? What could I have done to deserve that?

"The doctor scheduled Zoey for her second chemo tomorrow morning." Eden paused again like she was getting her thoughts —or her emotions—together.

"Yeah, so? And you're there to help her through. I'm fine with that. What are you getting at, Eden?"

"They canceled her appointment, Dan! They canceled her whole regimen and put it on hold indefinitely! Meanwhile, Zoey still has breast cancer, and the tumor could be getting bigger every minute!"

"Oh, no. Why would they do that?"

"Because of you, Dan! Because of you!" At that point, Eden broke down into long, drawn-out sobs, and I couldn't get another word out of her.

CHAPTER THIRTY-NINE
Jann

While Jann waited for the water to boil for her tea, she didn't want to pull more objects out of the bag just yet. Instead, she sauntered to her front door, unlocked the dead bolt, and proceeded at a slow pace to her mailbox that was on the street. Looking around, she hoped to find a neighbor that she could chat with to delay the inevitable. But it was a quiet afternoon, and no one was around to distract her. Grabbing her mail without looking at what was there, she returned to the house at a snail's pace. She closed the door behind her and dropped the mail on the little table by the door.

Jann reluctantly sat down in front of her coffee table and took a sip of the still too hot tea. She had stalled long enough, and now it was time for the inevitable. If Dan had confidence that she could handle this job, then she could handle it!

The first item she pulled out looked like a walkie talkie with an antenna and some kind of flexible wand attached. There was a yellow stickie note attached that said, *This is a "bug detector."*

That's all? What am I supposed to do with it? Then she remembered she hadn't finished reading the letter. The center of the letter contained a list of items. One of them was *bug detector.* Next to it, the text said, *Keep it in your purse. Use it every morning when you come in (making sure no one sees you), and every night when you get home from work, check your house. I hope you never find any, but if you do, the best thing to do is leave it where it is, so the person who set them doesn't know that you know. Then bluff your way through it, but say nothing important in front of it. (Obviously, but you knew that already.) You need to charge it before using it.*

She skimmed the list of items, and the listing for *cell phones* was at the top. Next to that, it said, *Jann, these are burner phones, not traceable at all. I have one already. Please secretly send one to Eden and keep the other one. But address the package to Zoey, and don't have your name or your address as the return. If you can get someone else to mail the package, that would be ideal. Be sure to include the charger when you send it to her. The fourth one, unfortunately, is broken. I don't know who I would have given it to, anyway. At this point, Marcus is out of the equation. All four phones are already set up to call each other.*

Hmmm, Jann thought. That's the first time Dan had ever shown any distrust in Marcus, even though she and Eden had always known what a jerk he was.

The carry-on was almost empty now. Putting her hand inside it, she pulled out the last of the equipment and some paperwork. She had no idea what it was. There was another yellow stickie note on the biggest piece. It said *surveillance equipment*. At the end of Dan's letter, he said there were instructions for each object in the bag. And he emphasized she was not to show the equipment to *anyone*. He had repeated that several times in the letter, including right at the very bottom.

Two hours and two cups of tea later, Jannika still couldn't figure out the instructions for the equipment. She had plugged in the bug detector to charge, and she thought she could handle that. And of course the cell phones were easy. But the instructions for the surveillance equipment were way too technical for her to understand. Frustrated, she wrapped up cell phone #2 and its charger for Eden. She included a letter explaining everything, addressed the package to Zoey, and left off the return address, because she couldn't think of what to put there.

Then, since the tea was ready to make its exit, she strolled into the bathroom. After she flushed the toilet, she turned on the water in the sink, and washed her hands and splashed cold water on her face. Maybe that would wake her up so she could concentrate better on the surveillance equipment's instructions. She should be able to figure it out. Of course she could! Jannika White was secretary to the President of the United States! She could do anything that she set her mind to do. And right now, she had set her mind on learning how to set up the surveillance equipment.

With a more confident attitude than before, she returned to the living room with her head held high, and every fiber of her being expecting to decipher the confusing instructions. What she didn't expect, though, was to find a man sitting on her couch by the coffee table where all the *secret equipment* was.

CHAPTER FORTY

President

I woke up with not only mild disorientation but completely overwhelmed with feeling horrible. Since I hadn't slept that long, the aspirin was still taking care of my headache and body aches—calming them down to a manageable level. So the horrible part was the bitter aftertaste of my conversation with Eden. What could she mean that it was my fault the hospital had canceled Zoey's chemo appointments?

Something moved beside me—something furry—and it was Bear cuddled up next to me, emitting a soft snore. My hand, on the other side of my body as Bear, still held the cell phone. I pushed the Eden icon again and braced myself.

"Hi, Daddy," said Zoey. "Mom's not ready to talk to you yet."

"Hi, darling Zoey. How are you feeling?"

"Still sore from the chemo, but otherwise, I'm fine. But how are you, Dad? I heard you have the"—she coughed—"dreaded virus."

"I'm a little sore, also, but otherwise feeling all right. Don't worry about me, I'm tough. Zoey, why did your mother say they canceled your appointments because of me? I have no idea what she means. I haven't talked to your doctors at all. What's she talking about?"

"Daddy, you're the President of the United States. And you had no idea that your presidential actions would have an impact on little ole me. It's not a big deal. I'm not blaming you."

"I still don't get it, Zoey. What are you talking about?"

"The National Emergency you declared. It called for all voluntary hospital services to be suspended, because they expect a big increase in cases of bat flu. According to the news, hospitals need to be prepared for more patients and also cautious about not spreading the disease to other people."

I heard yelling in the background. "Is that the kids?"

"No, it's Mom yelling that she still blames you, and she thinks you should call the doctor—as the President of the United States —and demand that they allow me to continue my treatments," Zoey whispered. "Ignore her, Daddy. She's not rational right now. Listen, I need to go or she'll grab the phone and yell at you. Give me a chance to talk to her, so if she calls you back in the next hour, it would be best if you wouldn't answer. Love you. Bye."

And she hung up without giving me a chance to say "I love you" back. That made me sad.

A few minutes later, Eden called. It was the first time in my life that I deliberately didn't answer the phone when she called. That made me sad, too. Bear knew something was up, because he gave me one of his little barks. It was like a question. I didn't answer him, either.

In the next fifteen minutes, Eden called five more times. Each time felt harder to just let it ring, but I trusted Zoey's advice and hoped that she would talk to Eden soon. Then I fell back to sleep.

The phone rang again, and before I even looked at it, I had decided to answer it, regardless. But it was Zoey, not Eden. "Hi, Sweetie. Is your Mom still mad at me?"

"A little, but not like before. I think I have her calmed down. She'll call you after a while. So please excuse the messages she left. It would be best if you would just delete them without listening to them. Honestly, Dad. That's highly recommended."

Zoey coughed. She had held the phone away from her, but I still heard it.

"I'll think about it, Zoe, but honestly, even if she's yelling at me, hearing her voice feels good to me."

"Not this voice, Dad. It's not hers. Oh! Hold on a second." A minute later, she returned.

"Something with the kids?"

"No, Mom is taking care of them right now. It's my toes. They're itching and driving me crazy. No big deal."

"Oh, okay. Oh! No! Zoey! Have you looked at them?"

"What's to look at? They itch. It's probably another side effect from the chemo."

"I don't think so, Zoey. Take off your shoe and look at them right now. It's important. Are they red and blotchy?"

"All right, Dad, just a minute. This is stupid, but I'll do it." A few seconds passed, and she came back on. "Yes, red from me scratching them, I'm sure. And a little blotchy. Like I said, no big deal."

"Zoey, sweetie, you've got bat flu. That was exactly my first symptom."

Zoey laughed. "Now you're trying to have one over on me, Dad. But, not funny."

"That's what I said to Jann when she told me. Then I called Dr. Stan in, and he agreed with her! He tested me and it was positive! Plus, you're coughing. I heard you. If you don't believe me about your toes, look it up on the internet. Or better yet, I'll have Dr. Stan call you."

"Daddy, you're serious? You're not kidding me?"

"No, sweetie, I'm not. And *having* Bat Flu is serious! And I think having cancer and having your immune system weakened makes you more susceptible to the more serious kind. Let me call him right now. I'll have him call you back right away. Bye."

I called Dr. Stan and explained everything to him. He told me that, yes, it was dangerous, and that he would be happy to call her. Then he asked me where she lived. I gave him all her information and hung up.

Now I not only had to worry about my beautiful little girl dying of cancer, I had to worry about her dying of bat flu.

Although what ultimately happened with Zoey surprised everyone.

CHAPTER FORTY-ONE

Jann

The man sitting on her couch wasn't a stranger, though. She knew him very well.

"Ricky? What are you doing here? You need to leave right now! This is all supposed to be secret!"

"Ma," Ricky said without even looking up. "First off, you need to keep your front door locked. Someone dangerous could come in. Second," now he looked up at me with the look of a kid going to Disneyland, "what are you doing with all this cool surveillance equipment?"

"You know what it is?"

"Sure. I learned about all of this when I was in the service."

Jann sat down beside him on the couch. "Great. Then you can explain it to me, because I don't get it!"

"It's no wonder you don't get it, Mom. These are advanced instructions for professionals—not for amateurs like yourself!"

"Well, that makes me feel better."

"Plus, you need to get this plugged in. But I'm more concerned about something else."

"What?"

He turned and put his hands on her shoulders. "Ma, seriously, you can't leave your front door unlocked like that. I was in juvie with guys who would take advantage of that, and they could hurt you."

She shrugged her shoulders. "Ricky, this is a safe neighborhood. Stuff like that doesn't happen here."

"It can happen *anywhere*, Ma! Promise me you'll at least *try* to keep that door locked."

"All right, I promise that I'll try to remember to keep the door locked." Then she picked up the bug detector and the power cord and plugged it into the side wall. "Okay, done. What's next?"

"What are you supposed to do with these?" Ricky held up the two cell phones.

"They're burner phones."

"I know what they are, Mom! Otherwise, they wouldn't be in with this other stuff. If no one knows about them, they're untraceable. One of them is broken."

"Yes, I know. There were three. One, I've already wrapped up to send to Eden, *secretly*, and one is for me. Since the third one is broken, it won't go to anybody."

"Are they already set up with each other's numbers, or do you need me to do that?"

"Dan said they're already set up for that. He has one, too."

"Ah, Mr. President himself." He held up some of the surveillance equipment. "So, where are you going to set this up? Did he tell you where to do it?"

"I haven't had time to even think about it. I've spent most of the time trying to figure out how all this works."

"All right. Let's get to work."

Rickey sat there with her for two hours, discussing every possible thing that she would need to know about the equipment, including every outlandish contingency that might arise. And even though he used simple language that was understandable, Jann still asked dozens of questions.

By the end of the two hours, she felt comfortable with the equipment, its versatility and what she would do with it. She and Ricky also discussed where she would put it in the West

Wing. He offered to help her set it up, but Jann thought that would just draw too much attention. If someone besides her was in the office that early, word would get around.

They decided to put one in the Oval Office. Although Dan wasn't there, since Marcus had sneaked in there before, she expected him to do so again. Then there was every chance that Marcus would have a meeting in the Situation Room. It was between the Situation Room and the Cabinet Room, and Jann thought that with Marcus's big ego, he would think it made him a bigger man if he had a meeting in the Situation Room. It was possible he would never go into the Oval Office or the Situation Room, but as Ricky said, with no way to know, those were two good guesses.

The last one would be more difficult, but she thought she could figure out a way to do it. She would put it in "The Beast"—the Presidential limousine that she knew Marcus would avail himself of every chance he got. And since all the bugs had GPS capability, she could keep track of where he went. She might have to talk to Dan about how she could arrange it, but she could call him on his burner phone, so it wasn't a problem.

After they finished the lessons, and they had tried the equipment and checked the bug detector, (her house was clear), Ricky said, "Ma, I can get you another device so you can stick it in Marcus's office."

Jann shook her head and shivered. "If I got caught in his office, I might not escape with my life."

Ricky laughed. "Now I know you're telling me a big one!"

She looked at him, and she could tell that he could see the fear in her eyes. "No, I'm not kidding, Ricky. I'm not kidding." She didn't want to tell him what Marcus had said to her earlier that day, because she was afraid of what Ricky might do to Marcus. But Ricky left it at that.

Ricky stood up and hugged her goodbye. "I've got to get home. Keesha and Jace are waiting for me. I stayed longer than I had intended." He walked toward the door. "Oh! Give me the package for Eden, and I'll have Keesha mail it tomorrow. And Ma, I had all of our mail forwarded here. Hope you don't mind."

She handed him the package and shook her head. "Course not, Ricky. I really appreciate you teaching me all this. And remember, it is an absolute secret. I hate to restrict you like this, but you can't even tell Keesha about it. But thank her for mailing this for me—though you can't tell her why."

He grimaced. "Yes, I know. I won't say a word. I'll just tell her that you can't get away. And you," he touched the tip of her nose, "keep that front door locked."

Jann nodded. Had she remembered to do that, everything probably would have turned out differently.

CHAPTER FORTY-TWO

President

When I got off the phone with Dr. Stan, I started to listen to one message from Eden. The first one started with her screaming at the top of her lungs, "Dan!" I had never heard her voice sound that aggravated. Anxiety seeped through it like water through a sieve. I didn't wait to hear any more; I pressed delete and then deleted the other messages from her as well. Zoey was right. I didn't need to hear that.

Then I turned toward Bear—who had his back to me—and spooned with him for an hour. Man, did I ever miss Eden. The emptiness of life without her was hitting me hard—even more so now that I was sick.

After an hour with no phone calls, I called Zoey. She answered on the first ring.

"Hello, Daddy. I'm sorry to say that you're probably right. Dr. Stan called and explained everything to me. And he told me I could go to a drive-up clinic not far from the house. Mom insists on going with me, so we had to wait for the kids to wake up— they were taking their naps. So, I'm about to get tested." She coughed.

"But he thinks you have it? You know, after talking to you, I mean."

"Yes, he does. He said my symptoms could result from chemo side effects, but corona toes being a side effect would be rare. Considering that I have a cough, too, and I'm tired and sore, he thinks I probably have it. Dr. Stan warned me it could be dangerous and to contact my doctor immediately if I have any shortness of breath."

"Oh, Zoey, I'm so sorry."

"He also spoke to Mom and explained everything to her. After their conversation, the first thing she said was that she would have to apologize to you. Dr. Stan told her that I most probably got the virus while I was at the hospital for my last chemo treatment, and had you started the Emergency Declaration earlier, that wouldn't have happened. *And* that she couldn't blame you for that, because he hadn't suggested it to you yet. So, no worries, Dad. You're now in the clear again." Cough, cough. "Sorry, Mom's got the kids in the car. Gotta go. Love ya. Bye."

"Love you, too, Zoey. Bye."

I stayed in bed for a few more minutes, trying to gather up my energy. Then I stood, shaking off the slight dizziness, and walked into the kitchen with Bear following. Joyce sat at the kitchen table reading a book. She stood up when she saw me.

"Mr., um, I mean Dan. How are you feeling?" Before I had time to answer, she scooped up something out of her med kit and put it close to my forehead. "Temperature's still normal."

"I'm feeling," I hesitated, trying to evaluate my body issues, "okay. Headache is better, body aches are still there but not horrible, and I'm tired. But nothing is any worse than it was before. And that smells great!"

"Dan, that's wonderful that you can smell that. Hopefully that means you only have a light dose of bat flu. I don't know what Dr. Patel would say, but in my experience, the people who can still smell and taste get through it easier."

"I hope that's true for me, Joyce, because I need to get back to work!"

"Easy now, fella. Today is your first day. You have a long way to go!"

After I cursed under my breath, I asked, "How long?"

"The day your symptoms begin—that was today, right?"—she didn't wait for me to answer—"the flu started two days before. So today is your third day. So you still have ten days to two weeks to, um, look forward to."

"I won't be looking forward to it!" Walking over to the oven, I reached out to open the door and see what was inside. But I had to stop because of a shout from Joyce.

"Dan! Wait! Don't touch the oven!"

Feeling aggravated, I turned toward her. "Why in the devil not?"

"Because I don't want to get this disease, that's why. I have to disinfect every single thing you touch, so if there is any way you can restrict what you touch, it will be better for everybody—well, me, anyway."

I put my hands in my pockets, stuck my bottom lip out like a scolded little child, and said, "All right. I understand. I don't want you to get it, either."

"And if you wouldn't mind not using the front bathroom, I'd appreciate that. I'll use the front one, and you use the one in your bedroom. Is that okay?"

"I guess it will have to be."

"Look, Dan, I hate telling the President of the United States what to do, and if you would prefer, I can follow behind you and disinfect everything you touch—"

"Honestly, Joyce, I don't think that's necessary. I can behave. But tell me, what's in the oven?"

"One of your favorites, meat loaf. Dr. Patel called your wife and got some of your favorite recipes. He thought you'd be more comfortable that way."

"I'm going to give that man a raise!" I said, laughing.

A shadow crossed in front of the kitchen window and I leaned against the sink to look out. It was Clive Holmes patrolling in front of the house. And I saw Jeff Egan in the distance talking to the Barclays—Steve and Sharon Barclay who lived here and took care of the place in my absence. Their house, smaller than mine, but still pretty, was out of my field of view.

What was in my field of view were my three beautiful horses: Star, Magic, and Dolly. Star and Magic were both solid black, except Star had a white star on his forehead, and Magic had a spot of white just above his right hoof. Dolly was a beautiful palomino.

And beyond the horses, I could see our dock jutting into Chesapeake Bay. And moored there was our forty-foot sailboat, the Ella Marie, named after Eden's mother who taught her to sail. When we were looking for a home close to Washington D.C., Eden said she didn't care where it was or what the house looked like; she just wanted to be on the water. My only requirement was a safe and comfortable place for the horses. This place was a great compromise. We both loved it.

Looking out at our beautiful grounds and the horses whom I loved so much, I decided that I felt well enough to go see them. So I headed toward the back door.

"Whoa, mister, where do you think you're going?"

"Just out to see my horses. I'll be right back."

"I don't think so! You need to stay inside and rest. Let your body recover from the disease that's raging inside your body."

"Who are you, anyway? Nurse Hatchett?" I pronounced it wrong, but knew she would know who I meant. "I'll just be a minute. What can it hurt?"

"You need to conserve all your strength to fight the infection. Dr. Patel said to make sure you stay inside the house."

"Dr. Stan said that? Really?" My shoulders slumped, and I returned to the window, putting my hands on the edge of the sink and leaning forward to see farther out of the window.

The horses were running in the field, and I sighed at their beauty and grace. Then I watched as Clive and Jeff crossed paths, spoke a few words to each other, and then continued their rounds. I felt so safe with them watching over me. Nobody could get through their tight net and watchful eyes. At least that's what I thought. But I was naïve. And I was wrong.

CHAPTER FORTY-THREE

Jann

Jann had gotten in extra early to make sure she was the only one in the office so she could plant the bugs. The first one in the Oval Office would be the most critical, because if Marcus came in early and caught her in there, she would have a hard time explaining herself. Of course, she could say Dan had wanted her to find something for him, but she didn't want a confrontation with Marcus. At all. If she never saw him again in her life, that would suit her fine.

So she was in and out of the Oval Office in less than a minute. She attached the bug underneath a table that sat to the left of the Resolute Desk by the window to the Rose Garden. Then she hightailed it back to her desk. After deep breathing for a few minutes to calm herself, she went downstairs to the Situation Room.

Although there were strict rules what could go into the Situation Room, they were more casual than formal, so Jann strolled in and attached the bug underneath the President's chair. It was secure and should catch all the conversation in the room. But, because of the sensors in the ceiling to prevent unauthorized communications—and bugging devices—she had to attach another device next to the bug, so it could block the sensors.

Ricky had found the device in with the bugs and had held it up to the light and said, "I've never seen one of these before! It's brand new technology, and I don't think it's even on the market yet. Where did Dan get this?" Then he had explained to her in detail how to set it up. After practicing a couple of times at home with Ricky coaching her, she was adept at the process. She had it attached and working in less than a minute.

After everything was in place, Jann returned to the Oval Office. The final bug, the one for the Beast, would have to wait until she was sure she'd be safe. Marcus could have plans for the vehicle in the morning and catch her there. That would not be good.

She listened for a minute and couldn't hear anyone else around. So she pulled the bug detector from her purse, turned it on, set it to *light* only—as opposed to light and sound—and walked around the room slowly like Ricky had showed her to do. Jann didn't expect to find anything, and she didn't. Even though she thought it was wasted effort, she did it because Dan told her to.

Sitting back at her desk and trying to quell her shaking hands, she took a sip of her almost cold coffee that she had brought in with her. She had never understood how something that was a stimulant could be so soothing. But it was—probably because it felt familiar.

Jann shuffled the papers on her desk and got to work. Even with Dan gone, she had plenty to do. And she might as well do it while she waited for the perfect opportunity to plant the bug in the Beast. A perfect opportunity that might never come, she mused. But she could hope. And she had a feeling that the bug in the Beast would be an important one.

She was deep in thought when footsteps came toward her desk. Looking up, she saw Isa rambling toward her. Isa stopped at Jann's desk and put out her palm within Jann's reach. Jann, still seated, gave her a high five.

"How you doin', woman?" Isa asked.

Jann took a deep breath of relief that it was Isa who had entered her office instead of Marcus. Not only was it good to see her, but she could protect Jann from Marcus, if need be! "I'm doing great, Isa, how 'bout you?"

Before Isa answered, more footsteps and Marcus entered the room. He looked at Isa and sneered, "What are you doing in here, Isa? Slumming?"

Isa turned half toward him and made a show of looking down on him, because she was so much bigger. "Why do you have to be such a total complete asshole *all the time*, Marcus?"

Marcus raised his hand with his forefinger pointing out when more footsteps approached the office. The sneer evaporated off his face, and his quintessential politician's smile replaced it. "Jon, good to see you! Come into my office; we have things to discuss." He put his arm around Jon Sharpe and led him down the hallway. Jon turned toward Jann and Isa and said, "Hello ladies," over his shoulder.

Jann thought how much more friendly he seemed with that little action. It was probably because Bear wasn't around, so he didn't have to be afraid. But she still thought he was a jerk, too, because of what he had done to the President. Dan wouldn't have bat flu right now if it wasn't for Jon Sharpe. Isa interrupted her thoughts.

"Now that you told me how Marcus tried to stop me from getting hired, I can treat him like the jerk he is. Do you believe how fast he went from asshole to politician when Jon came in?" She shook her head.

Jann laughed and held up her hand again for another high five, which Isa returned. "Well, I'm sorry he treats you so badly, Isa, but now I don't feel so alone!" She enjoyed the big woman's company, but with Marcus in his office with Jon, it would be the perfect time to get down to the Beast and install the bug.

Just then, they both heard a sound in the Oval Office and turned toward the door.

"Who's that? I thought President Indigo was sick. Is that why he used the other door?"

Jann scowled. "He wouldn't use the other door. And that isn't the President. He *is* sick. It's the asshole. He must have brought Jon in there to talk to him."

Isa shook her head. "No, he shouldn't be in there. It's not his office. Does President Indigo knows that Marcus goes in there?"

"Yup. I've told him." She almost let it slip about the bug in the office, but she kept that quiet. "Marcus does what he wants when Dan isn't here."

"That's just wrong," said Isa as she shook her head and walked away.

Jann couldn't understand what they were saying in the Oval Office. It didn't matter, though, that she couldn't catch their words. The bug would catch everything. At least, she hoped it would. The important thing now was getting the last bug into the Beast. And she had no idea how critical that action would be.

CHAPTER FORTY-FOUR

President

After Joyce left for the day and before I went to bed, I took the bug detector and went over every inch of every room in the house. Although I had to stop more than once to rest because I ran out of energy, I still got it done. And I found one. It was in my office. Whoever installed the damn thing must have thought I'd be hanging out in there while I was sick. Apparently, they haven't had this debilitating flu.

Tempted to rip the thing out, instead, I followed the advice I gave to Jann: leave it there and pretend not to know about it. The problem was that since I didn't check before Joyce arrived, now I wouldn't know if she put it there or if it was already there when she arrived. It's scary when you don't know whom to trust.

I woke up early the next morning to the sound of my phone ringing. It was Eden, and it felt so good to hear her soothing voice again. She had completely forgiven me and now was more worried than ever about Zoey, because Zoey's symptoms were worse than mine. Eden said that Zoey had spent most of the night coughing. And she had developed a fever, as well.

Now I was sick and worried, too. "Maybe you should call Dr. Stan," I told her. But she had spoken to him already, and he had told Eden that as long as the fever didn't get too high and no

161

shortness of breath occurred, there was no reason to go to the Emergency Room. He also told her to call him if she had any questions at all. That made me feel better.

Eden confessed she feared that she might lose both of us. I spent another few minutes consoling her and telling her we would both be fine, although I wasn't convinced of it myself. Then she had to go take care of Sage and Rose. They had become her responsibility once Zoey's symptoms worsened. We said *I love you* to each other and got off the phone. How I longed to hear her say that in person.

Bear licked my face, and I climbed out of bed and stretched. Should I get dressed or just put on my robe? What would be proper in a situation like this? After pondering the question for much longer than deemed necessary, I chose my robe. I was sick, after all, and she was a nurse. Decision made. Bear followed me into the kitchen, and Joyce leaned down to pet him.

After our talk yesterday, and watching Joyce disinfect the sink counter where I had leaned over to look out the window, I was careful not to touch anything and just sat down at the table at my usual spot.

"Good morning, Dan! You're up early this morning! Good morning, Bear! How are you this morning, Dan? Any better? Any worse? Do you need to report anything that I need to know?"

"Morning. Feel about the same. Slight headache, body aches, fatigue. I had diarrhea last night, but you don't need to know about that."

"Yup, I do. That's exactly what I need to hear about. Hey, would you like me to feed Bear? I bet he's hungry. Aren't you, big fella?" She scratched him on the scruff around his neck. "That food in the back, Dan? How much?"

"Two cups morning and two in the evening. And a dog biscuit."

"Great, I'll feed him while I'm here. One less thing for you to worry about and expend energy on."

On the table in front of my place setting was a wax-sealed manila envelope, marked in red with *For Your Eyes Only*. It was my Daily Brief.

"A secret service agent dropped that off for you this morning, Dan. Should I have given it to you right away?"

"No, Joyce. I'm sure if there was an emergency, I would have heard about it already. But thank you for asking."

Joyce fed both me and Bear, and afterward I retired to my bedroom to rest, read the Daily Brief, and to think about my conversations with Marcus and Dr. Stan the day before.

I had called Marcus late afternoon complaining that he hadn't checked in with me. He said that he was following doctor's orders, and that Dr. Stan had told him to let me rest. With a tone that sounded like he was placating me, he said that Dr. Stan's orders trumped my wishes. But Marcus being Marcus, he didn't say *Dr. Stan*, he just called him *Stan*. I had to correct him, which he always hated, but he tried not to show it.

Marcus told me nothing was going on and everything was under control. With an almost undetectable snicker in his voice, he said I didn't have to worry because I wasn't missed at all. I knew that was a lie. Jann for sure missed me. Who knew what Marcus would say to her—or even do to her—without me there to intervene.

When I got off the phone with Marcus, I wanted to call Dr. Stan to tell him I understood and appreciated his concern, but I wasn't dead, and a few phone calls wouldn't hurt me. I wasn't going to reprimand him—I had too much respect for him to do that—but him telling my vice president not to call me just wasn't right. So I punched in his number on my cell.

"Dr. Stan, Dan Indigo here."

"Mr. President! How are you feeling today? Is Joyce there?"

"She's here and a pleasure to be around. Thanks for sending her. And I'm doing okay. Same symptoms, but not any worse, so I take it that's a good sign."

"Yes, Mr. President, that is good. Let's see, your symptoms appeared yesterday, which means today is your fourth day. We often see worsening of symptoms on your fourth or fifth day, so if you're feeling the same today, that's a good thing."

"Listen, Dr. Stan, I don't know how to say this, because I appreciate your concern, but with all due respect, you should not be telling my vice-president not to call me when I specifically told him that he should."

"I don't know what you're talking about, Mr. President. The last time I saw Mr. Vice President was at your office yesterday, and you were present the whole time."

"So, you didn't tell him he shouldn't call me because I needed my rest—?"

"No, nothing of the sort. If you're feeling well enough to take a phone call, you'll know it."

"Oh," was all I could think of to say. Marcus had straight out lied to me and thought I was too sick to catch it. His actions were getting more and more questionable.

How I longed to talk to Eden about this. She had a clear head and would know what I should do about him. But I couldn't talk to her about Marcus until she received the burner phone. Little did I know that talking on that burner phone would lead to some excitement that I really didn't need in my life.

164

CHAPTER FORTY-FIVE

Jann

Hoping the two men—mainly Marcus, although she didn't trust Jon, either—would be in there for a while, Jann took the opportunity to leave the Whitehouse and walk as fast as she could the half mile to Secret Service Headquarters, where they kept all the Beasts. Although Marcus had his own Beast, she felt sure that with Dan sick, Marcus would choose to use Dan's, just to show he could.

There were several Beasts there—usually twelve—but Dan liked one particular one, and since he had talked about it before, she also felt sure that just being in *one* of the President's limousines wouldn't suit Marcus. It would have to be the President's *favorite* limousine.

He was that kind of guy. It surprised her that Marcus didn't try to horn in on Dan's wife again, but the way Eden always tried to avoid him, he might have already tried. Eden told Jann almost everything, but she seemed close-mouthed about Marcus. And it wasn't that Eden didn't trust Jann, because she said nothing to Dan about him, either. Jann didn't think she wanted to interfere with government business—at least not too much.

Jann made her way to the garage where they kept the limos. She had to show her ID a few times, but almost everybody knew her. She had been in the limos often enough or with Dan and Eden when they went here or there. Besides, she was the President's personal secretary—most everyone knew her or at least *of* her.

When it came time to get to the cars, though, it was a different story. "Jann," explained a secret service guy she didn't recognize, "we can't let you in a car on your own say so. It isn't done. We don't care if the President is sick or not. It's not done. Period."

Then Jann got lucky. She spotted Gavin Dennison on the other side of the garage. "Wait! Ask Gavin! He can vouch for me."

She expected the man to contact Gavin with a walkie-talkie. Instead, he turned in Gavin's direction and yelled, "Gavin! Come 'ere!"

Gavin talked a couple of more minutes, fist-bumped the guy he was talking to, and then sprinted over to where they were. "Hey, Jann! How's it going?"

"Hey, Gavin. Can you vouch for me, please? I just need to check Dan's favorite limo for something he left there." She had already decided what she would remove from the limo.

The man she had been speaking to spoke up, "Gavin, I've already explained to her I can't do that. You understand, right?"

Jann's hopes fell. If that didn't work, she didn't know what else she could do. Then an idea occurred to her. She just hoped it would fly. "Gav, call him! He'll verify for me."

Gavin looked at the guy, and the guy nodded and said, "If you can get hold of him, I'll take that as an official okay."

Gavin pulled out his cell phone, punched in the number, and pushed the *speaker phone* button.

Jann kept her fingers crossed—behind her so no one would see—that Dan would realize what she was doing.

"Mr. President? It's Gavin Dennison. Listen, I have Jannika White here, saying that you wanted her to check the Beast for something you wanted."

Gavin didn't ask a question, because that would be questioning Jann's veracity. He made it a statement that Dan could either agree with or not. The silence on the other end of the line was killing her. Sweat trickled down between her breasts. Then she heard Dan's voice over the speaker.

"Yes, yes, Gavin. That's fine. My old boombox in my favorite Beast. This sickness lasts a while, and I want my music. Please let her into the car."

Jann was holding her breath, but instead of expelling it in a rush so everybody knew how nervous she was, she let it out slowly through slightly parted lips.

"Great, Mr. President. Thanks, and I'll see you this evening."

"Goodbye, Gavin."

Gavin looked at the other secret service guy. The guy nodded and gave half a crinkled smile.

"I'll show her the car. Come on, Jannika. This way." He led the way down the line of identical Beasts. Gavin stopped in front of one, pointed to it, then led the way to the rear of the car. He slid in a key and opened it for her. "Voila, Jann!"

Jann stepped into the limo, searched around on the floor until she found the Boombox. As she was waiting for Gavin to open the car for her, she had fished the bug out of her purse and held it in her closed hand. Once inside, she slid it under the seat and secured it. She had completed the task! Jann exited the car holding the boombox and smiled at Gavin. "Thank you. Dan is so funny about this boombox, and he's probably had it since he was fourteen!"

Gavin shrugged. "Presidents, eh?"

Jann laughed along with him and then left the garage as fast as she could without looking like she was running away. Which she was. She couldn't wait to get back to the safety of the Oval Office. That is, *if* that was safe. As long as Marcus continued acting like he was more important than he was, anything was possible.

With Dan's beloved boombox in her hands, she walked straight back to the Whitehouse. Although she made a joke about it, Dan loved the stupid thing, and she wanted to get it back to him safe.

Jann walked into her office to find Marcus snooping around on her desk. There wasn't anything there worth snooping, though, because she always locked everything important away. But of course, having found him there doing something unsavory, he took the offensive.

"When the cat's away, the *mouse* will play, huh, *Jann-i-ka*? Out playing music on an extended break, are we?" He smiled his politician's smile at her, but it was tinged with a touch of malice.

He liked to draw her name out and emphasize all three syllables. Marcus probably thought it made him sound more authoritative than he actually was. In the seconds between when he said that and she answered, thoughts rampaged through her mind. Instead of answering back and mocking him like she normally would have, she was tempted to answer him in a patient and kind manner, as if she was talking to someone *normal*, instead of talking to the jerk Marcus. But then he would wonder what she had been up to, and she couldn't risk that. So she answered in her normal way.

"Marcus, if you weren't such a damn fool, you'd be dangerous. You don't recognize *Dan's* boombox that he's had since he was fourteen? You're even more stupid than I thought you were."

"What are you doing with it, anyway?" He tried to grab it out of her hands, but she pivoted out of his reach.

"Dan asked me to bring it to him on my way home. So keep your filthy hands off it, *Mr. Lucky!*" He especially hated it when she called him that.

"Why, you—" He took a step closer and had his fist raised.

Marcus wasn't a big guy. He was five feet nine inches, but he towered over five-feet-two inch Jann. She felt scared and held up the boombox so he couldn't hit her in the face.

"Um, excuse me," said a voice that Jann recognized. "Should I have bought tickets for this affair? I love a good boxing match." Isa had come in and put her big hand around Marcus's smaller one.

"Let my hand go, bitch!" he said and tried to pull his hand free.

Isa held onto it a second longer than she had to, then released him. Marcus turned and walked away, but both of them noticed he was rubbing his fingers as he went. Jann and Isa held their laughter until they heard him slam his door. Jann sat down still laughing, but she was shaking.

"Are you okay, Jann?"

"I will be in a minute. Thanks for rescuing me—again."

"No problem. Us girls have to stick together, right?" Isa held out her hand for a fist bump. Jann held a trembling fist up to hers.

"Phew. That was close. I wonder if he really would have hit me."

Isa tightened her mouth. "I'm sorry to say, Jann, that with President Indigo gone, I think he would have."

Jann shook her head. "I think you're right. I'll have to be more careful."

"Yeah, that would be a good idea." She started walking away. "I'll leave my office door open, just in case."

"Thanks, Isa, I appreciate it." Jann settled herself again, with the boombox settled on the floor next to her. She thought that she never wanted to be a real spy. It was dangerous! And she knew she would have to be extra careful with Marcus until Dan returned.

After her breathing returned to normal, she reached into her purse and pulled out the bug detector. She had been gone for a while. No telling what might have transpired while she was away on *spy business*.

Jann went to the door of the hallway that led to Marcus's office and listened. Nothing. She would have to be quick and cognizant of any noise that would indicate someone was coming. Starting at the perimeter of the room, she went over everything and then returned to her desk. Like this morning, she didn't expect to find anything. When she ran the detector under her desk, the light blinked wildly. Thinking it must be a mistake, she moved the wand behind her and the light went off. Under the desk, it blinked and blinked and blinked.

Dumbfounded, she just stared at it for a minute. Then the realization hit her. Someone had placed a surveillance device under her desk!

CHAPTER FORTY-SIX

The man

Closing his office door, he sat at his desk, opened his bottom drawer, and pulled out the catcher's mitt. Then he hugged it to his chest, swinging his body back and forth and saying "mmm-mmmm mmmmmmmm" as if he was holding a winning lottery ticket. In a way, he was. His goal was getting closer and closer—so close that he could feel it. Although he had no idea how it would happen, he knew that events would occur in his favor. That was the way it had been going, and he expected it to continue.

Dan Indigo could die of bat flu. Maybe the other people who stood in his way could get it, too. Or maybe he could just dispose of them like yesterday's trash. That's what they were, anyway. They meant nothing to him, just obstacles for him to get over. Whatever he had to do to get past them, he would do it. He knew that.

The words "Do something" echoed in his head. His mother had said that to him for years, and after a moment of weakness when he had shared that with his wife, she joined in and started saying it, too. At least she knew the proper times to say it—she never used it for mundane things like taking out the trash—only for more important things like when he suggested he might like to go into politics.

He relished the time he spent in the Oval Office. It had been his dream for so long. Today, he was an imposter in the Oval Office, but tomorrow, tomorrow he would be the owner.

CHAPTER FORTY-SEVEN

President

Since I had woken up extra early that morning, the phone ringing didn't surprise me, but who it was, did. The secret service agents who guarded me only rarely had occasion to call me on the phone. So it felt strange when I heard Gavin's voice. And when he asked about Jann wanting to get into the Beast, it took me a moment to realize what he was talking about. Luckily, I didn't question him, but figured it out myself after a few seconds. I don't know what would have happened to Jann had I not backed her up. But I did, and now I was certain she had put the bug into place.

And leave it to Jann to put it in my Beast instead of the one designated for the Vice President. She would know that Marcus's ego would entice him to use my Beast instead of his own. Good move, Jann!

It felt like it had been a long morning already. And as much as I didn't want to admit it, I didn't feel good. The headache had returned, and my legs ached something awful. In a moment of weakness that I refuse to regret, I called out to Joyce.

She came running. "Are you all right?"

"Yes, yes, just feeling the effects of this damned disease. Can I get a couple more aspirin from you?"

JK Lincoln

"Of course. Be right back," and her scrubs made a swishing sound as she left the room.

I took a deep breath and sank deeper into the bed. It felt good to lie down, and I felt grateful that I hadn't gotten dressed. Climbing under the covers for a good old-fashioned nap sounded damn good. Sleeping on top of the covers was one thing, but under the covers would feel like heaven.

Joyce strode in with the aspirin in a little paper cup and a glass full of water. "Here ya go, sir. Let me know if you need anything else."

"Joyce? You have a cell phone, don't you?"

"Yes, of course."

"If, um, if there was an emergency at the White House, and they couldn't reach me, they could always reach you, right?"

She sat down at the end of the bed. "Yes, Dan. And if you're wondering if it's okay for you to turn off your phone, I heartily endorse it. Get under those covers and have yourself a proper nap! It would do you good. Honestly."

"I'll do that. Thank you, Joyce."

"Do you want me to take Bear out to the kitchen with me?"

I put my hand on him and smiled. "No, I need him to keep me warm."

Joyce stood up, nodded, and said, "G'night, Dan." As she walked out, she closed the door most of the way.

After taking one last look at the phone, I turned it off and put it on top of the night table beside the bed. Then I opened the drawer and looked at the burner phone. There had been no reason to turn it on yet. Even if Jann could have mailed the other burner to Eden yesterday, she wouldn't have it yet. So it would be at least two or three more days before Eden received it. Frowning, I closed the drawer, took off my robe, and climbed into bed.

I woke up hours later with both arms around Bear, who had his head on Eden's pillow. She wouldn't mind. But it made me realize how much I missed her, as if I didn't realize that already. It made me want to call her.

174

I was sick, damn it. And when a man is sick, he needs his Mommy. And if his Mommy is gone, then his wife fits the bill. Yes, I know I'm the President of these wonderful United States of America and the most powerful man in the free world. But I'm also human.

My father, also gone, told me more than once that the key to being a strong and powerful man is realizing you are first and foremost a person. And people cry. Even strong people are sometimes weak. And both of those were okay. He also told me that the stronger and more powerful you are, the more you have to embrace your humanity.

So I'm embracing it. I'm sick and I need my wifey. Picking up my phone, I turned it on and found that Marcus had called multiple times, but had left no message. If it was something urgent about the state of the union, he would have left a message or called Joyce. There were no messages from Dr. Stan, so all must be okay on the bat flu front.

I called Eden. Although I couldn't discuss matters of state with her like I wanted to—because I couldn't trust the phone—we still had a great conversation. Until she received the burner phone, I would have to keep those other thoughts to myself. We talked for more than an hour.

What I didn't know was what was brewing at the White House and how much that would impact me in a very short time.

CHAPTER FORTY-EIGHT

Jann

When Jann first discovered the device under her desk, her first impulse was to rip the thing off and throw it away. But she remembered what Dan had told her: pretend you don't know it's there.

Her next thought was wondering who could have placed it there. The easiest and most logical person would be Marcus. But it could be Isa, although the more she got to know Isa, the more she doubted it. Isa was one of those people who acted hard on the outside, but who was soft on the inside. Jann liked Isa. She hoped it wasn't her. The other logical person was Jonathon Sharpe. He was around and probably wasn't with Marcus the whole time. And Jann still didn't trust him. If Bear didn't trust him, Jann sure wasn't going to. Jann considered dogs to be the best judges of character there are.

Considering she was gone for an hour, *anyone* could have come in there and she wouldn't know. Once she realized that, she put it out of her thoughts. Although she still had to be cognizant of its existence under her desk.

Jann was deep into work when footsteps approached her desk. It was Isa, who took her off guard so much that she ended up divulging something she hadn't intended to.

"So where is that—" Isa started, but Jann interrupted her by holding up her palm with one hand and held the index finger from her other hand to her mouth. Puzzled, Isa stood there and waited while Jann found some paper on her desk and hurriedly scribbled a note. *I found a bug in here, so watch what you say.*

"Oh! Sorry! I thought I was going to sneeze," said Isa, attempting to cover up the brief silence. "So where is that stamp you were going to give me? You know, the one for my brother's birthday card."

"Oh, I'm sorry, Isa. I was going to drop it off. Here, let me get it." Jann made a big show of opening a couple of drawers, hoping they would make enough of a noise for the bug to catch the sound.

While she rifled through the drawers, Isa wrote her own note. *Who put it there?*

"Here's the stamp, Isa." She looked at the note and shrugged her shoulders, then wrote on the notepad, *I was hoping it wasn't you!*

"Thank-you," said Isa while visibly struggling not to laugh. "How is Mr. President? Is he feeling any better?"

"I haven't talked to him today, but I hope so."

The two women heard quick footsteps in the hallway, and Marcus burst into the room. "What? I heard that! I thought you said Dan told you to bring him the boombox?"

"Boombox?" asked Isa.

Jann held it up for Isa to see. "Cool your heels, Marcus. He told me about it before he left his office yesterday, but I didn't have time to get it until this morning."

Marcus turned and started walking out of the room, muttering to himself. "I wonder why he didn't ask me to bring it to him."

Isa leaned over to say something to Jann, but Jann held up her palm again and handed her the pad and pen. She took it and scribbled, *That guy is fuckin' weird!*

Jann smiled and nodded, mouthing, *I know!*

Isa was just about to say something—goodbye is what Jann would have guessed—when Marcus returned to the room with one hand on his hip and the other with his finger striking the air. "You shouldn't be going over," he hesitated and glanced at Isa, "to, ah—"

"The residence?" asked Jann innocently. She knew why he hesitated. It was only she, Marcus, and the Secret Service who knew Dan was no longer in the residence. And Marcus didn't want to say anything in front of Isa. At least he had *some* scruples, thought Jann.

"Yes! You shouldn't be going there," he said, moving his finger in the air as if scolding her.

"Oh, Marcus," Jann said with obvious fake sincerity, "you don't want me to get sick. That is so sweet of you! Thank you. I didn't realize you cared."

Marcus narrowed his eyes, snorted, dropped his hand down to his side and stomped out of the room.

With a wide smile on her face, Isa said, "I think I'll return to my little office now." A couple of quiet giggles bubbled up from her as she walked away.

As soon as Isa closed the door to her office, Marcus came striding back in with his finger waggling in Jann's face again. "Look, you should not be the one to deliver that to Dan," he hissed.

"And who the hell should?" asked Jann. "You? Why would that be? It's a frickin' boombox. What—is—the—big—deal with you, Marcus?"

"Well, well," he stalled, because he didn't have an answer. "Give it to me!" He put out his hand as if expecting her to comply.

But she picked up the boombox and held it close to her chest. "This boombox ain't going anywhere until I talk to Dan! So don't even think about trying to get it from me!"

"I'm calling Dan right now!" And he strode off to his own office, where he slammed the door shut.

Jann sat there hugging the boombox to her. She knew some-thing would happen because of Marcus's reaction, but she didn't know it would create such turmoil in her life.

CHAPTER FORTY-NINE

President

After I got off the phone with Eden, I wanted to just lay there for a while before facing the world again. Talking to her had calmed me so much and almost made me feel human again. But as soon as we hung up, my phone rang, and it was Marcus. I didn't think I could put him off any longer, so I answered it.

"What's up, Marcus? Is there an emergency? I saw nothing urgent in the Daily Brief."

"Are you okay? What's wrong? Why didn't you answer? Have you gotten worse? Should I call somebody?"

He rattled off the questions, not waiting for an answer. You'd think that he might have even cared.

"Marcus, chill. I'm fine—well, not fine, but I'm doing okay and not any worse. I took a nap and then was on the phone with Eden. Nothing is wrong, and I wasn't deliberately avoiding you. So what's going on that's so important?"

"I don't think Jannika should come to the house!"

"She hasn't."

"She told me you wanted her to bring you that old-fashioned portable audio system you have."

"My boombox? Yes, yes, I asked her to bring it to me." That was close, I thought.

"Well, I don't think she should. We don't want anyone to know you're there and not at the residence, and I don't think it would be wise for her car to be there."

I thought I knew where he was going with this. "So, uh, who should deliver it to me, Marcus? Because I don't think if you drove up in the Vice-Presidential Beast that it would look very good."

"Oh, yeah, you're right. But it shouldn't be *her*!"

"All right, understood. Perhaps you're right." It didn't hurt to give in to him on this, because the boombox was only a diversionary tactic, anyway. "Just give it to one of my secret service guys at the residence. They'll deliver it, and nobody will be the wiser."

"But I—"

"That's my decision, Marcus. You don't want Jann delivering it? Fine. But neither will you. The secret service agents will make sure I get it with no extra cars around. Period.

"All right, Dan. Goodbye."

And then he hung up. I could tell he was disappointed, but oh well. He wanted so badly not only to deprive Jann of the chance to come here, but to show her up and come here himself. I didn't know why Marcus hated her so much. It was almost like she had something on him, and so he wanted to get rid of her because of it. If there was something like that, I didn't know about it.

My hour on the phone with Eden relaxed me and made me feel better. And five minutes with Marcus tensed me up and made me feel sicker. My head hurt.

As if the angel could hear my thoughts, Joyce appeared at the door. "Hello, Dan. How are you feeling?" She came to the side of the bed and used the thermometer on my forehead again. It flashed, and she looked at it. "Temperature's still normal. How's your head and body aches? Ready for some more aspirin?"

"I was trying to hold off, but yes, I would like some more, thank you."

She spilled two aspirin out of the bottle and into my hand, and handed me a fresh glass of water. "Can I get you anything else?"

"No thanks. I may walk around a bit and then lay down again."

"You mean walk around in the house, right? I'm still not going to let you go outside."

Looking at her with a pleading expression on my face, I felt like a teenager asking to use the car. "But I would feel so much better if I could just get closer to my horses."

"No, Dan, sorry," she said as she slipped out the door.

I climbed out of bed and put my robe on and then took it back off and got dressed. If I acted sick, then I would probably just get sicker. If I acted well, it may not make me feel any better, but I would *think* that I felt better, and that could make all the difference. Walking into my office, I stood before the window.

That window was at the side of the house that didn't face the horses. But if I opened it a little, maybe I could *hear* them. I unlocked it, lifted it up a couple of inches, and took a deep breath of the cold, fresh air. Then I heard them. Steve or Sharon must have moved them into the arena. Their hoofbeats were unmistakable. It sounded like they were chasing each other around in there. Although I could have walked to the kitchen window to watch them, just hearing them gave me a certain amount of peace.

Then I got a great idea! I hurried to my room to retrieve my cell phone to call the Barclays. Returning to the office, I wrestled with the screen to take it off the window. I pulled it inside, so it wouldn't be so obvious that I had taken it off—from the outside, anyway. Five minutes later, Dolly, Star, and Magic were all trying to stick their heads in the window at once. All three of them were nickering at me, and it made me want to weep.

When the cold started to get to me, I kissed each horse on the nose, thanked Steve and Sharon for bringing them out, and hurried to close the window before I froze to death. A minute later, I was under the blanket in my room trying to get warm.

And to rest. That small amount of excitement took all the energy that I had.

And in all the excitement, I forgot to lock the window, thank God, and that made all the difference in the world.

CHAPTER FIFTY

Jann

It had been more than an hour since Marcus stormed out, and Jann wondered why he hadn't returned yet. But when she went to the restroom, she carried the boombox in with her, just in case. Later, when Marcus sashayed back in with a big grin on his face and his hand out, she had it tucked under her desk.

"Talked to Dan. You are *not* to deliver it to him!"

"And you are?"

"I'll take care of it. Give it to me."

"I'm not giving it up until I talk to Dan."

"I told you what he said."

"No, you told me what you want me to believe. Have Dan call me, and I'll hand it right over, Marcus." She held up three fingers. "Scout's honor."

He took a step forward, but then his cell phone rang. His ring tone sounded like a funeral march. Picking it up, he tapped it and walked away, holding it to his ear. When he got to his office, she heard him close the door.

Since she didn't know how long she had, she grabbed the boombox and hurried out of the office toward the residence. If she couldn't deliver it to where Dan was, she could give it to the secret service guys stationed at the residence. They were there for show to continue the deception that the President was at the residence, but they knew where he really was and could deliver it to him. Not that he really wanted it, because the whole thing had been a ruse so she could plant the bug. Even so, it had to be played out.

When Jann got back to her office, she took her purse and stepped into the restroom. Once there, she pulled out the burner phone and texted Dan: *Boombox delivered to residence (by me). Guess what, Dan? I found a frickin' bug underneath my desk. I left it there, as instructed, & have been careful.*

Jann knew what a jerk Marcus was, but Jon Sharpe was still an enigma to her. While Marcus had dozens—no, hundreds—of strikes against him, Jon had only two: Bear always growled at him and Jon was the one who set up the dinner at the Air Force Base where Dan had caught bat flu.

The bug under her desk had made her give serious thought to who could have put it there. She still wasn't sure it was Marcus, though he was the obvious choice. The more Jann thought about it, the more she wanted to explore the possibilities. And she knew how. Ask Isa.

The irony, of course, was that Isa could easily be the one who did it. Her office was right there in the West Wing, and she had the opportunity. There was no motive, though. Why would she be interested in Jann's conversations? And there was something about Isa that made Jann trust her. Jann couldn't define it exactly, but it felt like Isa was "okay."

She remembered a time after she moved out of Dan and Eden's house, and she was looking for a place to rent for her and Ricky. Jann looked at a place, and it was perfect: right location, right price, clean, and just what she wanted.

When the owner, a big white man who looked like a boxer, asked her if she wanted it, she said yes, that she could forward him her references. He waved his hand and smiled at her. "I don't need references," he said, "I go by intuition." She and Ricky lived there happily for three years.

JK Lincoln

In that same way, she felt like she could trust Isa. If she was wrong, and Isa was the one who put the bug there, then it would not end well. But she was counting on her intuition being right. And with that in mind, she walked down the hallway and knocked on Isa's door.

"Come!" said the manly voice inside.

Jann opened the door and stepped inside, closing the door behind her. "Hi, Isa, I wanted to ask you about—" Stopping suddenly, she held up one finger and returned to her desk, where she unlocked the bottom drawer and pulled out her purse, re-locking the drawer afterward.

She closed Isa's door behind herself again, and after putting one finger in front of her lips so Isa wouldn't say anything, she reached into her purse and pulled out the bug detector wand. Carefully, she went over every inch of space in Isa's office.

Finding nothing, she put the detector away and said, "I just wanted to be sure. I have to ask you something."

"Sure! Shoot!"

Jann walked to the side of her desk and asked in a quiet voice, "You work with Jon Sharpe. What do you think of him?"

Isa raised her eyebrows and nodded. "I think he's very good looking—for a man!" She winked at Jann.

"But I mean as a person. Is he honest? Reliable?"

"Jann, dear, he wouldn't have gotten to where he is without those qualities. What is this about?"

"I don't know if you know this, but he's the one who set up the dinner at the Air Force Base. You know—the place where Dan caught bat flu."

Isa smiled. "I know the *whole* story behind that."

"The whole story? What do you mean?"

"Yes, Jon did that—after Marcus *told* him to. And when the President is away, and the Vice President tells you to do something, you do it. When he tried to explain that to Mr. President, he screamed at him and told him to get out of his office."

"I was there. I heard that part."

"It upset Jon, but he felt there was nothing he could do about it. And he told me that he'd feel like a tattletale if he went against"—she moved her head to the side to indicate Marcus in the office next door—"that jerk. Even with his politician smile and countenance, Marcus has a reputation for vengeance if someone goes against him."

"Seriously? I didn't know that, and I don't think Dan does, either."

"Well, someone ought to tell him because that guy"—she nodded toward Marcus again—"is dangerous."

Jann and Dan would both find the truth in those words in the not too distant future.

CHAPTER FIFTY-ONE

President

I woke up on the third day of my stay at home feeling the same. It disappointed me. Every day I kept hoping that I would feel better, but it wasn't happening. But it was a new disease, and I didn't know what to expect. I decided to call Dr. Stan a little later once he got into the office. Since there was nothing urgent, I didn't want to bother him at home.

The previous afternoon, Marcus had called me with an update. Nothing was going on. More and more people were getting sick with bat flu. Dr. Stan encouraged them to wear a face covering and not to get too close to other people. But some listened and some ignored that advice. Besides that, the country was running smoothing, according to Marcus.

Reluctant to get up, I stayed in bed snuggled up with Bear. For the following hour, I read the first Harry Potter book. I loved that series, and since I didn't have time to pick out new books for my time here, that's what I chose. When I finished the chapter I was reading, I put the book down and opened the drawer with the burner phone in it. It was driving me crazy not being able to talk to Eden about what I really wanted to talk to her about, so I picked up the phone and turned it on, planning to text Jann and ask when she had mailed the phone.

But when I turned it on, it immediately rang. All I saw on the screen was Caller #2. Following the instructions that Susanna Pollard had given me, I pressed the button to answer it, but didn't say a word. The idea was not to give the caller an idea who was on the other end of the phone in case the *wrong people* had intercepted the phone. Plus, I had no idea who *Caller #2* was. It should be either Jann or Eden.

How relieved I was when I heard, "Dan? It's me." Ah, my lovely Eden.

"Eden! You got the phone!"

"Dan, what's going on? What's with all the spy stuff? I mean, really, a burner phone?"

"That's what I wanted to talk to you about. But first, how is Zoey? I've been worried about her."

"She's not doing very well at all. She coughed all night long."

"Can't her doctor prescribe something for that?"

"He suggested codeine, but Zoe refuses to take it. So all she did was suck on lozenges until her tongue got sore."

"Have you talked to Dr. Stan? Does he think she should be admitted to the hospital?"

"He said definitely not unless she gets much worse. Her low grade fever is negligible and her breathing is fine. She can't smell or taste anything, but he said that's one of the normal symptoms. So how are *you*, Dan? I've been worried about you."

"I'm doing as fine as I can be with this dreaded disease. No fever, but I get headaches and body aches. I'm not better and I'm not worse. I think not worse is a good thing."

"I'm relieved to hear it."

"How are Sage and Rose doing? They can't spend any time with Zoey, can they?"

"I hold them up at the door so they can see that she's still here. That makes them feel better. But Rose asked me if her Mommy was going to die. That was disturbing."

"All right, let me tell you what's going on. When I found out that I had bat flu, Marcus and Dr. Stan were in the office with me. Marcus immediately asked about the 25th amendment.

189

Luckily, Dr. Stan defended me and said I was fine to remain in office. But it made me look at Marcus differently. I almost got the feeling he was just waiting for a chance like this to oust me from the presidency."

"Dan, I've tried to warn you about him from the beginning. But you kept saying he was your best friend and you would trust him with your life. You might have to reevaluate that."

"Yes, I know. After he said that, when I went back to the residence, I dragged out all the stuff that Joanna Pollard gave to me that night we had dinner together. I gave most of it to Jann and had her send the phone to you."

"Jann explained most of that in the letter that came with the phone."

"I still have a hard time believing that Marcus would do anything to hurt me. But I used to be one hundred per cent sure of that, and it has now slipped to maybe seventy-five per cent and falling fast."

"Listen, Dan, I need to tell you a story that will get it down to zero percent. I hope you understand why I've never told you before, and please don't get mad. When—"

"Wait! My phone just beeped; I think I need to plug it in. Hold on." I opened the drawer by my bed, but the only charger in there was for my regular phone. So I walked to the suitcase I had brought home with me and checked all the pockets, thinking maybe I had left it inside. It wasn't there. "Oh, no, Eden, I left the charger in the residence. I'll call you back. I have to reach Jann right away. Bye. I love you."

Hanging up quickly, I texted Jann. *I forgot the charger for the burner phone! Please retrieve it and then get it to me. I need it. BUT, you can't bring it here and you can't give it to Secret Service. Think of something. I'm counting on you.*

The phone died right after I pressed Send. Would Jann get the message? And what was Eden going to tell me about Marcus that she'd never told me before?

CHAPTER FIFTY-TWO
Jann

Jann drove in just before sunrise so she could get everything done and maybe get out of the office early, to give her less time with Marcus around. She sat down at her desk and thought about the burner phone in her purse. She hadn't even turned it on since Ricky helped her with the surveillance setup. An idea occurred to her. If she went into the bathroom with her purse, she could get away with at least checking for text messages.

Smiling happily, she locked the bathroom door behind her and reached into her purse. Instead of pulling out the cell phone, her hand came up with the bug detector wand. Jann thought it was a waste of time to check the bathroom, but why not? As soon as she turned it on, it began pulsating in her hand. "No! What sick fuck would put a bug in the bathroom?" she thought, without saying it out loud. That would blow the whole deal now, wouldn't it?

With the bug in the bathroom, she didn't dare check the burner phone—what if there was video, too? That bug made her more convinced than ever that it was Marcus setting the things, but in all honesty, she thought it could still be Jon Sharpe, or even, God forbid, Isa. But if it was Isa, she wouldn't have set a new bug in the bathroom. Alternatively, since she knew that Jann knew about the one under her desk, maybe that's *exactly* what she would do. It was all so confusing.

Now she had two bugs to report to Dan; and she had to wait until she got home to text him. There was no way she could take a chance doing it here. Maybe Isa's office? That was bug-free. No. Although she thought she could trust Isa, Dan had said that no one could know about the burner phones.

Ricky finding out about them was an accident. And besides, without his help, she wouldn't have been able to get all the surveillance work done. If there was anyone she trusted, it was Ricky: her own flesh and blood.

She flushed the toilet, although she had not gone, washed her hands and exited the bathroom to find Marcus sitting at her desk, pulling at her locked drawers. Thank goodness she always kept them locked.

"Oh! I didn't realize you were already in. I was just checking to make sure you kept your drawers locked up. You know. Security and all. That's my responsibility now."

"Marcus, my coat is on the back of my chair. Now get out of here."

"Don't get so touchy, Jann-i-ka. I was just doing my job." After giving the top drawer one last tug, he stood up with his politician's smile plastered to his face and walked out.

Hours later, with her head so involved in her work that she had no idea how much time had passed, Dr. Patel walked into her office. "Hi, Jann. I need to see Mr. Vice President."

Jann couldn't help it. She blurted out, "Why?" Then she made a show of pretending to slap herself across the face. "Sorry," and she held out both hands, palms up, like "whatcha goin' to do?"

Dr. Patel laughed and nodded. "I spoke with Mr. President this morning, and he suggested I talk to him."

"Oh, all right. His office is"—she was going to point the way to his office, but decided something else instead—"I'll buzz him for you."

"Mr. Vice President? Dr. Patel is here to see you." The next thing Jann heard was the clicking of the line. She expected him to come bursting out of his office and walking down the hallway to get Dr. Patel.

But that's not what happened. The next thing Jann knew, the door of the Oval Office opened, and with a huge grin on his face, Marcus strode out of there with his hand extended to the doctor.

"Stan! How nice to see you! Come in to *my* office."

Marcus led the way into the Oval Office, giving Dr. Patel a chance to turn around and look at Jann with a puzzled expression on his face. Jann just shrugged.

Jann could hear the conversation clearly, because Marcus had not closed the door. That must have been intentional—probably to show Jann that he could. Dr. Patel explained to Marcus that the virus had mutated, and that was not a concern in itself, because that's what viruses do. He said it was just discovered, and as of right now, he didn't know if it was more contagious or not, or more dangerous or not. They would know more in a day or two. Jann noticed that Dr. Patel was very careful about not mentioning that he had already spoken to Dan. Excellent choice, Dr. Patel! Jann had to give him credit for his political savvy.

There was nothing she could do about Marcus using Dan's office. She would text Dan tonight—on the burner phone—but she didn't think he could do anything since he was at home. Besides, he always let Marcus get away with more than he should because of their long relationship. But how soon would Dan be back? She wasn't sure how long bat flu lasted, but probably another week.

Who knew what kind of damage Marcus could cause, given another week? If Jann had only known—

CHAPTER FIFTY-THREE

President

Knowing I wouldn't find out right away if my message had reached Jann, I called Eden back on my regular phone. But aware that we might be "overheard," there wasn't much else to say—we had already talked about Zoey—and Eden had to get back to taking care of her and the kids.

Dr. Stan had called to report a new variant of the virus had been identified. I told him to report it to Marcus. There was nothing I could do from the ranch—although there was nothing Marcus could do, either. What do you do with an out-of-control pandemic? Everyone was already advised to wear masks and not get close to anyone else. Businesses were shutting down, restaurants were *to-go* only, and everyone who could was working from home. Although it was good to have the knowledge there was a new variant, did that knowledge really help us?

"Well, Bear, how about we get up and seize the day?" I didn't feel well enough to seize anything yet, but Bear wagged his tail, so I put on my robe and ventured into the kitchen. As I sat in my chair, Bear walked over and nuzzled the back of Joyce's hand as she stood at the sink.

I was used to seeing Joyce in my kitchen in the morning, but I wasn't prepared for Bill Clinton wearing a dress and scrubs. A very short Bill Clinton. Then Joyce ripped off the mask as she erupted into hilarious laughter and slipped on her usual surgical mask.

"Ha ha! I tricked you, didn't I? You wondered why Bill Clinton was in your kitchen preparing your breakfast! Admit it!"

"Well, I've met Bill Clinton a few times," I said, "but he's never been wearing a dress, and he's pretty tall."

Joyce kept laughing as she served me a bowl of steel cut oatmeal, served the way I liked it, with a little cream and a touch of maple syrup. Shaking my head, I looked at the envelope for the Daily Brief that had been waiting for me on the table. I wanted to check it out, but since I didn't know if Joyce was the one who set the bug in the office, I couldn't very well open it with her in the same room. So I put my hand on it and waited to go through it later.

"Would you like some aspirin today, Dan?"

"Yes, I would, please. I don't feel any better than yesterday, and I *hate* that!"

"Today is your fifth day of bat flu. Tomorrow is when we should see some improvement—but it won't be much."

"Any improvement would be good at this point." I shook my head. "But I shouldn't be complaining. My daughter has it, too, and she's really suffering. She's been coughing all night long."

"This is Zoey, right? Did I hear that she has breast cancer? I thought I heard that on the news somewhere." Joyce knitted her brows.

"Yeah, a president's family is always under the microscope. Nothing is private. She has breast cancer and had only one chemotherapy session before the hospital stopped all out-patient activity.

Joyce nodded, tightened her lips, and turned away. There was something ominous in the way she did that. It scared me.

After finishing my breakfast and thanking Joyce, I returned to the bedroom carrying the Daily Brief with me. Bear followed at my heels.

The aspirin dulled the pain of the headache and body aches, but did nothing for my fatigue. I climbed into bed with a pillow propped up behind my back, so I could read the Brief while sitting up. It was mostly routine political information with a little on the progress of a bat flu vaccination, updates on how many cases of bat flu in the country—too many—and how the investigation on the bat flu origin was going. It wasn't that different from the day before or the day before that. And hopefully it would stay that way until I was back in my bloody office.

When I finished the Brief, I called Dr. Stan again to find out how he did with Marcus, or if he had found out any new information on the variant.

"Dr. Stan. Dan Indigo again. I wondered if you found out any more information about the new variant or if it's too early to tell."

"I was about to call you, because I found out one thing you won't be happy about. You've got it."

"Bat flu? I know I have it! Tell me something I don't know!"

"No, Mr. President. You're not understanding me. You have the *new variant*. And unfortunately, so does Zoey."

"How can you even know that? I haven't seen you in days."

"We did a DNA test off your bat flu test. You know. When they stuck the long Q-Tip up your nose. Same with Zoey. I was in touch with her doctor and had them test it. You both have the new variant."

"Is that bad or good?" I asked.

"No telling yet. It doesn't seem to make people any sicker, but it may be more contagious than the original."

I thought about Joyce's knitted brows. "Tell me, Dr. Stan, how is Zoey? Be honest."

"I won't lie to you, Mr. President. It's not good. She has two serious comorbidities."

"Comorbidity? Does that mean she's going to die?" My heart sank, and a breath escaped me.

"Comorbidity means there are other conditions occurring with the primary disease. In Zoey's case, she has cancer and she

196

had one chemotherapy treatment. The problem is that chemotherapy suppresses the immune system. It can decrease the number of white cells and other immune cells that the body needs to fight the main disease."

"But she only had that one treatment."

"Well, that's good as far as the bat flu, but not good for the cancer. It's a risky situation, Mr. President. I'm monitoring her closely. I've already spoken to Eden today. Getting through the fifth day without getting worse is a good sign. And Zoey, although not any better, is not any worse, either. Although she's having major coughing issues, she's not having any trouble breathing. So I'm guarded but hopeful."

"Oh, thank God," I said. And to myself, *my little girl might make it.* But the truth was, nobody knew. This was still a new disease, and now an even newer variant.

"There's something else I'd like to talk to you about, Mr. President. And it's none of my business, but with you laid up like this, I feel it's my duty to say something."

"Please speak freely, Dr. Stan. I respect your opinion, whether or not it's your business."

"You asked me to go see Mr. Vice President to inform him of the new variant. And I did that."

"Yes, I was wondering how that went."

"It went fine, Mr. President, but he was in the *Oval Office!* And when I walked in with him, he said something like, 'Come in to *my* office.' It didn't feel right, Mr. President."

Still holding the cellphone to my ear, I stared off into the distance—which wasn't too far, because I was in my bedroom staring at the door. "Dr. Stan, while I appreciate the information, I think getting Marcus out of there would be a mistake. It would be tricky and complicated. And then where would I be? In a situation where the President and Vice President were butting heads. With Marcus, sometimes it's better to go along with his bullshit. And believe me, Dr. Stan, I know it's bullshit." At that moment, I realized that if Marcus was monitoring my phone, then Dr. Stan had just made a huge political blunder. Not to mention that Marcus wouldn't appreciate what I said, either.

We hung up after that, but I have wondered long and hard if that wasn't one of many mistakes I made that ultimately put me in that horrible position in that horrible place. Would getting him kicked out of my office have changed anything?

CHAPTER FIFTY-FOUR

Jann

By midafternoon, Jann had gotten her daily work done and caught up on some of her backlog. She looked up when she heard a loud voice. It was Marcus, and she could hear him screaming even though he had closed his office door. She couldn't hear the words, just the raised voice. Briefly, she considered getting up and walking a few steps so she could hear, but she discounted that idea. She was already on his shit list and no reason to risk him getting even angrier.

But she had an idea. With him occupied, she could get a quick peek at the burner phone. Maybe Dan had texted her something important or something she needed to know. Fumbling inside her purse, she turned it on and immediately turned the sound off so no one could hear the opening tones. There was a message there, and it was from Dan. He had forgotten to take the charger for the burner phone, and he needed it. Jann knew she could easily get the charger from the residence. That would not be a problem. But she could not bring it to him, and because no one could know he was using a burner phone, she couldn't give it to the secret service guys to deliver to him.

Then how the hell was she to get it to him? Mailing it to him would be too risky. No, it had to be something else. But she had no idea what that might be.

Her first job, however, was retrieving the charger from the residence. She locked up, took her purse to carry the thing in, and walked over there. The secret service guys stationed at the door were glad for the diversion. They knew the President wasn't really there, and they were there just for show. So they let her in without question, because she was a frequent visitor and a personal friend of Dan and Eden's.

She searched all the places she could think of where someone might plug in a cell phone: living room, kitchen, she even checked the bathroom. The bedroom was an afterthought, but then she chided herself for not coming up with that sooner, because if he was keeping it a secret, it would have to be out of public view.

Jann had wondered why he couldn't use the charger from his regular phone, but when she picked it up, she saw it was completely different. She clutched her purse tight to her on her return to the Oval Office, as if she was carrying a treasure.

At the end of the day, she still didn't know how she would get the damn thing to Dan. He said in the text he was counting on her, and she hoped his confidence wasn't misplaced. How could she get something to him—something that wasn't even supposed to exist—secretly? It was an incredible dilemma.

Driving home, she called Ricky. He had helped with the surveillance equipment, knew about the burner phone, and she trusted him. It was Friday, and sometimes he worked late, but hopefully, he wouldn't mind.

"Hey, Ma, what's up?"

"Ricky, I need to talk to you. Can you come over after work?"

"I'm on my way home now. Can't we just talk here? Keesha has dinner waiting."

"Um, no." She should have expected that answer, but she wasn't prepared for it. "I need to have a face-to-face conversation with you. It's important."

"Oh. Nothing's wrong, is it?"

"No, honey, I need some advice on something personal."

"Tell you what, Ma. You call Keesha and explain. If I call her, she might get upset, but if you call, she'll understand!" He laughed.

"Sure, Ricky, I'll see ya soon."

An hour later, Jann was home, clothes changed, dinner in the oven, mail retrieved, and almost to the point of panic worrying that she might let Dan down. She had never smoked cigarettes in her life, but at moments like this, she thought a cigarette might help her cope.

Jann heard Ricky come through the front door. "Ma! You need to keep that door locked! Did you know there was a serial killer active a few years ago who targeted his victims by whose house was unlocked? Please! Keep it locked."

"I'm trying to remember, Ricky. But I've left it unlocked for so long now. I only remember about half the time."

"Well, half is better than none. Make it a habit, then you won't have to remember. So what's going on? Issues with the surveillance equipment?"

"Sit down. I need you to help me brainstorm."

"No, I need to get home to dinner. Shoot. Let's do it quick."

Jann explained the dilemma to him, and he nodded his head the whole time with his eyes wandering upward like he was taking it all in. He repeated to her all the ways she couldn't use, and at the end he said, "Honestly, it seems impossible. Can't you put it in a disguised package and give that to the secret service agents?"

She shook her head. "They have to open every package that goes to the President."

He hugged her and walked toward the front door. "All right. I know the parameters. Let me think about it and get back to you. Love you, Mom."

"Love you, too, Ricky."

If Ricky couldn't come up with something, Jann didn't know what she would do. Dan was counting on her, and she was counting on Ricky. What she didn't know was that she wasn't going to like his idea very much—

CHAPTER FIFTY-FIVE

President

It had been two days, and I had heard nothing about the charger for my burner phone. I knew I had given Jann an almost impossible task. She had never failed me before, but even *I* couldn't think of a covert way to get it to me.

But I felt grateful that the dreaded disease had all but left me. I was almost back to my old self. Although I still felt like I was sick, I didn't have to take aspirin anymore for my headache and body aches. The headache was only a hint of its former self. My legs still ached, but less than before. Now I was spending more time in my office and less time in my bedroom. Only a few more days, and I would return to the residence and the Oval Office.

My daughter, Zoey, was better, too,—not cured, and not as well as I was—but at least she had gotten no worse and was on her way to recovery. That was a huge weight off my mind. I'd spoken to Eden at least twice a day and had even spoken to Zoey once, but her coughs had punctuated our conversation. But she was better, and Dr. Stan had said she was now out of danger—at least from the virus. The cancer was another story.

While in my office, I was always cognizant of the bug. I didn't know who put it there or why. My guess was Marcus, but it could as easily have been Joyce. And the why was even more confusing. Although my father always used to tell me that the more information you had, the better off you were. In my life, that seemed to be true. But it still didn't tell me the *who* behind the bug.

Now that I was in my office more often than in my bedroom, my wonderful caretakers, Steve and Sharon, would come by the window with the horses to see if I was available. If I was in there and not on the phone, I would open the window so the horses could poke their heads in. Since I had taken to keeping some carrots with me in there, they were even more eager to stick their heads in.

And I would pet them, and kiss them on their noses, and inhale their wonderful fragrance. Eden called it equine perfume, but I would not be caught saying something like that. That didn't stop me from enjoying their scent, though. The smell of a good horse was enough to calm a man's soul. So I left the screen off and the window unlocked. The ranch was way out in the country, and no one knew I was here, anyway.

My days were routine now and maybe not *comfortable*, but they were *familiar*. Still, I longed to be back in the White House. But I'd read the Daily Brief every day, spoken to Marcus a couple of times a day, and nothing untoward had happened either with the virus or the politics of the world. At least nothing that I had to worry about.

Dr. Stan would check up on me every day to make sure I was progressing in the right direction, and I'd ask him the truth about Zoey. I feared Eden and Zoey might make everything more palatable to keep me from worrying, but they hadn't so far. And Dr. Stan would also tell me about the progress with the vaccine, any new variants that were out there, and if anything else needed to be done to keep the infection rate in the United States down to a somewhat manageable level. So far, everything was as copacetic as it could get in the middle of a worldwide pandemic.

So, there I sat in my kitchen enjoying a cup of chamomile tea that I had made myself, since Joyce had already left. It was dark, and I was enjoying the quiet, the gentle sounds of the wind, and my horses in the background. Bear lay at my feet, as usual.

When he pricked up his ears, I paid no attention because there were always many sounds on a ranch. I had just placed the cup back on the saucer, when suddenly, a tattooed black arm wrapped around my chest to hold me in place while the other hand clamped itself over my mouth, so I couldn't move a muscle and couldn't make a sound. Black dreadlocks hung down over my shoulders, and a deep voice said, "Don't even try to move." I had never felt so afraid in my entire life.

CHAPTER FIFTY-SIX
Jann

As her friend from college, Saul Goldstein, used to say, Jann was plotzing. She had cleaned her entire house, including vacuuming twice. After sorting through the hall closet, she did the same for her bedroom closet. Then she forced herself to leave the house to deliver all the clothes she had collected to the Humane Society Thrift Store. When she returned, she hoped to find that Ricky had stopped by and left a note, but there was no sign of him.

Jann was so disappointed in him. She knew he wouldn't or couldn't call because the whole thing was so secret. But a responsible man would have attempted to get word to her that he couldn't think of any way to get the charger to Dan. Although she knew that any kind of solution was a long shot, she would not give up until she had asked Ricky. Now that she had, and he had failed her, that meant she had failed Dan. And she felt bad about that. Really bad. Of course, it hadn't been twenty-four hours yet, and maybe Ricky would still come up with an idea. Perhaps she shouldn't be so hard on him. He was a family man now and had a life of his own. Cut him a little slack, she told herself.

But because she was beside herself with wondering, she finally broke down and used her burner phone to call Eden. Jann had known Zoey since before she was born, so when Eden answered the phone, instead of blurting out what the trouble was in her heart, she asked about Zoey. After all, some things were more important than other things.

"Hi Eden. How is Zoey today?"

"She's doing better every day, Jann. Dr. Stan says she's out of danger now—at least from the bat flu." What was unsaid is that she was still in danger from the cancer.

"That's good. I'm glad to hear it."

"Jann? Something is up. I can hear it in your voice. Come on. Fess up," said Eden, who knew her as well as Jann knew herself.

"It's Ricky. You know how Dan's burner phone died? He assigned me the task of getting the charger to him. But I couldn't bring it over there, give it to secret service, or mail it. There weren't a lot of other choices. So I asked Ricky if he could think of any. He said he would think about it, but I haven't heard from him! I didn't want to push him, so I haven't called. But it's been almost twenty-four hours and still no word from him."

"I'm so disappointed in him. I guess he isn't any more responsible than he was when he was a kid."

"Jann, you're not being fair. It's less than a day! Ricky has his own life. He has a family. Give him a break and give him some time. And for God's sake, don't call over there."

"I hope you're right, Eden. I just feel like he's let me down when I was counting on him."

"Don't be silly. It sounds like an impossible task. Given those parameters, I don't know how you could get it to him. That's probably why Ricky hasn't responded. It's impossible."

"But he should have at least told me. Although he couldn't call, he would have to stop by."

"See there? That's a good reason. It's the weekend! That's family time! Give your son a break and don't be so hard on him. Listen, Jann, I hear one of the kids crying. I'll talk to you later. Love you."

"Love you, too, Eden. And thank you. I'll try to chill."

But she couldn't. She took out the bug detector and swept the whole house for bugs, but didn't find any. Then she took it out to the car and checked that. Nothing. Since she hadn't listened to the recordings on the surveillance equipment, she checked that. Marcus had been in Dan's Beast, but it was boring conversation. She still listened to every word just to pass the time.

Jann started dinner, but her heart wasn't in it, and while browning the hamburger for a casserole, she burned it. She cleaned up the mess, tossed the hamburger, and made herself a sandwich. Still hungry, she decided a good dessert might make her feel better, so she made a Devil's Food chocolate cake and frosted it with coconut pecan frosting. It was more satisfying than the sandwich had been. When she had cleaned up, she decided she couldn't stand the suspense any longer.

She took out her regular cell phone and called over there. Keesha answered and said he wasn't there. When she asked when Ricky would be back, Keesha was vague. And it sounded like she was *deliberately* vague. That made Jann even more suspicious. Was Ricky getting himself into trouble again?

CHAPTER FIFTY-SEVEN

President

I was trembling with fear until I realized something. Bear had stood up, looked over my shoulder, and was wagging his tail with love in his eyes. What?

The arm and the hand came away from my body, and the voice said, "Ah, you noticed that your dog loves me." Then he stepped out in front of me where I could see him.

He was tall and solidly built. As he petted Bear, I tried to figure out who he was, because I didn't have a clue.

"You don't recognize me, Dan? It's me, Rick. Well, you knew me as Ricky."

It took me a minute to even figure out who Ricky was, because I hadn't seen him in more than a decade. "Jann's son?"

Ricky smiled as he continued to pet Bear. He shrugged. "You guessed it. It's been awhile, hasn't it?"

Jumping up, I hugged him to me. "Ricky! I've missed you so much. Why did you ever go away?" It had been so long since I'd seen him, and felt like so long since I had touched anyone, that I not only couldn't let him go, but a couple of tears might have slipped down my face. Suddenly, I pushed him away. "Oh, wait! I probably just contaminated you. I'm still contagious for a few more days. I'm so sorry!"

"Don't worry, old man. I've already had bat flu—before it was even a thing."

"Old man?" I balled up my fist and held it in the air between us. "Why I ought to—"

But I couldn't finish the sentence because Ricky balled up his fist and held it up right next to mine. His was almost twice as big —made my hand look almost like a girl's. We both laughed then and couldn't stop laughing.

Tears ran down my face again, and I didn't wipe them away. Reaching out, I took his big hand, which was still in a fist, in the two of mine. "I have missed you so much, Ricky. You were like a son to me—no!—you *were* a son to me. And I'm sorry to say that I was closer to you than my own son, which hurt him very much. Why did you disappear from my life for so long? It hurt me very deeply."

Ricky looked down but didn't take his hand away. "I felt so embarrassed, Dan. I knew I had let you down. What I wanted more than anything else in the world was to make you proud of me. After everything you did for me and my mom—and all I could do to repay you was to get into trouble."

Ricky wouldn't look up, and he tried to pull his hand away, but I held on. He could have pulled out of my grasp, but he didn't.

"Ah, Ricky. You were at the wrong place at the wrong time. I understood that. You got unlucky. Did I ever tell you about the time that I had a similar thing happen, but I slipped out the back door before the cops arrived?"

Ricky looked up hopefully, but he didn't believe me. So I held up my right hand with three fingers showing. "Scout's honor, Ricky. True story. You can ask Eden. I'm not sure your mom knows or not. It's not something I advertise. It wouldn't look too good if it got around." I squeezed his fist and let it go. "So why now? What are you even doing here, and how the hell did you get past my secret service guys?"

"Oh! I almost forgot!" He stood up, pulled something out of his black jeans, and handed it to me.

"My charger! Thank you! Your mom came through, after all. I was beginning to worry. I didn't know how she was going to get it to me with the restrictive parameters that I placed on her."

"Well, she told me about it, but coming here myself was my idea. She doesn't know I'm here."

"Thank you. I appreciate it. How did you get past the guys out there?"

"I spent a lot of time on your boat! Friday night after Mom told me, I sneaked on and watched how the guys worked. So tonight, I knew when I should come across the property. Then I checked the house and found the screen off that window and discovered it was open. That made it easy."

I silently thanked God for my neglecting to lock that window. "How are you going to get out of here? Getting in was"—I chuckled—"easy, but how are you going to get out?"

"I was hoping you would have an idea about that."

Nodding, I said, "How about you spend the night, and I'll get up early, call the guys over, and engage them in conversation while you go out the front?"

"Sounds good."

"So—you know about the burner phone, did your mom tell you about the surveillance equipment, too?" I must have had a funny look on my face or a funny tone to my voice, because Ricky stepped right up to defend Jann.

"It wasn't her fault, Dan. I came into her house while she was trying to figure it out. She couldn't, so I helped her. That was *professional level* equipment. And the instructions were for a professional."

"Well, I'm glad you helped her then," I said, and I meant it. Then I told him what Marcus said about the twenty-fifth amendment, and the bug I found in the office, and how I didn't know whom I could trust. And I told him there were few people in the world that I felt certain I could trust, but I knew I could trust Jann, and I knew I could trust him.

"Really?" he said in an almost little boy's voice. "You still trust me after all this time away?"

211

I nodded. "I would trust you with my life." Little did I know that the day would come when I would have to do exactly that.

CHAPTER FIFTY-EIGHT

Jann

Jann passed a restless night. She kept going over and over in her head what kind of trouble Ricky could have gotten himself into *this time*. Although she hated when she had those kinds of thoughts, she couldn't help it. Since Ricky had been away for so many years before moving back here, she realized she didn't know him very well at all. He seemed to have a good job and to have straightened out his life after that little blip with the law, but maybe he met some nefarious characters when he was in juvie and still hung out with them or something. There was no way to know.

Although, since Keesha came into his life, he seemed to have changed. Jann felt strongly that it was Keesha who talked him into moving back to the East Coast. Jann didn't know exactly why Ricky had stayed away from her all these years, but she thought his embarrassment over what happened had a lot to do with it. Keesha helped him over that, and Jann felt grateful for that.

It was just after sunrise when her doorbell rang. Putting on her robe, she moved to the door, looked out the window, and then flung the door open. "Ricky! Where have you been? I've been so worried!" Jann was so ecstatic over seeing her son that she threw her arms around him and wouldn't let him go.

"At least you had the door locked this time, Ma!" He struggled to get free from her embrace, but she held him tight. "Come on, let me go. I need to text Keesha—she'll be worried, too."

"When I called Keesha, she was very vague—almost like it was on purpose."

"It *was* on purpose. I couldn't tell her what I was doing, but luckily, she trusts me. And she was on strict instructions not to give you any information except that I wasn't home. Glad to know she succeeded in evading your questions!" He tilted his head down and started tapping on the screen of his phone.

A noise on the coffee table made Jann break her embrace. She turned and retrieved the burner phone from the table, where it had vibrated to alert her to an incoming text. Picking it up, she tapped the message icon. It was from Dan, which confused her because the extra charger was sitting on the table next to the phone. *Jann, thank you for getting my charger delivered! Please thank Ricky for me! I appreciate it! I'll be in touch.*

She turned. "Ricky? What's this about? I don't get it." Jann held up the charger. "How can it be delivered? It's right here."

But Ricky wasn't listening. He was still texting on his phone. After he pushed the Send button, he looked up to see her waving the charger around. "Oh! Yeah! I took care of it for you."

"But the charger is still here!" She gave it a shake to make sure he saw what was in her hand.

"Remember the fourth burner phone that had a broken screen? I took it home to repair it and took the charger along, too. So I gave him that charger."

"But how did you get into the house to give it to him? The secret service wouldn't have let you in."

"No, and you said it had to be kept secret from them, anyway. I spent a very cold day and night on Dan and Eden's boat. Then I sneaked close to the house. Dan had left a window open, so I climbed in." Ricky laughed. "Dan was pretty surprised to see me."

"Yeah, I'll bet. You were a skinny little seventeen-year-old when you left here."

Ricky nodded. "It would have scared him worse, except that Bear wagged his tail at me and gave everything away." He looked down and couldn't meet her eyes. "We had a long talk and ironed everything out. I think—I hope—I've healed the rift between us."

"Why didn't you tell me what you were going to do? I went crazy trying to figure out why you didn't contact me and say that you couldn't think of any way to do it." This time, Jann looked down. "And I had bad thoughts that maybe you got yourself into trouble again."

Ricky came over and put his arms around her. "Oh, Ma. I will not get into trouble again—at least not voluntarily." He took her by the shoulders and looked into her eyes. "I promise you, I will not embarrass you ever again. I will only make you proud."

Little did each of them realize that he *would* get himself into trouble again. But it was the good kind of trouble.

CHAPTER FIFTY-NINE

President

When I woke up yesterday morning—a little past dawn—Ricky had already left. How he got by the secret service agents again, I'll never know. Ricky! How great to see him. It had been so many years. He was truly like a son to me, and then he left without even a goodbye. I understood his shame and his reticence to talk to me for all those years, but even so, it hurt something fierce.

Seeing Ricky made me miss my own son, Douglas, who had no room in his life for me. It wasn't like I didn't know why. Oh, I knew why. By the time he was old enough for me to spend any quality time with him, I was already in the politics machine with not much time for my family. Thank God Eden never left me. That would have killed me. What I did to Douglas, though— there was no excuse for that, and if he never forgave me, I would completely understand. I wouldn't like it, but I would understand.

The rest of the day was as normal as being sick at home could be. And since it was a Sunday, there wasn't much going on at all. Marcus called, even though nothing was going on. He was being so nice that it scared me. Although maybe I was being too suspicious about him. Still, somebody put a bug in my office. Who else could it be? Jonathan Sharpe? Besides Bear always growling at him and him sending me into that restaurant to catch bat flu, there wasn't much against him. That was enough, though.

Although Joyce had been the picture of exemplary service and gave me no reason to suspect her, she could still be the one. That was only because I had neglected to use the bug detector before she showed up. But I would not feel guilty about that, because I was sick that day. Very sick.

Now, on my seventh day at home and the ninth day of my disease, I felt almost human again. I almost felt good enough to do my workout, almost being the key. My calves still had a slight ache, and I had the remnants of a headache. Mostly, I had every reason to think that I'd be back in the Oval Office by the end of the week and raring to go. Then I got the phone call from Dr. Stan that rocked my world.

"Dr. Stan, good morning!"

Immediately, I noticed a catch in his voice. "Mr. President. Good morning. I'm afraid I have some bad news. How bad it is exactly, we still don't know yet. But this is the latest information, and it isn't good at all."

"All right, tell me." I hadn't talked to Eden yet, so I asked, "It isn't Zoey, is it?"

"No, no. She's on par to recover quickly. But this affects her as well as you."

"What? Just tell me."

"You know the new variant I told you about? The World Health Organization has named it bat flu2. It looks like everyone who has that variant—that you and Zoey both have—don't get completely over it. Everyone has recovered from the symptoms in the regular ten days to two week's time, but, and this is a huge but—they are still contagious after they recover. It's called *asymptomatic*. It means although a person feels normal again, they still have the disease and can still spread it to others."

"So what does that mean for me?"

"It means, Mr. President, you cannot return to the White House until we figure out more about this variant. You will still be contagious even after you feel back to normal. So you shouldn't be around other people."

"This is horrible news, Stan!" It upset me so much, I called him by his first name for the very first time. "I was counting on being back at the Oval Office by the end of this week. Are you sure about this?"

"It's been checked and re-checked. Doctors in England, France, and Spain have confirmed our findings. The World Health Organization has called it a *variant of concern*. I'm sorry, Mr. President."

I took a deep breath, set aside my feelings of *poor me*, and stepped into my presidential shoes. "This affects many people, doesn't it? How many in the U.S. do you think have it?"

"Thousands, I'd guess, but at the rapid pace it's spreading, I would say it will be in the hundreds of thousands within a week."

"Oh, my God."

"I know."

"Does Marcus know yet?"

"I wanted to tell you first."

"Thank you. I appreciate that. But you need to tell him sooner rather than later."

"I have a bad feeling about telling him, Mr. President."

"What do you mean?"

"I mean, I was there when he wanted to invoke the twenty-fifty amendment. Don't you think he has even more reason to now?"

"Not really. I'm almost back to normal again right now. Just because I can't go into the Oval Office doesn't mean that I can't carry out my presidential duties."

"I know that, and you know that, Mr. President, but—" He left the rest unsaid.

This had gotten out of hand. I didn't know how it could possibly get any worse. But it did.

CHAPTER SIXTY

Jann

Monday morning, Ricky had to drop his car off at the mechanic, and Keesha needed the car for some errand, so they picked Jann up and dropped her off at work so they could use her car. Keesha didn't need it until later that afternoon, but they all decided it would be better to get the car in the morning rather than have to navigate getting it from White House parking.

At her desk, Jann counted the days of Dan's illness and hoped he would be back by Friday. It would be easier navigating Marcus's weirdnesses with Dan being back.

It was still early when Dr. Patel appeared asking for Marcus again, but this time he had a serious expression on his face. "I'll get him for you, Dr. Patel."

Jann buzzed Marcus, and a few minutes later, the door of the Oval Office opened. He had a big smile for Dr. Patel until Doc said, "It's serious, Marcus." That was probably what made Marcus close the door instead of leaving it open like before—which disappointed Jann because she wanted to hear what was serious.

She was so curious that she took her purse out of the bottom drawer and began fiddling with the surveillance equipment, half ready to hook it up and listen to what was going on, when the door burst open and both men marched out. Marcus closed the door without locking it, the dumb shit, and Dr. Patel stopped in front of her desk.

He knew, as everyone in the Oval Office knew, that Jann was a personal friend of Dan's and Eden's. So he said, "In case you haven't talked to the President today, Jann, it's bad. We've found out more information about the variant he is infected with. It stays contagious even after the patient has fully recovered."

Dr. Patel leaned forward to whisper to Jann. Always cognizant of the bug attached to her desk, her first impulse was to stop him, but she didn't know where he stood. Maybe he was an ally of Marcus. But when the first words coming out of his mouth were, "I know how Marcus treats you—" she held up one hand to stop him and put a finger to her mouth. He straightened back up and tilted his head as if he were trying to ascertain the meaning of her actions. She wrote on a piece of paper: *end that sentence and then say goodbye.*

"—but he means well, Jannika. Listen, it's time for me to get back. Bye!"

"Bye, Dr. Patel," she said as she silently stood up and led him into the cabinet room. There was no reason to believe that a bug would be in there, but she would check later. Since she knew the bathroom and her desk were bugged, the cabinet room was the safest place she could think of on short notice.

"There's a bug attached to my desk and another one in the bathroom. While I don't know who set them, my first guess would be Marcus."

Dr. Patel nodded his head. "I know you're close to the President, so I'll tell you this. When I spoke to him this morning, I told him my concern about what Marcus might do with the information. He ignored my concerns."

"Dan always minimizes the threat that Marcus might pose."

"But just now—after I told Marcus about the variant—he said he was going to hold an emergency cabinet meeting in the Situation Room. I'll attend, but it might be a good idea to let Mr. President know. I feel as if I've said enough already." He turned and headed toward the door. "I better get back now and prepare for the meeting. I don't know what Marcus is planning, but I doubt it will be anything good."

"I agree with you, Dr. Patel. Thank you for telling me, and I'll let Dan know."

Jann returned to her desk. She didn't know how soon the meeting would start, but she needed to be ready. She didn't think Marcus would allow her to sit in on the meeting, as she had done when Dan called a meeting. But it might be worth it to see his response. The surveillance equipment would record everything, so she wouldn't miss anything.

Less than an hour later, she heard Marcus leave his office. She had to time it just right. Standing up, she started down the hallway when Isa's door opened. "Ah, Jann. You going where I'm going?"

"Probably. Where are you going?"

"The Situation Room. Although he didn't invite me, I'm going to try to get in. I think it's important that somebody stand up for the President."

"I agree. There's no way Marcus will let me in. Why don't you use that to your advantage and slip in while he's forcing my exit?"

"Good idea. Hopefully that other door will be unlocked." She held up her arm again, palm out, and they did a high five. "I'll let you know what I hear."

"Thanks, Isa." What was going on or what they suspected was going on made the two women tense. They walked in silence the rest of the way.

Marcus greeted each member of the Cabinet as they walked into the room. Isa and Jann waited until he turned toward the inside of the room. Isa quickly walked around to the other door, while Jann started walking into the room, with her purse in one hand and a pad and pen in the other, as usual.

When he saw her, his politician's smile morphed into a snarl. "Wait a minute, you! You're Dan's secretary and you don't belong here. Not anymore."

It sounded ominous, but Jann had to play the part. She wanted to give Isa plenty of time to get into place. "I just came to take notes, Marcus. I won't say a word."

He put his hand on her shoulder and gave her a none-too-gentle shove. "You don't belong here. Now go back to the ghetto where you belong."

Turning back to the room, he looked around, then turned back to her. "Goodbye!" He gave her another shove and closed the door in her face.

Jann didn't see Isa wandering around anywhere, so she felt confident that she got in. That was good. Whatever Marcus was planning wasn't good for Dan, and whatever wasn't good for Dan was not good for her, either. When she reached her office, she put the pad and pen on the desk and dug into her purse for the bug detector. First, she covered the area where she and Dr. Patel had been standing in the Cabinet Room when they had their conversation. Nothing. Then she covered the rest of the room and found nothing at all.

Hurrying back to her desk, she opened her purse and pulled out her iPod, which was strictly for cover. After hooking up the ear pod to the surveillance equipment, she turned it to live. The meeting had already started, which she expected, so the first voice she heard was Dr. Patel's.

"—still capable of performing the duties of his office. He—"

"Shut your damn mouth, Stan! I brought you to this meeting for your medical experience! You're not a politician!" Marcus said.

Dr. Patel raised his voice and spoke again. "My patient, the President of the United States, is in no way incapacitated or—and I quote the constitution *for your convenience*, sir—'unable to discharge the powers and duties of his office.' The only issue with him is that while he is almost over the bat flu, he will still be contagious after he's recovered—as I've already told you. But if you push it, *Mr. Vice President*, I can clear him right now to return to *his* office."

It surprised Jann that Dr. Patel stood up to Marcus that way. Then again, he didn't have to worry about the political side of things like the rest of the people in that room did. He was a doctor more than he was a politician.

"It's clear," said Dana Ogham, the Secretary of State, "the President can unquestionably perform his duties. So we have settled the Twenty-fifth Amendment discussion. Let's move on. What was the second thing you wanted to talk about, Mr. Vice President?"

"The second thing concerns—excuse me a moment. Stan? The rest of this discussion does not concern you. Would you mind leaving us so we can get on with the business of running this country? Please."

Jann could imagine Dr. Patel fuming, but she didn't hear him say a word. She heard a scuffling of a chair and a door opening and closing. Of course he would have the courtesy of not slamming the door. He was a good guy.

"Now we can get on with important matters," said Marcus. Jann thought he sounded like the pompous ass that he was. "The second matter also concerns bat flu. In my Daily Brief this morning—perhaps some of you have read it, too—there was more information on the origin of bat flu. Victor?"

Victor Galloway, Director of National Intelligence, answered. "Yes. The intel that we have gathered has confirmed that the so-called bat flu originated in China. It is still under investigation and whether it was an accidental release or deliberate has yet to be determined."

"Thank you, Vic," said Marcus.

"Excuse me, Mr. Vice President, but if I may speak up here," said General Bryce Skora, Chairman of the Joint Chiefs of Staff. "I know Mr. President did not approve, but I know you take a more *enlightened* view."

Jann thought she was going to barf at the blatant obeisance of Skora. And when Marcus murmured "yes," oblivious to it, she had even less respect for him than she already had. But she guessed that when you craved respect like Marcus did, even a phony showing of it felt good.

"Since China has proven to be the origin of bat flu, and regardless of whether or not it was deliberate, I think they need to be punished, and I think we need to be the ones to punish them. After all, if you run someone over with your car, whether or not you did it on purpose, the person is dead. And with bat flu, thousands of people have already died. This could be biological warfare, and I think a first strike is in order!"

Even Marcus couldn't swallow that one. He cleared his throat, but before he could speak, Isa spoke up. "How about if we go to Defcon 4 while we gather more information? Because, ladies and gentlemen, *we* had a hand in this."

"What?" gasped General Skora. Jann heard his hand hit the table. "What could you possibly mean?"

"Yes, explain yourself, I-sa," Marcus said with deliberate reproof.

"We—that's the United States *we*—have been sending money to that lab for several years to research, *jointly,* coronaviruses. Gain of function, to be exact. Therefore, *we* are partially responsible. And if you want to know what gain of function is, it means it increases the virulence of the virus. If you had allowed Dr. Patel to stay, he could have given you a more thorough explanation."

"Look into this, Vic," said Marcus.

General Skora pounded on the table again. It came through the surveillance equipment as if Jann was sitting right there. "It doesn't matter! *They* are the ones who let it escape—or whatever happened. We should go to Defcon 3. My boys are ready!"

Calm down, General, thought Jann. You don't want to have a heart attack right at the table. She pictured him with his triple chin and bloated belly—not very becoming a General.

"All right, all right. I think going to Defcon 4 is a good idea while we do more research. And we will revisit a first strike in a couple of days," Marcus said calmly, as if what they were talking about was some innocent little maneuver. That man was in *way* over his head. And that was dangerous.

Jann couldn't figure out why Isa was the one to suggest going to Defcon 4. But the more she thought about it, the more she realized that by doing that, Isa had defused the situation. Defcon 4 meant increased intelligence gathering, which wasn't a big deal. Without Dan here to supervise or control Marcus, there was no telling what Skora and Marcus would do. She had heard enough. Digging her burner phone out of her purse, she texted Dan and suggested he better do something before the entire country was plunged into war.

CHAPTER SIXTY-ONE

President

When the text came, I was outside with the horses. I had seemed so much perkier today that Joyce cut some carrots for me, put them in a plastic bag, and said I had ten minutes out there. It had only been five. Jann's message was brief—I'm sure she wanted to get it to me as soon as possible. *Mtg in Sit Rm. 25ᵗʰ Amnd not accepted. But . . . now at Defcon 4. Do something.*

So Marcus held a meeting in the Situation Room and tried to get the Twenty-fifth Amendment to go through again, but failed. Then, probably the General—because he mentioned striking China before—got the group to go to Defcon 4. Granted, that was just more intelligence gathering, but it wasn't a signal I wanted to send to the world. At the end of her message, she included a phone number, which I assumed was for the General.

I gave the horses the rest of the carrots and hurried inside. I wasn't going to call on the burner phone. When I came into the house mumbling to myself, Joyce stopped me.

She looked at her watch. "You're early. Are you feeling poorly again?"

"No, business calls. But I still have five minutes left. Maybe I can go out again later?"

She just smiled and put her hands on her hips, without answering.

Keeping the burner phone in my pocket, I retrieved my regular cell from the bedroom and closed the door. As I started to tap out the number, I realized this was a conversation *the bug* should hear. Opening the door, I crossed the hall to my office and closed that door.

General Byrce Skora answered a gruff, "Hello!"

"Hello, General. It's Dan Indigo here," I said in a pleasant manner.

"Oh! Hello, Mr. President! I, uh, heard you were feeling better."

"Much better, General. I'm pretty much over it now." I paused. He didn't say a thing. "So I understand the country is now in Defcon 4. I find that interesting since I made myself clear that I did not want any action taken against China.

"I'd like to tell you something important, General," I continued, and then I screamed into the phone. "I don't care if they tell you or if you hear that I am dead! Until you touch my cold dead body, you are NOT, I repeat, NOT, to initiate any kind of action against China."

Then, back in a pleasant voice, "Even a little one. Do you understand me, General?"

"Yes, sir. I do, sir."

"And you better damn well make it your business to get the Defcon level back up to 5."

"Yes, sir. Right away, sir."

But I knew he wouldn't. He was Marcus's man now, and until I was back in the Oval Office, it was like talking to a wall.

"Goodbye, General." I didn't wait for him to reply. I just hung up the phone. Hard. Of course, with a cell, it does not have the same impact of slamming a hand phone down into its cradle. They should invent something like that—a *hang-up-on-you* app. It would sell off the virtual shelves in no time.

I was mad as a hive of pissed off hornets, and I wanted to calm down before I called Marcus. Because I *had* to call Marcus. He instigated all this bull shit.

"Marcus, it's Dan."

"Hello, Dan," he answered in a neutral voice, as if he hadn't just tried to rip the presidency out from under me.

"So I understand you tried to invoke the twenty-fifth amendment again. You do understand that I'm much better now and almost ready to come back to work? Right?"

"With all due respect, Dan, you're still contagious. It wouldn't be proper for you to return to work now. That's why I did that. I thought I was doing you a favor."

Marcus didn't respect me—never had. Why did it take me so long to realize that? How should I play this? I decided to do something that I hadn't done with Marcus in the past—get tough. "Do me a favor? Seriously, Marcus? Do you think I'll believe that bullshit? Do you think that this disease has affected me mentally?"

And at that moment, I realized something I had never accepted about myself before. I *was* smarter than Marcus. All those years when he told me he was smarter than me, was him pretending or wishing it was true. But it wasn't. And I was a fool to listen to him. Eden had tried to tell me that for a long time. I wasn't a fool anymore.

Before he could answer, I started talking again. "And Defcon 4? Really? You were at that meeting where I distinctly remember telling General Skora no on striking against China. And yet you allowed him to do that? What kind of fool are you?"

"It was *your* Chief-of-Staff who suggested it. Not me."

"Oh." I'd have to check with Jann on that part.

"Mr. President, you know that I always have your best interest at heart. You've known me too long to think otherwise. I'm trying to take care of things the best way I know how until you return to the Oval Office."

Mr. President? Marcus had never, in all the years I had been in office, called me Mr. President. And to call me that now while it was just the two of us on the phone? Dangerous. I knew I was in for trouble, but I did not know much or how soon. I should have been more vigilant. Famous last words. And they almost were.

CHAPTER SIXTY-TWO

The man

He hung up the phone and smiled. He had played it well—been his most obsequious, and that stupid bastard didn't realize a thing. This complicated matters. Obviously, that fucking Indian Patel told him about the twenty-fifth amendment discussion. But who would have told him about Defcon 4?

Although the bugs he had set up hadn't given him any new information—yet—it was all right. He'd figure it out for himself. Although he had heard Dan's side of the conversation with Bryce Skora, that didn't tell him who told Dan about Defcon 4.

Sitting back in his chair, he pulled the catcher's mitt from the bottom drawer and started hitting his fist into it. One, two, three, four. One, two, three, four. His first guess would have been Jann, but he hadn't allowed her into the room. So who could it be? In his mind, his eyes roved over everyone sitting at the table. Could it be Jonathan Sharpe? No, that imbecile did everything he told him to do and was too afraid not to. He wouldn't have had the balls.

It was the bitch! Isa the whore! That's all right. He'd take care of her. She may be bigger than him, but he still had power over her. He had power over everyone! One thing was for sure though: the fact that Dan found out about today's meeting meant that he'd have to move up the timeline. That's all right, too. The sooner Dan was completely out of the picture, the better. Glancing upward, he shook his fist and said, "I'm *doing something*, dammit! I'm *doing something*! Tonight's the night!"

CHAPTER SIXTY-THREE

Jann

Jann hoped Dan had gotten the text she had sent to his burner phone. There was no way to check, though. She couldn't text him on his regular phone because if either phone—his or hers—was traced, it would show up. And that would give away the secret of the burner phone. It was another one of those dilemmas for which she had no suitable answer.

So she was grateful for the diversion when Isa appeared at her desk, holding up a sheet of paper that said *Come into my office and bring your wand-thingy.*

Jann knew she meant the bug detector, so she unlocked her purse from the bottom drawer and brought it into Isa's office, closing the door behind her. Isa held up her finger to her mouth before Jann could say anything, and then Jann went to work. There was nothing; the office was clean.

Isa stood up and motioned Jann into the corner of the office, away from the wall Isa shared with Marcus.

"I want you to know I took a bullet for you today," said Isa in a whisper.

Jann shrugged. "Took a bullet? What do you mean?"

"Marcus came in just now, fuming. He accused me of telling Mr. President about Defcon 4. I held up my right hand about to swear that I didn't, when I realized it must have been you, and you must have a bug in the Situation Room! Right?"

There was no way Jann could deny it now, especially since Isa had indeed taken a bullet for her. Marcus wouldn't let that go. He'd find a way to get her back. Jann nodded. "Yes, I do and yes, I did. How could I not? Marcus could start World War III!"

"You understand why I suggested Defcon 4, right?"

"Absolutely. With Skora pushing him, Marcus could have easily agreed to Defcon 3. It was a brilliant move, Isa. Good work."

Isa put one hand in front of her waist and another hand behind her back and took a deep bow. "So where else are there bugs?"

Jann didn't hesitate for more than a second. If Isa was pretending to be on the *right side*, it was an elaborate ruse. "In the Oval Office, because I know how Marcus loves to go in there when Dan isn't here, and in Dan's favorite Beast, which Marcus also prefers to use instead of his own. They're exactly alike, but Marcus thinks he's getting something over on someone."

"Have you gotten anything from either one?"

"Marcus was in the Oval Office with Dr. Patel this morning, but it was only about what's changed about Dan's variant. I can listen to it when I get home. And I've never heard a thing from the Beast—at least nothing worth anything. But with everything that went on today, one never knows. I'm just glad that Dan got the message I sent him earlier—I wasn't sure if he did or not." Jann realized too late that she just intimated there was another method of communication, but Isa didn't seem to notice.

"And I was glad to help. I know there will be some retribution involved, but it had to be done. I have no regrets." Isa walked back to her desk.

Jann headed toward the door. "Thanks again, Isa. I appreciate it." She returned to her office, locked up her purse, and felt satisfied that Dan had gotten her message and had acted on it.

There were no more surprises that afternoon, which Jann was grateful for. There was only so much excitement she could take.

But she got an unwelcome one at 5:15, when she should have been heading home. Ricky and Keesha were supposed to call her about when they would pick her up. Instead, Ricky called to say he had been delayed at work. He said a thirty minute job had turned into a three hour job, and he was still working on it.

"It's a leak in the static system," he had explained. When Jann didn't respond, he added, "That's what sends outside air pressure to instruments that monitor airspeed and altitude."

"It's all right, Ricky. You know where I'll be. Just call first."

"Ma, I can have Keesha come pick you up and then she can come back for me after she drops you at home."

"No need for her to do all that extra driving, Ricky. I'll be patient. I have plenty to do here. Just let me know."

Jann didn't know it, but her patience—and boredom—would end up saving a life.

CHAPTER SIXTY-FOUR

President

The last vestiges of a beautiful sunset had disappeared, and it was full dark, but still early. Joyce had left after dinner, and I sat alone in the living room with Bear at my feet. I had just gotten off the phone with Eden, and everything was going well in Pennsylvania. The kids were fine, although lonely for contact with their mother, and Zoey was much better. But she didn't feel as well as I did. Although her timeline for the disease was the same as mine, her symptoms had been worse from the beginning. That's why it had been so scary. There was no telling about the cancer, but her bat flu was almost gone now. I'd be glad when Eden could return home. I didn't begrudge her staying there to help Zoey, but I missed her very much.

Life had gotten so complicated. Not the disease—I felt almost human again, with the headache gone, the aches gone, and the fatigue on the way out—and yet I couldn't go back to the Oval Office. Try as I might to handle things from the ranch, it just wasn't working. I needed to get back, and I needed it bad. It was almost like a wish. Click my heels three times and I'd be back at the White House.

So, with that in mind, it was like a wish come true when Marcus appeared at the door saying he had made a decision—

despite what Dr. Stan wanted—and was bringing me home. He was an unlikely fairy godfather, but that's what it felt like at the time. That's my only excuse for not knowing what he was up to. I wanted to believe. I so wanted to believe.

And I know there were red flags, but they were only in the last couple of weeks or so. Marcus had been my best friend since high school. We had gone to college together. We had become lawyers together. We had gotten into politics about the same time. When we lived in the same town, we always socialized. Eden wasn't always comfortable about that, but I figured it was because she had dated Marcus before me.

At least I thought that until I caught him cornering her when he and his wife were over for dinner one time. He had Eden backed up against the wall in the kitchen, and he was holding her arms above her head. I heard Eden say in a quiet voice, "Get your hands off me or I will scream." She said it calmly and firmly, like she wasn't scared, but she was firm about it. And I heard Marcus say, "If you scream, I'll claim you hit on me. Plus, you don't want to ruin the close friendship between me and Dan, do you?" As I was about to step in, Eden brought up her knee, hard—because it doubled Marcus over—and shoved him out of her way and left the kitchen.

I suppose that should have been a red flag, but Eden handled it well, and it never happened again—maybe because Eden never put herself in the position to be alone with him again. Anytime Marcus was over, I watched her. Even now, Eden avoided him whenever she could. So many politicians get caught up in the whole *sex* thing, so I couldn't hold that against him. See what I mean? I made excuses for Marcus all the time and spent years defending him. It made sense that in this vulnerable time in my life, I chose to believe him.

And the chance to go back *home*—back to the White House— was a greater lure than all the red flags were a warning. So when Marcus said he was going to take me home, I went.

"Hey, ole man," he said when I opened the door. "I've come to take you home," were his exact words.

He stepped forward and tried to hug me, but I stepped back. "I'm still contagious, Marcus."

"I don't care!" And he drew me into a big bear hug and patted my back. Bear, at my heels, growled at him and bared his teeth, which, looking back, is probably why Marcus hugged me—to provoke that response from Bear.

"I assume you only have like a small suitcase? Go pack it up and let's go! Time's a wasting!" He looked nervous, but it never occurred to me to wonder why. More red flags that I ignored.

Hurrying into the bedroom, I packed my bag. As I packed, Bear stood at the door, guarding. I grabbed my cell and stuck it in the back pocket of my jeans. But the burner phone was being charged inside my nightstand, and I forgot it. Luckily.

I strode into the living room with a big smile on my face and Bear at my heels. "All right, already! Let's go *home*!"

Marcus had a look of genuine concern on his face—well-rehearsed—but concerned. "Oh, Dan, sorry ole boy. You know how the dog is around me. I'll have him brought to you later."

"No problemo, Marcus. I'll just have one of my agents bring him over."

"Oh! Sorry! I already sent them back. They'll meet us there. I have my two guys in the car."

"Oh," I said, suddenly worried—not for myself, but for Bear.

As Bear growled, Marcus put his arm around me and led me out the door. "Don't worry. I promise that I'll take care of Bear." Then he led me out to the Beast that I recognized as mine, not his.

We climbed into the back and as the car pulled away, Marcus said, "It feels good to be going home, doesn't it, Dan?"

"I can't tell you how wonderful it feels, Marcus. Thank you so much for doing this."

"And I'm about to make it even better." He reached forward and pulled a cup of steaming hot cocoa from the cabinet. "I know how much you enjoy your hot cocoa. Your favorite." He handed it to me. "Enjoy."

I took a sip, and it soothed me. After taking a few more sips, I was so soothed that I fell fast asleep. Of course, the drug that Marcus had slipped into the cup helped that along.

CHAPTER SIXTY-FIVE

Jann

Jann felt panic surge through her body. She had beaten on Isa's door for several minutes, with tears streaming down her face, all the while knowing Isa wasn't there. Then she returned to her desk and broke down crying and sobbing and crying some more.

Thirty minutes before, Ricky had called to say he would be at least another hour. Jann told him not to worry about it, because she had plenty to do. She didn't, though, because she was all caught up with work. So she set up the surveillance equipment on her lap—no one was around, but you couldn't be too careful —and the iPod as cover on her desk. What she heard from the Beast's bug shocked her.

"All right, he's asleep now. The hot cocoa worked," Marcus said. "He should be out for a few hours. So drop me off and then deliver him. When he wakes up, tell him I left him a letter under his thigh. I guess I owe him at least that. Or not." Marcus laughed and Jann heard laughter from the front seat.

"What should we do with the dog? Leave him?"

"No!" Marcus was emphatic. "Kill the dog!"

Jann was overwrought. As a last desperate action, she called Dr. Patel and even tried him at home, but couldn't reach him. She didn't know where the men were to *deliver* Dan to—but if she was to save Bear's life, she must get to him before they do. There was no time to waste. Even if she called Ricky to send Keesha with the car, it would take too long. It had to be now. And there was no one else to call. Who could she trust?

She tried to calm herself to clear her head. Maybe she could think of a solution if she was calm. When she heard footsteps in the hallway, she prayed it wasn't Marcus. If he took one look at her, he would know that she knew. And that could be fatal. Jann didn't know what was going on, or why Dan was asleep and being *delivered* somewhere, but it didn't sound good. If the cocoa had poison in it, he could be *delivered* to a landfill somewhere. If he's just asleep, why and where would they be *delivering* him to? How could she know?

The man came into view. It was Jonathan Sharpe. He took one look at Jann's face and hurried to her side, putting a hand on her shoulder. "Jannika? Are you all right? Is there anything I can do?"

She looked up at him, tears streaming down her face, and she thought of Isa saying that it wasn't his decision to send Dan into that restaurant. Still, Jon did Marcus's bidding, whether or not it was his idea. He could still be on Marcus's *side*. Not to mention, Bear always growled at him, and Bear is the one who needed rescuing. And yet, in a moment that felt like perfect clarity, she decided to trust him. It didn't make sense, but sometimes things that are *right* don't make sense.

As she was about to tell him what she needed, she remembered the bug. Shaking her head, she wrote on a notepad, *After I speak, say goodbye & quietly go into the Cabinet Room.* "I'm fine, Jonathan! Just leave me alone! Goodbye!" She said it harshly, as she had intended.

His eyes got big, he nodded, and said, "Okay, bye! Sorry I asked." Then he walked down one hallway noisily, got halfway and removed his shoes, then returned and strode into the Cabinet Room. Jann followed him in.

"What was that about?" he whispered as they reconvened in the far corner.

She wiped away the tears in her eyes and said in an unhurried voice that belied the urgency of the situation, "I'll explain everything later. But can you give me a ride to Oceanview?" When Jon nodded, she added, "For me—and a dog. The President's dog."

Jon did not hesitate for even a second before answering, "Yes, of course. Whatever you want, Jann. Let's go."

Jann got her purse, cleaned off her desk, and locked up. As they walked to Jon's car, they were both silent. Before they got in, Jann said, "Keep a lookout!" Then she went over the whole car with her bug detector. His car was bug free. "Okay, let's go! We're in a hurry!"

They got into the car and Jon turned to her. "All right. Are you going to tell me what all that was about?"

"I just checked your car for bugs. And the reason we talked in the Cabinet Room, instead of at my desk, is because, believe it or not, there is a bug on the underside of my desk."

Jon nodded his head. "Let me take a wild guess who put it there. Marcus Lowry."

Jann turned toward him and took a deep breath, deciding to be honest. She hoped he wouldn't turn the car around and refuse to rescue Bear. "Funny you should say that. I thought you were on his *side*. Because, you seem to do his *bidding*." Not waiting for him to speak, she plowed on. "I know it wasn't your idea for the President to go to that restaurant where he caught bat flu, and yet you made the call when Marcus told you to."

Jon took several deep breaths before answering, and Jann noticed his knuckles were white on the wheel. It was like he was hanging on for all he was worth. He shook his head. "I want you to know that I *love* Mr. President. I voted for him, I support him, and I would do anything for him. Except, being honest here, he is a good man, but he is blind to anything that concerns Marcus Lowry."

He looked at Jann. "That man is dangerous." Jon spit out the word. "That man is the *devil*. Crossing him is like kissing your political career goodbye. You have no idea how much power that man wields—some that the President has inadvertently given to him and some that he has just grabbed.

"Had I to do that incident over again? I would probably still do it to save my butt, but I would warn the President in advance so he could find a solution instead of going ahead with it. I'm sorry. It's like all this happened because of me." He hung his head for a minute, then picked it back up to avoid a car that was slowing in front of them.

Jann nodded, taking it all in. If anyone knew about Marcus's grab for power and how the President ignored the warning signs, it was her. She reached out her hand and patted Jon's, still tight on the steering wheel. "I understand. Completely.

"And as far as that man being the devil," Jann shook her head, "you have no idea." Then she related to him about Dan being *asleep* and being *delivered* to some unknown place. And Marcus's comment about Bear. "That's the kind of devil he is."

"All right, we're on our way to save Bear, but how can we save the President?"

"Good question. We have to know where they've taken him first. There is a GPS on the bug that I placed in the Beast. So, if they don't move him to another car, we'll know exactly where he is. We need to wait and see where they take him." Jann turned to look at him. "In the meantime, how is it you have always been so afraid of Bear, and now you're willing to rescue him?"

Jon glanced at her and laughed. "It's a long story. I'll start with why I was afraid, and then why I'm not anymore." He told her a harrowing story of when he was a teenager, a large German Shepherd—the same color as Bear—attacked his little brother. He had to beat the dog off with a rake. The dog turned on Jon and got in a couple of bites before the neighbor pulled the dog off. Every time he saw Bear, all he could think about was beating that dog off with a rake. "I think that's why Bear always growls at me." He shrugged. "I wasn't only giving off fearful vibes, but *mean* ones, too. And I couldn't help it."

"How did you get healed from that? And so quickly? It doesn't make sense."

Smiling, he turned toward her and winked, then he squirmed in his seat like he couldn't wait to share his story. Jann hoped the story would last until they arrived, because worrying about Bear was driving her crazy. She welcomed any distraction.

"My daughter. Chloe. She's ten." Then he followed up the harrowing story with a sweet, heart-warming one. His daughter, Chloe, did not want a poodle or a yorkie. Instead, she insisted on a German Shepherd. And worse than that, the puppy she picked out—that she fell in love with—had an *encumbrance*. It was the pick of the litter. The breeder would only sell her if they took the mother, as well. The breeder was getting out of the business and wanted the puppy's mother to go to a good home. His daughter and his wife talked Jon into it, and they brought home Beauty, the puppy, and Maisie, the mother dog. Maisie *adopted* Jon, following him around everywhere. And Jon fell in love with her.

They had reached their destination. Jon parked in front of the ranch house. It was dark inside. "Let's go in. If they haven't already done it, they could be back any second," Jann said.

Side by side, they walked up to the house. They found the front door unlocked. Jann turned the handle, not knowing if Bear would greet them at the door or if he was already dead.

CHAPTER SIXTY-SIX

President

I woke up groggy and confused. Since the brain fog in my head hadn't lifted, I waited until I felt like I had my bearings before I said anything. The vehicle I sat in was moving fast down a two-lane highway. The vehicle was the Beast. I closed my eyes to concentrate. Everything was coming back to me. The Beast! Marcus had picked me up and was going to bring me home—to the White House. Looking out the window, even in the dark, I knew I was nowhere close to home. Where was Marcus, anyway?

"Hey, where's Marcus and where are we going?"

"We already dropped Marcus off, and there is a letter for you that he left back there."

I looked around and found it under my thigh. Picking it up, I turned it over to see that the unsealed envelope, addressed to *Dan*, was in Marcus's handwriting. Before I even opened the envelope to read the letter inside, I had a sick feeling in my gut. Although I didn't know where they were taking *me*, what scared me was that I had left Bear at the mercy of Marcus—who hated him. My own life may or may not be in jeopardy, but I knew that Bear's was.

And as my head cleared, I realized—or remembered—that I had forgotten to lock the front door of the ranch house. What possessed me to think I could trust Marcus to take care of Bear? I was just thinking of myself and how much I wanted to end my isolation. And that selfishness might have just cost Bear his life. I had to force myself to do deep breathing to keep from vomiting right there.

Opening the envelope, I slid the letter out and read: *Dan: Although I deceived you, it was necessary. You are not the only one with the variant that causes you to be continually contagious.*

The country cannot afford to have all those contagious people going back to work and infecting other people. Something had to be done, and I knew you wouldn't do it.

Those people need to be put somewhere—separated—until science has an answer or a cure, or a vaccination is available. The somewhere is in the Fema camps that have been set up and are ready to receive them. I will speak to the Cabinet tomorrow about having martial law declared. That will enable us to pick up every person who has tested positive for the variant and transport them to the camp. In order for all of this to transpire in an effective and expedient manner, it was necessary for you to arrive there first to demonstrate to the people there is nothing to fear.

Don't worry. You'll only be there for a week or two, and then I'll have you brought back to the White House in seclusion. I promise you I'll have you out of there soon. Remember, Dan, this is for the good of the country—and I know that's what's important to you.

He had signed it *Marcus*. With all that bullshit in the letter, I was surprised he didn't sign it love. Oh, I knew full well he intended to have people shipped to the Fema camps. At least that part was true. And it was also true I would not have done that. But putting me in the camp first to demonstrate there was nothing to fear? No. That was a convenient way to get me out of the picture so he could seize power.

The days of me seeing Marcus in a positive light were gone. Finally, I saw him clearly for what he was: a wannabe dictator. As far as me only being here for a week or two? I knew damn well I would be lucky to see the light of day again. He'd probably keep me alive for a while. How long that *while* would be was unknown. In the meantime, I needed to come up with a plan. But until I arrived at the camp and saw the layout and how things were handled, I couldn't even begin to think of a plan.

The sick feeling in my stomach grew worse as I came to a painful realization. Zoey had the same variant I did. Therefore, she would be rounded up and sent to a camp like the others. I couldn't allow that to happen, and *that plan* must be enacted immediately. I lifted up my butt to retrieve the cell phone that I had put in my back pocket. It was gone. Marcus had removed it and with it any attempt for me to communicate with the outside world. As I sat there, helpless, something popped into my mind: the bug that Jann had placed in this vehicle.

Taking the letter back out of the envelope, I read it over quickly to make sure that I wouldn't be divulging any government secrets to the two goons in the front. They were goons—not Marcus's usual agents. I had never seen them before. But first, I had to make Jann realize I was sending her a message. Then I thought of how to do it.

I looked out the window and started tapping on it frantically. "Hey! Did you see that? It looked like an old man wearing white robes walking alone out there!"

Both goons in front laughed. One of them said to his partner, "Must be the drugs. Or maybe it was God."

They laughed again, and then the one driving said under his breath, "He'd need God's help to get out of this place."

"Well, must have been a *mirage* then!" I said, knowing Jann would get my meaning—the Mirage was the name of the store where Jann had met Eden so many long years ago. Then I picked up the letter and said, "Hey, did y'all hear what Marcus is planning to do? You better hope you don't catch this virus." Then I loudly and distinctly read every sentence of the letter so Jann could hear it. If she wasn't listening at that moment, I hoped she would hear it later. And I prayed she would hear it in time to save Zoey the humiliation—or worse—of going to a Fema camp.

CHAPTER SIXTY-SEVEN

Jann

Jann sat in her office in the dark, listening. Jon had texted her on the burner phone that Marcus had scheduled the Cabinet meeting at six A.M. Instead of holding it in the Cabinet Room, he planned to hold it in the Situation Room because Marcus deemed it a critical situation. Typical Marcus.

The meeting had an unusual and unexpected start to it. And it was very clever. She had to give Marcus credit for that. Instead of trying to beg for acceptance and convince people of his cause, he had Corrie Corrigan announce it at her early morning press conference, as everyone in the Situation Room listened.

Scientists have determined that anyone infected with the new variant of bat flu, called bat flu2, is still infectious even after the individuals have recovered. Because of that, it has become necessary to segregate the infected portion of the population so as not to infect the rest of us. We expect a certain amount of confusion and resistance to this mandatory step to protect the people of the United States, so Vice President Marcus Lowry has asked every governor to declare martial law as of this minute. First, National Guard will gather up all those who have tested positive for the new variant. Then they will be transported to a comfortable, but out-of-the way location. Then, everyone

who had bat flu but not been tested for the variant, will be tested, and a
determination made at that time about their future arrangements.

*To allay any anxiety about the separation camps, please know you
have nothing to fear. In accordance with proving to the general population that the camps are safe and pleasant, late last night, President Dan
Indigo was voluntarily transported to one of the camps at an undis-
closed location. He is alone there now, but the camp will soon be filled
with people like him. And he very much agrees with these measures to
keep everyone safe.*

Corrie hesitated, and Jann could imagine tears running down
her face. Jann also knew that Corrie did not write this speech.
Never in a million years would she have said *people like him.*

Corrie continued. *Our scientists and doctors are all working
overtime to find a solution to this crisis our country is now experienc-
ing. Until we have a cure or a vaccination available, these people will be
treated with the utmost of care and consideration to make up for their
inconvenience.*

*This morning, Dr. Patel has provided new information that will be
of interest to you. Scientists have discovered that everyone who had the
original version of bat flu are immune to the new variant. You must
agree that is very good news.*

*Rest assured we will keep everyone apprised of any new development
with the virus. Thank you and goodbye.*

From the sounds Jann heard, she surmised by the footsteps
and unanswered questions that Corrie had walked away before
anyone had the opportunity to ask anything. It wouldn't surprise Jann if Corrie was breaking down right now and crying her
eyes out. News of Dan in a separation camp, as Marcus called it,
would make many people cry. And only a few people—Marcus
and his minions—happy.

The rest of the Cabinet meeting was dull by comparison to
Corrie's speech. Since Marcus had the forethought to announce
his actions *before* the meeting, there wasn't much discussion
before all had agreed it was imperative that action be taken.
Marcus's exact words were, "If we cancel the plans for the separation camps now, it would make the government look like the

248

right hand doesn't know what the left hand is doing. It would be dangerous for our country to go a different direction than what was announced in the press conference."

After rhetoric like that, how could anyone disagree? The discussion that followed was brief and meaningless. Dan would stay in the camp, and all over the country, busloads of people would begin arriving today.

Jann removed the earplug from her ear and put the bug equipment back into her purse. She had heard what she needed to hear. Now, in the relative silence before people returned to their offices, she could process what had occurred the previous night.

When she and Jon had opened the door of Dan's and Eden's ranch house, Bear was at the door to greet them. Jann had fallen to her knees, thrown her arms around him, and cried into the thick fur around his neck. Bear sniffed at Jon and wagged his tail tentatively until Jon knelt down and Bear licked his face. There was no growling. Then Jon kept a lookout while Jann did a quick search of the house. In Dan's bedroom, she found the burner phone plugged into the wall behind his nightstand. She grabbed the phone and charger and hurried back to the front of the house. It would be dangerous if Marcus found out about the burner phones. Since Dan didn't need it anymore, and since Jon was obviously on the *right side*, she gave it to him.

"Let's get out of here before his guys come back to kill Bear. I'll leave the door open a little—maybe they'll think he escaped."

Jon dropped Jann and Bear off at Jann's house with the admonition that it would be safer if Bear didn't stay there. It might be one of the first places where Marcus would look.

Earlier, when Jann had texted Ricky that she had a ride home, she offered to cook them all dinner. But Ricky had said that Jace was too hungry to wait, so they had gotten him a Happy Meal, which had indeed made him happy.

Since Jann didn't know if Ricky had his burner phone with him, when she texted to tell him she had gotten a ride home, she said that it was fine if he took Keesha and Jace home before returning her car. She hoped he would understand that she needed to talk to him alone. Just in case, though, she also texted his burner phone and said *please come alone.*

After eating dinner, Jann and Bear sat huddled up on the couch awaiting Ricky's arrival and hoping he got the gist of her message. He did. When he came in a couple of hours later, he felt so tired from working a twelve-hour shift that he sank down on her couch on the other side of Bear.

"I got your message," he winked at her, "so what's up, Ma? And what's he doing here?" He stroked Bear's fur.

When she told him about Marcus having Dan *abducted,* Ricky's hands formed fists and his face got red. "So you want me to go rescue him?" He stood up, his hands still in tight fists. "I'll go right now!"

"Ricky, we're not even sure where he is."

"Yes, we know exactly where he is. Where is the bugging equipment? It has a GPS."

"I forgot about that. But there is something that's more important than rescuing Dan right now. He should be safe for a while, although I'm sure Marcus will try to *dispose* of him at some point. But he sent me a message while he was being abducted. It's important."

Ricky sat back down on the edge of the couch, still upset. "What could be more important than rescuing Dan, Ma? Tell me!"

"Ricky, it's Zoey. She's in danger."

"Zoey?" His fists loosened and his demeanor softened. "Why is Zoey in danger?" Ricky had always considered Zoey his little sister. And like a big brother, he had protected her, he had teased her, and he had loved her fiercely since the day she was born.

"She not only has breast cancer, but she has the same variant as Dan. So they will pick her up just like everyone else who has it. And then they will transport her to one of the *separation camps* —probably not the one where Dan is."

Ricky nodded his head. "Then I need to rescue her first."

"As soon as humanly possible."

They discussed strategies and where Zoey would go after she was rescued—*if* she was rescued. By the time Ricky left that night, they had finished hammering out a plan. It was risky, and Ricky would need help, but *if* he got there in time, he and Jann both thought it might work. It was a big *if*.

When Ricky walked out her door, he took Bear with him to keep him safe, in case Marcus suspected that Jann had something to do with Bear's disappearance. Then Jann left the house for the first step in their plan. It might still work if this part fell through, but if Jann could make this happen, everything else would go much smoother. So she had driven over to Dr. Patel's house.

That was all last night. Jann looked at her watch. Ricky's plan should be well in motion by now, but she still hadn't heard from him. He was supposed to call as soon as he had Zoey safely tucked away—or not.

CHAPTER SIXTY-EIGHT
President

I woke up disoriented because of either the drugs from the night before or the lack of sleep. It took me a long time to get to sleep in the bunk bed that I was *assigned*. Although, not exactly the one that was assigned—they wanted me to sleep in the bottom bunk, but I insisted on the top. After ten minutes, they stopped arguing and let me have it. In this place of absolute non-privacy, it felt a little more private.

When the car arrived at the camp the night before, the gates to the place were wide open, like they were expecting me. Which they were. Instead of driving inside, Marcus's goons escorted me to the gate where three men waited for me.

When one of the goons said, "These men will be with you now," I played dumb and said, "Where's Gavin and Derek? They were supposed to meet me here." The goon replied, "These men are Bob Haines, Ted Kenyon, and Vincent Boyd. Two of them will be with you at all times. You'll be safe with them, I assure you. They've all had the virus, Derek and Gavin haven't."

In such a nonsensical situation, it made sense. Of course, at that point, I thought it was fifty fifty if the three men would protect me or try to kill me.

There were flood lights showing the way to a large canvas tent. They *allowed* me to use the outdoor restroom before we entered. Inside were rows of bunk beds, but in the center of it was a cordoned-off area that held two sets of bunk beds—for my three companions and me. At first I wondered why they hadn't sectioned off one end of the tent, and then I realized that if I tried to get away from them, it would be easier to catch me if they kept me in the middle.

After we got the bed situation settled and I lay down, sleep wouldn't come. All I could think about was Zoey, Bear, and Eden —what would Eden think when I didn't answer the phone? She might think I had died or something! I hoped Jann had heard what happened. If so, she would not only try to rescue Zoey, but she would call Eden and calm her down. Jann was one of the few people who could do that. And after hearing that Marcus had abducted me, Eden would be just this side of hysterical.

When the disorientation left after I had awoken, I slid off the top bunk to find one of the agents awake and standing guard— in an empty camp. Maybe that's why there was just one awake. I said good morning to him, but he just nodded and didn't speak. He watched me, but all I did was get in the aisle of the bunks and drop down to do my pushups. I continued with as much of my exercise routine as I could without equipment, and then I improvised to get in a good workout. But before I had finished, a bell rang.

The two sleeping agents jumped out of bed and started getting dressed. The one standing guard said to me in a gruff voice, "Get dressed. It's time for breakfast."

My two escorts for the day were Vincent Boyd and Ted Kenyon. They again *allowed* me to use the portable bathroom, probably because Ted had to go, too. And I say *allowed* because it felt like they were instructed to watch my every move. And I watched theirs, as well, because I knew I had to formulate an escape plan before it was impossible to leave at all. I thought Ted used the facilities at the same time I did because there was no one else in the camp besides me, but as soon as others started arriving, that probably wouldn't happen. There was a six-foot-wide multi-faucet sink across from the bathrooms. I used the sink to wash my hands, but Ted didn't.

The *mess hall*, I don't know what else to call it, was in another large canvas tent. I had noticed many tents spread around the camp in my brief tour from the sleeping quarters to here. We sat alone at a four person table separated from the rest. There was no question they were expecting me, and Marcus did well in planning all this out. I had to give him credit for that. Breakfast was nothing to brag about and nothing to complain about. The portions were large, and I ate everything on my plate, because I had to keep my strength up if I was going to escape this place *alive*.

After we finished breakfast, the two men wanted to take me back to my bed. "Absolutely not!" I said in my presidential voice. "What? Do you expect me to sit around all day doing nothing? I want to see the place!"

"Sorry, not possible," said Ted Kenyon.

I stood with my legs apart and my arms folded across my chest. "I'm not going back in there."

Ted grabbed one arm. "Take his other arm! We'll get him in there."

"Let him walk around. What will it hurt? There's no one here." said Vincent Boyd.

"They're supposed to be arriving today."

"They're not here yet. Chill Ted. It's not a big deal."

And so we started walking around the enclosure. It was large, maybe fifteen or twenty acres. The twelve foot cement block walls surrounded it all. There was only one gate—in the front. There had been a second gate on the opposite side of the grounds, but it had been removed and replaced with more large blocks. They looked newer than the rest.

"Hey, either of you guys know why they removed the other gate?"

Since Vincent had been the one who allowed me to walk around, I thought maybe he would be easier to get along with, but instead of answering my question, he said, "Shut up! We're not here to answer your damn questions!"

So the men weren't just taciturn, they were downright rude. That would be the last time I entertained the thought that one of them could be of any help to me. Marcus was paying them too well.

As we walked around the perimeter, I counted fifteen large canvas tents the size of the one I slept in. They surrounded four more large tents with a picture of a knife and fork on them—the *mess halls*. In the very center, though, were two medium sized concrete buildings and between them a metal Quonset hut. I wondered what those were for but wasn't going to ask the two jerks with me.

Halfway through our walk, a man in a security uniform drove a quad by. A few minutes later, another guy in a security uniform drove a quad in the other direction. Ten minutes after that, Vincent got a message on his portable two-way radio. I couldn't hear what they said, but I heard him say, "Yes, we're on our way." Then he grabbed my arm—hard—and turned me around toward the center of the compound. "This way!"

"Hey!" I said, roughly pulling my arm away. "Can't you talk? Just ask me nicely, and I'll do it. No need to bruise my fucking arms!"

"I'm not paid to talk."

"Obviously," I said, but he had let my arm go, and that's all I cared about. Where we were going, I didn't know, but I hoped it wasn't to my death. The way things were heading in this bizarre scenario, I couldn't be sure of anything—except for one thing: I was not safe with these men.

CHAPTER SIXTY-NINE

Jann

As Jann waited in painful suspense for Ricky's phone call, she realized she didn't feel any kind of foreboding—at least for Zoey. For Dan, it was a different story. When she had called Eden on the burner phone last night to tell her of the kidnapping, Eden had reacted badly.

"He's going to kill him! Marcus will kill him! I just know it!"

Jann had calmed her down as best she could, saying they would just have to rescue him before that happened. But first, she told her, they had to rescue Zoey. And she told her the plan she and Ricky had come up with. Eden offered to call Dr. Patel to beg him to cooperate, but Jann had warned her about the risk of Marcus listening in on the phone call and upsetting everything. That's when Jann told her she was on her way right at that minute to see Dr. Patel and tell him what they needed him to do. With no hesitation, Dr. Patel had agreed.

But waiting for the phone call from Ricky had made her more and more uneasy. She checked her watch a dozen times and opened her purse to make sure that the burner phone hadn't turned itself off or something. When she didn't think she could wait a moment longer, she felt a vibration in her lap. Even with no one around, she didn't dare remove the phone from her purse.

After locking up her desk, she hurried out of the White House —taking a longer, more remote route so no one would see her— and made her way to the grounds of the Washington Monument. It wasn't until she passed the National Museum of African American History and Culture that she turned onto the lawn, looked around to make sure no one she knew was around, and pulled the burner phone out of her purse. It was a text message, but it was from a number she didn't know, so it wasn't from Ricky. That scared her. Had something gone wrong?

She tapped the icon, and the message appeared. *Good news, Jann. Zoey's doctor in Pennsylvania saw the news this morning, knew what I was trying to do, and helped! He said it went smoothly with him running interference, and he had subsequently signed her release papers, so it would all look natural, and no one would report her missing. This is my daughter's phone. I'll pick one up today. If you need any more help with anything, Jann, just ask. I hate what's going on.* He signed it *Stan.*

Although she felt a little relief from the message, she still wondered why Ricky hadn't called yet. If it had gone so well, they should be in the clear by now and should call her. Should she return to the White House to await his call or stay where she was? She walked around, holding the phone in her hand and willing it to ring. And when it did, she was so thrilled that she dropped it on the manicured lawn. Picking it back up, she tapped Accept and said, "Ricky? Everything okay?"

"Chill, Aunt Jann. It's Zoey. We're safe." Since she was a toddler, Zoey had called her Aunt Jann. And Jann liked it.

"Oh, thank God."

"I know you're wondering why it took so long, but Ricky wanted to make sure we were out of Pennsylvania and safe before calling you. Everything went smoothly. The doctor even helped! It was so cool! He nodded to Ricky, and when I wheeled Ricky out in the wheelchair, he nodded to me while he kept the nurses busy!"

"Wait. What? *You* wheeled *him* out?"

Zoey laughed. "Yes, I wheeled him out! It was Ricky's idea, and I thought it was brilliant. He had brought me a pair of nurse scrubs, and I slipped them on. Ricky took off the ones he had worn to get into the room, and then he got into the wheelchair that he had brought. And we were both wearing surgical masks, of course. It was perfect! Everything went off without a hitch, and we were on the road in no time."

"Oh, I'm so relieved, Zoey. I'm so glad it worked and you're both safe."

"Ricky wants to know if we should come in now, or wait a few hours."

Jann wasn't ready for that question, and she knew she should have been. When would be the best time to sneak Zoey in—right past Marcus's nose? Now or later? In a few seconds' time, she assessed the matter and thought that with the outrageous news he had announced, he would be busy with questions for most of the morning. And if not, she could enlist Dr. Stan to help, and maybe even Isa. She made her decision. "Now! How soon will you be here?"

"Where do you want us to meet you?"

You'd think that with all that time Jann had that she would have figured out where to meet them. But she hadn't figured it out at all. "How about Lafayette's Statue in Lafayette Park?"

"We'll text you when we arrive in about thirty minutes. See ya soon!"

"Love you, Zoey."

"Love you, too, Aunt Jann."

Jann pressed End on her phone, sank down onto the grass, and couldn't stop crying. She still didn't know how she was going to get Zoey into the residence. And what if Marcus caught her? Both she and Zoey, and probably Ricky too—bat flu or not —would all be sent to the separation camp.

CHAPTER SEVENTY

President

We had almost reached the metal Quonset hut when it started to rain. Hard. Vince knocked on the door, and without waiting for an answer, we walked in. There was a small office to one side, but we went through another door into a bigger office with a computer set up in the middle. Ted gave me a shove toward it. I sat down in the chair and moved the mouse. The dark screen lightened up and there was Marcus looking back at me.

"Very tricky, Marcus. I'll have to give you credit for this one."

"Ah, Dan. You know you wouldn't have done what needed to be done. And by the way, more people will arrive at your camp today."

"All right, so with me in here, you've convinced them it's safe, so they won't give you any resistance. Now when do I get to leave?" I knew Marcus was not about to let me leave. He had me where he wanted me—away—and he would not lose that advantage. It would only be a matter of time before he had me removed—permanently.

"Oh, a few more days or a week or two at the most. Just enjoy your time there."

"It's not easy, Marcus, with these two jerks you've assigned to me."

Marcus laughed. "Oh, give them a chance, Dan. You're just not used to their style yet. And none of your boys had the virus, so it had to be these three. Stop complaining, old man. It could be worse."

Old man. We were the same age. "When can I talk to Eden?"

"No talking, Dan. Sorry. Right now, we're keeping the location of the camps a secret. I'll let you email her—a couple of times a day. Short emails. No long involved stories from either of you."

Marcus always commented on how Eden and I talked to each other. He and his wife didn't seem to have that kind of communication. "Eden would be grateful if she could see me, Marcus, you know, make sure I'm all right and all." I knew he'd want to make Eden grateful.

"Ok, Dan, I'll let her see you. Come back here in a couple of hours, and I'll have it arranged."

"And what about you giving me reports on the state of things? You know, like you were doing when I was at home."

Marcus laughed again. "There's not much you can do from there, now, is there? With no phone? No access to the internet without my permission. Don't worry. I'll take care of everything to your satisfaction." He hesitated and then continued, "When you get back here, I can guarantee you'll be perfectly satisfied with the way I handled everything. We'll talk again tomorrow. Bye."

And his image disappeared before I could ask him where the hell I was. Not that he would have told me, even if I had asked. And he *guaranteed* I'd be satisfied when I got back. It was getting more and more clear that Marcus planned for me *never* to get back. So how the hell was I going to get out of here before Marcus decided I was no longer useful?

Ted interrupted my reverie when he gave my shoulder a shove. "Come on, *old man*. Time to get out of here and take a shower."

He had been standing right behind me when Marcus called me that. I stood up slowly and faced him. We were the same height, but I had a little weight on him. If we hadn't been alone in that big room with no witnesses, I might have elbowed him in the stomach. Yes, two against one, but I didn't think either one would do that—at least not at this point. But they were Marcus's men, so I could be underestimating their capacity for abuse. Regardless, I got right into his face and said, "*Don't* call me that again."

Surprised, he stepped back. Then he grabbed my arm and shoved me toward the door. A shower sounded good. We walked out of the Quonset hut and into the adjacent cement building. It contained locker-style showers, or should I say, prison-style showers? At the far end of the building, there was a heavy canvas curtain separating me from the rest of the building. How long did it take Marcus, I wondered, to set this all up? The idea scared me.

There were benches on the side, with a pile of towels, just out of reach of the water. I removed my clothes and got into the shower. There were industrial dispensers of soap and shampoo on the wall. The two men stood on the inside of the canvas curtain and watched me as I washed my hair and my body. You'd think they'd have the common courtesy to look away, but they didn't. Did they think I would try to escape? Through the concrete walls? This was getting old fast.

After I dried off and got dressed in my same clothes, they escorted me back to the sleeping area. I followed without resisting, laid on my top bunk, pulled out my Harry Potter book, and started reading. It gave me an idea. I memorized what I needed and kept reading.

Later, after a bathroom break and more exercises, there was a change of guard. Vincent Boyd lay on his bunk looking at his phone, and Ted Kenyon and Bob Haines escorted me back to the Mess Hall for lunch. It wasn't horrible is all I can say. As we stepped outside, I heard a sound. The front gates had opened, and through them I could see a bus unloading people. There were both men and women, but very few children. So it had begun. Two more buses unloaded as I watched in horror at all the people pouring into the camp.

It was still raining, hard, and there was mud everywhere. One of the quads I had seen before had gotten stuck to the right of the gate, and several men were trying to get it unstuck. I heard a sound and Ted turned his back and spoke into his portable radio. "It's ready. Let's go." And he gave me a shove toward the Quonset hut.

Finally, I thought I could talk to Eden! But that's not what happened.

CHAPTER SEVENTY-ONE
Jann

Jann looked at her watch and forced herself to stop crying. She had to come up with a plan and she had to come up with it quick. Making up her mind, she stood up and hurried toward the nearest big box store. It was not too far out of her way, and it was something she needed to do.

Not long after, she came out of the store with her purchases: packing tape, a small notebook of paper, and ten prepaid cellphones. She sat on a bench in an out of the way place in Milian Park, determined the numbers for each of the cell phones, wrote her number, Ricky's number, and Jonathan Sharpe's number on a piece of paper, and attached it to the back of each cell phone with tape. Then she packed everything back up and marched on to her next destination.

As before, when she visited the Secret Service Headquarters, Jann showed her ID again several times before she got to the garage. She saw no one she knew until she got there. With Dan gone and the residence empty, Dan's agents were probably enjoying the time off. Starting to get discouraged, she saw Gavin at the other end of the garage. Instead of waiting for the agent beside her to contact him, she couldn't help herself: she screamed at the top of her lungs, *Gavin!*

He had been in animated conversation with another guy, but when he heard her calling, he came trotting over. "Jann, what's up?"

"Gavin, can we go someplace to talk?" She didn't know who she could trust and who she couldn't. She didn't even know if she could trust Gavin. But she had to start somewhere, because if she was to make things right again, she couldn't do it alone. She needed help.

Gavin shrugged his shoulders at the agent Jann was talking to and led her out of the garage and onto the street. "All right, Jann. What's going on? I watched this morning's press conference, and while I understood it and the reasons behind it, I didn't understand why Mr. President didn't tell us himself. That wasn't like him."

"It wasn't like him, because it wasn't him! Marcus kidnapped him last night, Gavin! He drugged him and took him to that place against his will!"

Unconsciously, Gavin put his hand on his gun. "Where is he, Jann? We'll go get him!"

With a slight smile on her face, because it confirmed that she had done the right thing, she held up her hand. "Wait a minute, Gavin. Marcus, I'm sure, has everything in place to stop you from doing just that. It would probably be a fatal mistake, for you *and* for Dan." Considering his words, she added, "Who's we?"

"Eric, Justin, Derek, and Jeff."

Jann went through Dan's agents in her head to figure out who he had left out. "Not Clive?"

Gavin moved his head in a strange side-to-side manner that wasn't exactly a no. He held up his right hand. "I know Clive would always do his job and take a bullet for Mr. President. I am certain of that. But—he voted for Marcus. So would he try to rescue the President when the man he voted for was in charge?" He shook his head and shrugged. "I just don't know."

Jann reached into the bag she carried, pulled out five cell phones, and handed them to Gavin. "Take these. One for the five of you. Clive doesn't need to know. Marcus has bugs everywhere —including my desk. Since he doesn't know about these burner phones, they're safe from him. I taped three numbers on the back: mine, Ricky's, and Jonathan Sharpe. Jon helped me rescue Bear last night after Marcus was going to kill him. I trust him."

"Who's Ricky?"

"My son. He's rescuing Zoey right now." She glanced at her watch.

"Oh! Zoey! That's right, she's got the same variant, doesn't she? Mr. President mentioned that to me."

Dan had always had a close relationship with his agents, often having long personal conversations with them. But she didn't wonder why he would not trust them completely. He had trusted Marcus so long when he shouldn't have, that now he was going the opposite direction and not trusting anyone. It was understandable, but inconvenient. Luckily, Jann could fix it.

Before she could respond, Gavin continued. "So,"—he looked at his watch—"too early for her to be at a camp, so he rescued her from getting *sent* to a camp. Very smart, Jann."

"She's who I want to talk to you about, Gavin. She needs to go someplace safe—someplace Marcus would never think to look." Jann looked up at him. He was tall, dark-haired, and built like a football player. "I'm thinking the residence would be the best place.

"Eden is bringing the kids there today, but Zoey will have to stay away from the kids. Five-year-olds are too young to keep a secret. So Zoey will stay in Bill Clinton's old saxophone room— it's sound-proofed." Grimacing, she looked up at him with pleading eyes. "Can you somehow get her in there without being seen? She'll arrive within the hour."

Gavin laughed. "That's the easiest assignment I've ever been given!"

Jann's sigh of relief could have almost been heard on the next block. The weight off her shoulders was immense. She wouldn't let Dan down. "Thank you."

"I'll call the other boys right now." He pulled out his regular phone.

"But not Clive, right?"

"No, not Clive. Where will we meet her?"

"Layfayette's statue."

"Perfect. It's close to the Secret Service area at the White House."

Jann couldn't stop herself from giving Gavin a quick hug. "Thank you, Gavin. I wasn't sure I could pull this off or not."

"Fear not, Jannika White! Secret Service to the rescue!"

"How're you going to do it?"

"Let's just say this. There is more than one way to skin a cat and more than one way to get into the residence. Add to that, five savvy Secret Service Agents who know that area as well as their own homes. We'll take care of it. Now, how soon do we meet Zoey?"

"About twenty minutes."

"Let me get on the phone then and get the boys over here." He put his hand on Jann's shoulder. "Your job is to keep the Vice President busy while we do this."

Jann nodded. But she didn't know what she would have to do to keep Marcus busy. And the risk of not keeping him busy— was deadly.

CHAPTER SEVENTY-TWO
President

We walked into the back room of the Quonset hut, and I sat down at the computer, eager to get started. But when I moved the mouse, it was Marcus's face that appeared. "Marcus? I thought I was going to talk to *Eden*? Where is she?"

Marcus tried to swallow his smile but was unsuccessful. He was in charge and he knew it. "What I said was, 'I'll let her see you.' So look over the top of the monitor and you'll see a video setup. You can tape a brief statement that you are alive, healthy, and"—he coughed to suppress a laugh—"happy. Just this one time. Then you can email her a couple of times a day, but keep them brief, too. I know how you can go on and on with your writing."

That comment brought me back to our college days when he'd be busy with a date or something with his fraternity brothers and would ask me to write his essay for him. Idiot that I was, I wrote it. Then he would often complain it was too long! Why did I think for so long he was smarter than I was? The only evidence of that was how successful he was at getting me to do his work for him—and him telling me all the time how smart he was.

The current situation pissed me off, but in my vulnerable position, I couldn't complain. "Fine, Marcus. I just want contact with Eden. Oh, and one other thing. Your three goons you have *protecting me* are literally *shoving* me around. I can't imagine that you told them to do that, did you?"

He looked surprised when I told him that. The two guys with me, who had been right behind me listening in, stepped back when they saw Marcus's face. So he hadn't told them to treat me like that. I could only surmise one thing with that new information. They knew how this situation was going to end. What they didn't understand was Marcus didn't want *me* to know how it was going to end, and with that in mind, they were supposed to pretend to be nice—or at least neutral—toward me. Good. I was glad I mentioned that.

"No, I did not, and I will take care of it. I promise you. Now go make your brief recording and send your brief email. You won't be in there for long. A week at the most."

"Thanks, Marcus." I was thanking the man who had kidnapped me. Stupid, but I had to pretend, or I'd never make good my escape—if that was even possible.

"I'll get back to you later, or" a weird hesitation followed, "oh, no!" And then the screen went blank.

"All right, let's go over here now," said Ted in a gruff voice. He wasn't much nicer than before.

I walked to the video setup and sat down on the chair facing the camera. Bob walked behind the camera. Nodding to him, I said, "I'm ready.

"Hi Eden. Marcus wanted me to tell you I'm alive and healthy and happy. Not sure about that last one. I'll be emailing you later today, so if you could let me know how Zoey is, I'd appreciate it. I'm worried about her. I hope you're—"

"Thirty seconds to go, *Dan*," said Ted, pointing to his watch.

"I hope you're doing ok. No need to worry about me. I'll be fine. I've been through tougher than this. I think!"

"Ten seconds."

"I love you, Eden. Hope to see you soon." I heard the camera click off, possibly before I got the "soon" out.

We walked outside, and the rain was still a heavy downpour. The buses had left, but people milled around everywhere like lost souls. Since they were here in this God forsaken place, that's exactly what they were. Lost.

The two men pointed me back toward the tent with my bunk in it, but I stopped. "Hey, how about I go back in there and send Eden an email now? That way we don't have to come out in this rain again?"

Bob nodded and said, "Yeah, let's get it over with."

Back into the Quonset hut we went with me leading. I sat at the computer, went into my online email account, and typed in Eden's email address. Bob and Ted were both standing behind me, reading over my shoulder. It didn't matter, because I knew someone would censor the email, so I made it as innocuous as possible. If they took out the wrong sentence, it could mess up the whole secret message.

Hi again, Eden. I miss you so much. I wish I could have seen you before I got sent here. Although it's not too bad. How's Zoey? How's Bear? Plenty to eat here, including 52 green peas for lunch! There are about fifteen barracks-like tents, and I get three meals a day. More people came today. I saw about 225 people milling around the camp, but only maybe five children, one was a cute little girl about four. She reminded me of Zoey when she was a child. They have a couple of quads here. I got a look at the first one, and it looked like it had about 320 horsepower—probably not enough to get through all the mud from the rain we've been having. Marcus said I'd be home in a week, so six days to go. In the meantime, one is a lonely number. I miss you.

"Enough already," said Ted. "End it."

I'll write again tomorrow. I love you, Dan.

Although I pressed send, I knew damn well it wouldn't go straight to her. Someone would censor it, unfortunately. No question that her return emails would be censored, as well. But that was all right. I had gotten my message across in an innocent email. Hopefully, Eden could figure it out. The secret message in the email was *Where am I.*

CHAPTER SEVENTY-THREE

Jann

Jann walked toward Lafayette Park, while Gavin contacted the other guys. She took out the burner phone and called Eden to let her know everything was proceeding as planned.

"Jann? Is everything okay? Did Ricky get Zoey?"

"Yes, but I thought you'd already know."

"Zoey and I talked about it and decided I should leave when she got admitted, so no one could implicate me in the escape."

"Good idea. Ricky and Zoey will be here soon, and Dan's agents will get her into the residence. I just have to keep Marcus busy."

"Be careful, Jann. You know what an asshole he can be. Hey, which agents? You know Clive voted for Marcus."

"Yes, Gavin told me. He'll be left out of this adventure. How come everyone knew about Clive but me?"

"Oh, he's a good guy, but Marcus—I don't know how he found out—was always saying that Clive voted for him and not Dan."

"Where are you, Eden? If you left after Zoey got admitted, then you should already be here."

Eden laughed. "I'm traveling with two five-year-olds and a dog. When Sage has to go, Rose doesn't, and when Rose has to go, Sage doesn't. So double the amount of potty stops, plus snacks, plus breakfast."

"Oh! Okay. When do you think you'll get here?"

"About another hour. Hold on." A few seconds passed. "All right, the kids are sleeping. Do you remember me showing you Bill Clinton's music room? The sound proof one? I think that's where Zoey should stay. The kids can't know that she's there. Five-year-olds aren't the best at keeping secrets."

"Yes, I know, I thought of that. And I already told Gavin about the room. I'll tell Zoey, too."

"Thanks for everything, Jann. I got a couple of emails from Dan. One was just weird or cryptic or both. I'll have to study it to figure it out. The second one was a video, which I haven't had time to watch."

Jann wanted to say *at least he's still alive*, but she didn't think that was appropriate. "I'm glad he's okay. Listen Eden, I need to make a couple more calls before Zoey arrives. I'll stop by the residence later."

"I love you, Jann. Thanks again."

"Bye, Eden. I love you, too."

Jann tapped in the number of Dr. Stan's daughter's phone. It rang and rang, and just when Jann wondered if he had given it back to her, he said, *Hello?* in a timid voice.

"Dr. Stan, it's Jann. I—"

"Wait, Jann, let me call you back on my new burner. Bye."

The phone rang in fewer than ten seconds. "I had already plugged your number into it. What's up, Jann? Is Zoey all right?"

"That's what I'm calling you about. She'll be here in a few minutes and Dan's agents will get her into the residence. Can you help me keep Marcus busy? I'm afraid to be in his office alone with him."

"I don't blame you! The man can't be trusted. Of course I'll help."

"Thank you, Dr. Stan. I'll text you when she gets here, and if we both head over there, it should be perfect timing. As long as

Marcus is in his office, that is. If he's wandering around at some unknown place, then I don't know what we'll do."

"Tell you what, Jann. I'll go over there right now to make sure he stays there. And didn't you say Isa is on Mr. President's side, too? I'll enlist her to help me. And if Marcus is loose somewhere, I'll let you know."

"Great. I'll see you soon, Dr. Stan, and I'll let you know somehow that it's all clear."

Jann sat back, took a deep breath, and stole a glance at her watch. Zoey should be there in ten minutes. Then she heard "Aunt Jann!" and saw Zoey running toward her with her arms open, and Ricky coming up from behind, smiling. Jann stood up and put her arms out, but Zoey stopped six feet away. "Air hugs only, Aunt Jann. I think I'm contagious for another day or two." Zoey was wearing a red wig, and Jann wouldn't have recognized her except she called out her name. She barely had time to process what was happening when Derek Moran and Gavin came out of nowhere.

Gavin squeezed Jann's arm. "We'll take it from here, Jann. You know what you have to do."

"Already done. But I'll go now to supervise!"

The three of them turned to go when Jann remembered. "Wait! Zoey! Your Mom said the best place for you to be is Clinton's sound proof music room. She said you had to stay away from the kids."

Zoey nodded. Repeating her mother's words, she said, "They're not great at keeping secrets. Got it, Jann. Love you!"

And Gavin and Derek led her away.

Jann rushed back to the Oval Office taking a different route. She had to make sure Marcus was occupied. Yes, Dr. Stan said he would handle it, but Marcus may have already been out. Would Dr. Stan remember to let her know? What if Marcus was just coming in and would see Clive and Derek leading Zoey into the residence?

Jann hurried into the lobby entrance so she could walk right by the Vice-President's office. Her heart turned to stone. The door was closed, and she heard no voices coming from within. Where was he? Where was Dr. Stan? Putting her ear to the door just in case they were speaking softly, she still heard nothing. What would Marcus do if he discovered Zoey? Send her to the separation camp? Probably. Dejected and downright scared, she walked slowly toward her office.

CHAPTER SEVENTY-FOUR

President

After the email and video business, the two goons took me back to my bunk. That was fine. It had been an emotional day, and I felt tired. Laying in bed, I thought about all that had happened, but before long I fell asleep. Since the canvas tents didn't block much noise, a loud sound from outside woke me. I felt disoriented enough by not only a mid-afternoon nap, but by being here at all. So it took me a minute to figure out what the sound was. It sounded like a tractor!

I climbed off the bunk in my quest to run out of the tent when a powerful arm grabbed me and held me back.

"Where do you think you're going, mister?" said Bob Haines.

Pulling myself out of his grasp, I said, "I want to see what that sound is."

"You're staying right here where you belong."

"No. I'm not staying right here. And it's *not* where I belong. I'm going out to look, and you can either come with me or fight me. But I do not intend to obey like a meek little lamb while you try to subjugate me." A beat, and then another, while he just looked at me, wondering if I meant what I said. "Are you coming or not?"

I walked through the tent while Bob Haines and Ted Kenyon followed. It was still raining but not as bad as before. There by the gate, a big tractor moved back and forth along the fence line. It was scraping down the ground and moving the mud from the inside perimeter. They were probably doing it so the quads could still make their rounds, but it wouldn't work. The path they just carved out would be solid mud again if this rain kept up. They needed horses, not quads, to get the job done. It was too cold and wet to stand out there gawking, but I stayed long enough that the scene made me smile.

Something I've always believed is that you have to make the best out of any situation. So I started thinking about the tractor. I had one for the ranch and enjoyed using it. The tractor made me think of those big excavators with the bucket on the end of a long arm. I'd always wanted to try driving one of those. It was funny—maybe not funny, but unusual—most people dreamed of seeing sights and traveling the world, but I'd done all that, even before I was President. My dream was to drive an excavator. Silly, I know, thinking about that as my life was held in the balance.

In the balance of what, I wondered. In the balance of Marcus's deranged whims was the answer to that question. But when I stood up to the two men about the tractor, I had made a decision. I refused to play the victim. Sometimes when you allow yourself to slip into the victim role, the people around you step into the bully role. I wasn't all that sure that's what happened here with my three *goons*, but from here on out, I would fight them at every opportunity. I wouldn't fight for the sake of fighting, but if the situation called for it, I was ready.

Marcus had already shown that he didn't want them to hurt me or to act like they would be hurting me—killing me actually —later, so although standing up to them was not without risk, I still felt like I would be fairly *safe* doing it. If *safe* was the right word to use when you're trapped inside a separation camp.

Through the incessant driving of the rain—I was grateful that it wasn't cold enough for snow—I laid on my bunk, thinking about the day and my two brief encounters with Marcus. That morning, he had said that he'd have me out of here in a week or two. But after lunch, he had amended that to "a week at the most." That meant I had little time. Whatever his timeline had been, he had moved it up. In the short time I had been here, I had found no vulnerabilities that I could use to my advantage. It wasn't just my bully guards. The place was designed so no one could escape. I wondered then if I would make it out in time. Was there even a whisker of a chance that I could escape from this fortress? Since I wasn't giving up, I would keep searching for a possible opening. But I had to admit, it wasn't looking good.

CHAPTER SEVENTY-FIVE

Jann

Jann smiled as she thought about what had happened a few hours ago. When she found Marcus's door closed, her heart started racing and her vision got cloudy. Feeling like she was going to faint, she grabbed the frame of the door. She took a deep breath, and using the wall, she made her way to her office —and a happy surprise. The Oval Office door was wide open, and she saw Dr. Stan and Isa inside conversing with Marcus. *Conversing* was putting it mildly, because Dr. Stan was yelling at Marcus, who had a grim look on his face. Realizing that all was okay, Jann almost fell over with relief. Sitting in her chair, she had put her face in her hands, and it was all she could do to keep from crying. Zoey was safe.

Dr. Stan and Marcus continued to go at it, but Isa wandered out and leaned down to Jann. "Everything fine, I trust?"

Still feeling the reassurance of seeing Marcus no where near the residence, Jann had smiled, but she couldn't even squeak out an answer. Isa nodded and retreated to her room, leaving Dr. Stan and Marcus alone in the Oval Office.

Jann had heard something about war and bat flu, but before she could get a handle on the conversation, her cell phone dinged—her regular phone, not the burner phone. She pulled it out to check the message, and it was from Eden.

They had arrived and were safely ensconced in the residence. The children and Tika, the shepherd, were all tired, not to mention Eden felt exhausted from driving and stopping a dozen times on the way, so she thought it would be better if Jann didn't come over today. Eden said she'd call her later after a nap.

Jann had already started texting back, *I understand*, when another text arrived from Eden saying she had her agents back, and they were actively guarding the doors. That was excellent news, thought Jann.

Then Dr. Stan had walked out of the Oval Office with an upset look on his face, and as soon as he got clear of the door, he turned to make sure Marcus wasn't following, and held up his hand with fingers pointing to his ear and mouth indicating he'd call her later. She drew another breath of relief, which didn't last long.

A few minutes after Stan had left, Marcus came out of the office with a scowl on his face. He slammed the door behind him and passed Jann without acknowledging her presence. But when he got to her door, he hesitated and then turned around. Pointing a finger at her, he said, "And I'll see you later!" Then he stomped off.

Fat chance of that, Jann had thought, and she packed up her belongings and left the other way past the Cabinet Room. She made a quick stop at the Press Room to drop off a burner phone for Corrie. Dan trusted her, and Jann did, too.

Now, hours later, here she was at home, cutting up potatoes and celery for the pot roast that was already in the crock pot along with the carrots. Ricky would go get Keesha and Jace and bring them back here. Jann smiled as she worked and then realized she hadn't checked the mail yet. She put the last of the potatoes and celery in the crock pot, wiped her hands on the towel attached to her apron, and walked out the front door to get the mail.

She shuffled through the envelopes on her way back into the house and stood inside the entranceway, sorting the bills from the junk mail. The door behind her opened, and she turned around to see who it was, thinking it might be Ricky. It wasn't.

It was Marcus, standing there in his expensive suit, with a shit-eating grin on his face. He looked her up and down. "Look at this! You got dressed up for me!"

"Get out of my house, Marcus! I don't know what you're doing here, but get out now!"

"I don't think so, Jann-i-ka. I came to collect what you owe me." She was about to speak when he pulled a gun from inside his jacket. "Now get down on your knees and open your mouth." When she didn't move, the smile faded from his face, and he waved the gun around, its tip in the air. "Now!"

Jann was so shocked that her mouth fell open of its own accord. She stood there, gaping at him, not believing what was happening.

"You got it half right, bitch! Now get down on your knees!" He pointed the gun at her, and with his other hand fumbled inside his zipper.

Still too stunned to move, Jann stood there, staring at the gun. Then she heard footsteps in the hallway.

"Put the gun down, Mar-cus!" Ricky came out from the bathroom with a gun drawn and pointed toward Marcus.

"What do we have here? A boy with a play gun. Drop the gun like a good little boy and I won't shoot her."

"You always did like to refer to me as 'her boy' when I was growing up. I didn't like it then, and I don't like it now. Put your gun away. I won't tell you again."

Understanding dawned on Marcus. "Oh, she's your mother. You have grown up!" He took a closer step to Jannika, grabbed her and put the gun to her temple. "Now what are you going to do, *boy*? Put it down or I shoot your mother."

Ricky nodded. "You shoot her and I shoot you. It's as simple as that. Now let her go, put that thing back in your pants, and get the fuck out of here."

Jann couldn't see Marcus's face, but she felt him tighten his grip on her. "And what are you going to do if I don't?"

Ricky, never taking his eyes or his gun off Marcus, reached into his back pocket and pulled out his cell phone. "I'll call 9-1-1 and report that someone was in the house trying to rape my mother, and I shot him."

Marcus started laughing and pressed the gun tighter on Jann's temple. "As soon as your shot goes off, my two agents, who are waiting outside the door, will rush in here and take you out."

Then Ricky laughed. "That may well be, but I'll have already made the call, and the proof will be that before your guys get in here, I will shoot your dick off as proof of the rape. If you had put it away like I told you to, you wouldn't have to worry about that."

Marcus loosened his grip on Jann, but didn't let her go. It was like he was trying to figure out what to do to save face. But he couldn't think of anything.

"Now let her go, put the gun down, and get the fuck out of here. And next time you threaten somebody, it might be more effective if you take the safety off your gun."

Marcus loosened his grip on Jann to look at the gun in his hand. Ricky seized the moment and karate-kicked Marcus sideways. Marcus ended up on the floor as the gun flew out of his hand. Ricky kicked it out of Marcus's reach.

"Now crawl over to the gun and pick it up by the barrel, then stand up with your hands in view."

Marcus lay there for a minute, not moving, until he must have decided he didn't have much of a choice. He gingerly picked up the gun by the barrel, as instructed. Standing up, he moved his hands to put his penis back into his pants.

"No! You leave it out and walk out that door as it is. I want the world to see what a fucking pervert you are!"

Marcus narrowed his eyes and walked toward the door. As he opened it, he turned around. Looking at Ricky first and then Jann, he said, "You will pay for this! *Both* of you!"

Ricky sprang to the door as Marcus closed it, and bolted it after him. Then he turned to Jann, hugged her, and whispered, "We have to get out of here now! You have two minutes to pack a bag! Now!"

Jann ran to the bedroom, collected sleeping clothes, some underwear, a couple of changes of clothing, and some comfortable shoes. She wouldn't be returning to work now, so she didn't need any work clothes. When she returned to the living room, Ricky had her purse, the rest of the surveillance equipment that didn't fit into her purse, and the crock pot ready to go.

"I've already called a cab. It should be here in just a minute."

"Why a cab? We have my car."

Ricky looked at her without saying a word, and she immediately understood. Marcus knew her car, and he would have his guys looking for it. Then they heard a honk in front of the house.

"I need a minute to leave food and water for Sneezy!"

"Who?"

"The cat!" Jann said as she poured out several days food into Sneezy's dish.

"Hurry!" said Ricky.

In another minute, she and Ricky were in the cab. The driver was foreign—Jann didn't recognize the accent—but he was friendly. And when Ricky told him someone might try to follow them, the driver said, "Ah, I know what to do!"

He made a sharp right turn, throwing Jann and Ricky into each other, and then followed a circuitous route for the next hour. When they were sure no one had followed, the driver returned to the neighborhood and dropped them at the street in back of the one Jann and Ricky lived on.

As they walked the rest of the way to the cottage, they constantly looked over their shoulders, knowing that if Marcus found them, the *least* they could expect would be death. But it could be much worse than that.

CHAPTER SEVENTY-SIX

President

Another day of imprisonment faced me. I had done my exercises and had climbed back into my bunk to wait for breakfast. Vince was standing next to me when his radio went off. He was so close that I could hear it. "*All of you* come to the shower building right now. You're first."

"Right away, sir," he said into the mic, and then to me, "Let's get going." And then in a quieter voice as I got off my bunk and started toward the door, I heard him say, "*All of us.*"

At first, the optimist in me thought how kind—they were letting me shower before the rest of the camp. How soon I found that I was mistaken. Way, way mistaken.

All three goons, Bob, Vince, and Ted, walked me out. No other people had moved into *my* tent yet, and I wondered how soon that would happen. The answer waited for me as we exited the tent. It was still raining. Hard. I looked toward the main gate, and I had been right. The quads were stuck in the mud again. But the gates were open and a large bus was bringing more people in.

"Let's go." Bob put his hand on my shoulder and directed me toward the cement shower building. At least he didn't shove me this time. Things were improving.

I thought one of the men would break off to use the restroom outside our tent, but all three accompanied me into the cement building and toward the canvas separation curtain. Walking through the makeshift door cut into the canvas, there was a woman standing there next to a small table. She looked like either a nurse or a doctor, dressed in pink scrubs and wearing a surgical mask. Did I have to shower with an audience? Whatever. Or maybe they were giving us some kind of vaccination for the close quarters in the camp? I approached her and started taking off my shirt.

"No need for that, sir. I just need your ear."

Unlucky for me, I didn't see the instrument in her hand. It was not a syringe. It was an ear punch made for punching holes in cow's and pig's ears.

"This shouldn't hurt for long, sir." Next thing I knew, I had a burning pain in my right ear. She was rubbing something on it with a piece of soaked cotton. "Just hold this on it until it stops bleeding. It shouldn't take long."

I reached up, and there was a piece of soaked cotton on either side of my earlobe. And the cotton wasn't too thick for me to feel the large hole in my ear. That's when I noticed the ear punch.

Looking behind me, I saw that Bob, Vince, and Ted were none too happy about being next. Before I moved away from the table, I noticed a stack of flyers on the edge of it. I picked one up, folded it, and stuck it in my pocket while I waited for the deed to be done to the three men behind me.

The cotton I held on my ear had soaked through, and I felt blood dripping down my neck, so I grabbed more cotton balls that were in a bowl on the table next to the flyers. When the three men finished, we walked through the cement shower building that now had lines of people waiting for the same *treatment* we got.

I turned to go to the mess tent, but Ted said, "Breakfast is delayed because of *this* garbage!" He took his bloody cotton and threw it on the ground.

Without thinking, I held out my handful of cotton that I had gotten from the bowl. He took one, pressed it to his ear, and said, "Thank you." That surprised me. At least he was polite.

Two of the four of us used the restroom facilities, and then we returned to our bunks. The far side of the tent was filling with people. I pulled the flyer from my pocket and read it. Only one paragraph long, it said that the reason for the earmarks was because we were all still contagious, and since science didn't know yet for how long, it was prudent to make it as apparent as possible, so no one else got exposed. I wondered if Marcus had come up with that one or one of his stooges.

As I lay in bed with my stomach growling, I thought about what I wanted to say to Eden at my next opportunity. She hadn't written yesterday, and that worried me. But I had to remain steadfast in my belief that she was okay. I was certain that had something happened to her, Marcus would have flaunted it to get me riled up.

Then I heard a noise from outside, filtering in through the canvas tent and the constant drizzle. "Hey, guys," I called out, "can you use your radio to find out what's going on out there?"

"Why should we?"

"Because if you don't, I'm going to go out there and see for myself!" What with the blood loss and empty stomach, I didn't feel like going out to check, but they didn't need to know that. Next I heard was someone mumbling into his radio.

"They're building a barn. They're bringing horses in here to patrol because the quads keep getting stuck."

Yay, me. Even the thought of having horses around made me feel better. I may be cold and wet, I may be a prisoner, I may be facing death any day now, but if I had horses, then I would be okay. Of course, I didn't exactly *have* the horses. Who knew if *the boys* would even let me go see them? No! That's not the way to look at it. I will *make sure* I get to see the horses. It was so easy to slip into victim mode—even for a president—at least in this situation.

As I lay there, my mind drifted back to what I would say to Eden. One thing was for sure: horses or no horses, my secret message to her for the day would be: *get me outa here.*

CHAPTER SEVENTY-SEVEN
The man

Marcus sat in the chair behind the Resolute Desk in the Oval Office and smiled. Soon—this office, this country, *this world*—would all be his. And he could do whatever the fuck he wanted to do with it. The first thing he would start with would be that wood! If he was cold, he could turn up the heat. He didn't need wood and the spiders that came with it! And why wait?

"Men! Men!" He called to his secret service agents. He didn't know their names, nor did he need to. They worked for him. And he didn't need to buy their loyalty with kindness. All he needed to do was buy their loyalty the old-fashioned way—with cold, hard cash. Marcus had made a science of buying people; and he was *always* the highest bidder.

When the two agents came in half a second later, Marcus said, "Get all that wood out of here! Now!" They took turns carting it out to the Rose Garden to be taken care of later. After finishing, they dutifully stepped out of the Oval Office. He had trained them well.

Marcus felt so good that he was finally *doing something*. Now he didn't have to listen to his mother's voice—and his wife's—saying, "*Do something, Marcus, do something.*"

There was still the issue of the black bitch and her son to deal with, but he would deal with that after eliminating Dan from the picture. And that operation was imminent! Although he still had to find the damn dog and kill it. Somehow, it had gotten loose before the men could get back there to deal with it. But by God, he would have that dog found and killed for all the times it had growled at him.

That damn Indian Patel had to butt his nose in, but Marcus had fixed him. He laughed when he remembered telling Patel that he would reconsider action against China if Patel could find valid evidence within three days. Marcus's laughter intensified knowing that action against China would happen in *two* days. That would serve Patel right—that know-it-all meddler.

In two days, the world would be his! Now that everything was in place, he needed to write the script for the press conference. And after giving thought to it, he didn't think Corrie Corrigan was right for the job. In a falsetto voice, he said, "Hello, I'm Corrie Corrigan and I want to tell you what a momentous day this is." No, that would never do.

With a piece of paper in front of him and a pen in his hand, he began to write. *Ladies and Gentlemen of the Press and our wider television audience.* Giving the boot to Corrie Corrigan had made him realize that he should have a television audience as well. If he could put it out on satellite, he would. He'd have to remember to ask about that. He continued writing. *Today is an incredibly momentous day. This morning, our military, led by General Bryce Skora, has bombed three major cities in China, including Shanghai and Beijing. And for its part in unleashing bat flu to the rest of the world, Wuhan has been completely obliterated. About the only thing left there now are some fortune cookie crumbs.* He laughed to himself at that and then crossed it out. Thinking again, he wrote it back in.

The second momentous event to occur today was that due to an unfortunate incident at the separation camp where former President Dan Indigo was being detained, he is now dead. One of the other inmates killed an agent protecting him and critically injured the other. Then he shot the President in the head at point blank range. Doctors declared former President Dan Indigo DOA at the separation camp's medical clinic. So I stand before you as the next and final *President of the United States.* He didn't write *final* but in his heart he knew it was true.

CHAPTER SEVENTY-EIGHT

Jann

Jann woke up but didn't open her eyes. She enjoyed doing that in the morning to plan her day before she opened her eyes. Then a few moments of gratitude about where she had come from and where she was now, and gratitude for the people who had propelled her there—that would be Dan and Eden. Sleepily, she stretched her arms outside the covers and opened her eyes.

The room looked unfamiliar, and she turned her head to see dark eyes looking back at her. Dark eyes and a big smile. Jace. "Hi, Gramma! You slept in my room last night! In my trundle bed!"

"I sure did, Jace! How 'bout some cuddle time?" She patted the bed beside her and held open the covers for Jace to crawl in.

As she lay there, arms cradled around the small boy and rocking him gently, she got a sick feeling in the pit of her stomach as the day before came back to her. Marcus in her house, Ricky protecting her, the taxi ride, sitting on Ricky and Keesha's couch with Jace on her lap, and Ricky and Keesha hugging her from either side. And Bear lying on her feet, helping to ground her. How would she have made it otherwise? They held her like that while she sobbed and sobbed, thinking of what might have —what almost—happened.

The conversation at breakfast was subdued, with no one mentioning what had happened the day before. Until Jace asked, "Are you going to sleep in my room again, Gramma?"

Keesha tried to shush him, but Jann said, "No, Keesha, it's all right. We can't ignore it forever." Then she turned toward Jace and put her hand on his little arm. "No, baby, I think I need to sleep in my own bed tonight."

Ricky's raised voice shocked Jann. "Oh, no, you won't! No, Ma, no. You're not going home again until that lunatic is gone."

"And when will that be, Ricky? Tell me that. When will that be?"

"After I rescue Dan from the separation camp."

No one said a word for several minutes until Jace dropped his fork on the floor. Jann leaned over to pick it up. "What about work, Ricky? You have a family now."

"And what would my family think of me if I don't do the right thing? I told my work before I left to get Zoey that I needed some time off." He nodded his head and balled up his fists. "Rescuing Dan is my job now."

Jann had an unusual reaction to his statement—half fear, half relief. "How are you going to do that, Ricky?"

"I have some ideas. But, I need to run them by the boys first."

"The boys?"

"My motorcycle group—Riders Protecting Children—you know, the ones who protect little kids in court, before and after. I can't do it alone, Ma. I'm not Rambo!" Jann and Keesha laughed, which broke the tension. "And I'll need help from you—information—from all your White House connections."

"Anything you want, Ricky, it's yours."

After breakfast, Jann cleaned up and watched Jace, so Keesha could get some of her studies done. Her mind traveled between what happened the previous night and Ricky saying he would rescue Dan. She tried to get the former thoughts out of her mind. It wasn't until she was drying her hands and getting ready to hand Jace off to Keesha that she realized both her phones—her regular iPhone and the burner phone—had been stuck in her purse since before leaving her house. Where was her purse, anyway?

"Keesha, do you know where my purse is?"

"In the front closet, Mom." It had taken a while for Jann to convince Keesha to call her *Mom*. And now hearing it made Jann feel good.

Opening the closet door and pulling out her purse, Jann reached in and pulled out the two phones. They both had multiple calls on them. The iPhone began to ring. It was Eden. Oh, no! She was supposed to call her back last night. Jann grimaced, but didn't accept the call. Instead, she punched in the number on her burner phone.

"Jann! Oh my God! Are you okay? I thought maybe they took you to a camp! I've been frantic. Where are you? I would have come to your house, but in the current circumstances, there was no way I could risk it. Are you okay?" Eden sounded on the verge of hysteria. You couldn't blame her, though, thought Jann, her husband in a separation camp and her best friend missing in action.

In a calm voice, Jann said, "I'm fine, Eden. Hiding out, but safe."

"Hiding out? Why?"

And then Jann told her every disgusting detail of what had occurred—or rather, what had almost occurred. When she finished, she was sobbing again.

"Jann, it's all right, honey. You're safe. He can't hurt you now. It's okay." When Jann had calmed down, Eden said, "You know, that's what I haven't told you. When I was going out with him, he did the same thing to me. Luckily, Dan arrived home as Marcus was unzipping his zipper. Marcus said, 'If you say one word, I'll blow your head off.' I pushed the gun away from my temple, stood up, and walked out of the room. As I was going out the door, he held the gun up and pulled the trigger. It just clicked. 'See?' he laughed and said, 'It wasn't even loaded.' It surprised him when I wouldn't see him again."

"Did you ever tell Dan?" Jann asked.

"I was about to a few days ago, but with everything going on, I never got the chance."

There was a minute of silence while both women processed the conversation. Then Jann asked, "How are the kids and Zoey? Everything working out okay?" But before Eden had said a word, Jann's phone buzzed. She looked at the display and said, "Oh, shoot, Eden. It's Dr. Stan. He had something to tell me about Marcus. I better take it."

"Talk to you later, Jann. Bye. I love you, and I'm glad you're safe."

"Dr. Stan. Good morning. What's going on?"

"I wanted to tell you what happened with Marcus. Sorry I didn't call last night; I just couldn't get away. We have three days, Jann! Just three days!"

"Three days for what?"

"Before Marcus and that war monger General Skora start World War III. They're planning on bombing China for starting bat flu! I told Marcus there was no conclusive evidence that they did, but Marcus wouldn't listen. He said I had three days to present him and Skora with substantial proof it didn't originate in China. I've got Isa helping me research. See what you can do on your end, Jann. Good luck and goodbye."

When the call ended, Jann sat there for a moment, holding the phone in her hand. What could she do to stop this? One thing was for sure: it didn't matter how much evidence Dr. Stan came up with. Once Marcus had made up his mind, nothing would deter him from following through with his plan. So why the three days?

The answer brought with it a sick feeling that traveled through her body. Marcus would keep Dan alive just long enough to see the end of the world as we know it. World War III would change everything. And after Dan saw that—Marcus would kill him. It made Ricky's endeavors to rescue Dan that much more important.

To get her mind off all of that, she called Eden back to find out about Zoey and the children. They weren't on for more than a few minutes when another call came in. "Ah! Eden, Ricky is on the line, I have to take it. Love you, bye."

In just a few minutes, Ricky gave her a list of all the information he needed. It was varied and seemed strange to Jann, but she wrote it all down. Most of it would be easy to find, and even the information about Dan's separation camp shouldn't be that difficult to find, thanks to the GPS on the bug she had planted.

She retrieved her computer from the closet she had found her purse in and set to work, emailing Ricky the information as she found it. By late afternoon, she had finished everything and emailed Ricky everything he had wanted. It was only then she realized she had forgotten to mention to him about bombing China and the three day *time limit*. Better not to worry him, anyway. She didn't want to put any more pressure on him than she had to. He had a big job ahead of him and God only knew how he could pull it off and not get himself killed.

Jann sat on the couch with Bear's big head in her lap. As she petted him, she tried not to think about anything bad in the world; she just wanted to focus on the smooth feel of his coat beneath her fingers.

Keesha walked into the room with Jace hanging on to her leg. Looking up at her, Jann's smile disappeared from her face. Keesha looked like she had just seen a ghost. Jann pulled herself to the edge of the couch. Was it Ricky? Keesha knew what was happening was dangerous to Ricky. Had he been caught already, before he had even gotten started?

"Keesha, tell me. What is it?"

"Ricky called. They're going in tomorrow."

CHAPTER SEVENTY-NINE

President

It had stopped raining. It was almost the end of a very long day. First the big hole punched into my ear—which still throbbed— then, after a late breakfast, I sent Marcus a quick email hoping to find out what had happened the day before when he disappeared. Then I emailed Eden. She had responded to my first email, but didn't answer my secret question. Nor did she mention Zoey or Bear. I wondered how much of my secret message she had received, or if it had been obliterated during censorship.

Then a shower after everyone had cleared out of the shower building. Ted and Vince started standing in the room with me while I undressed. But this time, I surprised them. I grabbed a towel from the bench, got it soaked through with water, and threw it at them. "A little privacy, please!" When the sopping towel hit them, they stepped to the other side of the curtain— which didn't matter, because there was no way for me to get out or anyone else to get in.

After that, lunch, and when we finished eating, I saw them move the horses into the newly constructed barn. The four of them looked like some kind of draft horse cross, maybe Percheron. They were beautiful. Horses gave me such peace.

It was then time for my second email message to Eden and to see if she had answered my first one. But when I mentioned it to Ted and Vince, they said they had gotten instructions "from the top" that I was cut down to only one email a day. When I asked who was at the top, they laughed. "Marcus?" I asked, "then let me video him."

"Nope! None of that, either," said Ted.

"All right, let's go see the horses." It was getting close to dinner, so I wouldn't have that much time with them, but some is better than none.

"No way. We're not walking over there in the mud."

I pulled myself up to my full height and spoke slowly. "Ted, Vince, I've had a hole punched in my ear today, and I've been restricted on my emails to my wife. I *want* to see the horses. You can either come or not, but I am going, and if you try to stop me, we will have many witnesses to your abuse." Looking around, I nodded toward the knot of people that had grown bigger and bigger as the day progressed. They had been following us since this morning when they realized they were sharing the camp with the President.

The two men relented but complained about the mud all the way to the barn. As I started walking in, they followed. I turned around and said, "Why are you following me in here? There is only one door. If you don't mind, I would like some time alone with the horses."

"I don't know," said Vince in an exaggerated, slow voice.

"Look around. There is nothing in here that you need to protect me from."

"One of those horses could kick you," said Ted.

"You let me worry about that." When they still hesitated, I looked around the barn until I spotted what I hoped to find. Yes, there it was against the far wall: a fork. No, not as in pitchfork and not as in a utensil to eat with. This was the horsey version of a pooper scooper. I walked over, picked it up, and walked back toward them. When they looked agitated, thinking I might attack them, I said, "Look, it's plastic." Then I walked into one of the open stalls where a horse had been. And there, right in front of me, was what I was looking for. I picked up the fresh horse poop—mmmm, I loved that smell—and started walking toward them.

"What are you doing?" asked Ted.

"I'm encouraging you to leave me alone in here. I'm experienced and a pretty good shot at this." I held up the overflowing fork and motioned for them to leave.

"You wouldn't!" said Vince.

"And why the fuck not?" I said as I tossed the whole forkful all over them.

They screamed like a couple of sissies and left me alone in the barn, which is all I wanted all along. I spent my time with the horses petting them and brushing them down. But it wasn't long before one of the two men called out, "Dinner! Come out now!"

"I'll come out when I damn please," I said as I walked to the open barn door. I didn't think there was any way that either of them would put himself in a "vulnerable" position in the barn again. It surprised them when I walked out. "Come on. Let's go. I'm hungry."

They grumbled about their suits all the way back to our canvas tent. This time, we had to walk through people to get to our bunks, although canvas "drapes" hung between our beds and everyone else's. Vince and Ted walked on either side of me with their outside arm held at a right angle like they were showing off their muscles. But they were trying to block any interference from the other *inmates*. The two men changed their clothes, and then we all ate dinner without a word spoken between us. Our table was still isolated, so I couldn't talk to anyone else either.

After dinner they wanted to go back to the bunks, but I insisted on taking another walk around the perimeter. I needed all the exercise I could get. Besides, the sky was slate gray with a pinkish undertone close to the horizon. It was beautiful.

We walked and walked until something in the sky drew my attention upward. It was a red-tailed hawk, and it was so majestic and so wonderful to see during my confinement. Its beauty caught me so off guard that I said, "Look at that!" as I pointed up to the sky. Vince and Ted, equally caught off guard, looked up where I pointed.

Then a hand tapped me on the shoulder. I turned around to see a smiling man that I recognized as one of the tight knot that had been following us around most of the day. He grabbed my hand and shook it up and down. "So nice to meet you, Mr. President!"

Vince and Ted had a hissy fit and chased the man away, threatening him. With what, I didn't know, because something else had captured my awareness. I stuck both hands in my pockets, hoping it didn't look suspicious. Because whoever the man was who had shaken my hand, had placed a note in my palm.

CHAPTER EIGHTY
Keith Enright

Keith Enright sat in the parking lot at the truck stop near Springfield, Virginia, holding his cell phone. When Jeni answered, he said, "Jen, I'm in Springfield getting ready to take off," trying to keep the excitement out of his voice.

"Be careful, Keith. I'm worried about you."

"Oh, sweetie, I'll be fine. I've already delivered there once, and I was safe."

"That was before the inmates arrived."

"Jen, they're not inmates, they're only people who were unlucky enough to catch bat flu2. And you know, I could have been one of them."

"Oh, you're right, Keith, you're right. It's just the connotation of *separation camp* that makes it sound dangerous. Just call me when you finish, okay? It will make me feel better."

"Sure thing, hon. Love you, bye."

He put the phone away and thought about what she said about the separation camp. Yes, the connotation of being in one was that you were a bad person and had done something wrong. But those poor people had done nothing wrong. They were just unlucky enough to catch the new variant. There, but for the grace of God go I. He wished he could do something for those people, but he was no hero, just a good ole boy truck driver.

Keith looked up out of his reverie to see a big black man walking toward him. He had long dreads and an earring. Although it was cold out, the man didn't wear a jacket, and Keith could see tattoos on his bare arms.There was something familiar about him, and he was smiling.

Keith opened the window as he approached and smiled back. The man stepped up on the running board of the truck and said, "Keith! How you doing?" Then his large hand produced an even larger gun and pointed it right at Keith's face. "Move over. I'm driving."

Keith complied. Keith was scared, but more than that, he was curious. "You look familiar. I think I know you."

The man turned toward him and grinned. "It's Rick! You knew me as Ricky!"

"Ricky! Hey! How long's it been?"

Ricky nodded his head. "More than a decade."

Keith put his hand on Ricky's shoulder, even though the other hand still held the gun pointed toward him. "Hey, Ricky. Didn't we promise each other way back then that we'd never go back to the joint? What happened? Why are you in trouble again? I never saw you as the criminal type." Keith remembered the promise very well—and the friendship. "Remember when we met?"

Keith remembered it. He had found several white tough types who had cornered Ricky and were taunting him—their way of prepping someone before they beat the crap out of them. He had intervened and saved Ricky. Of course, back then Ricky was a skinny kid of seventeen, not the large man he was today. But after that, they were best buds. And the time came when Ricky had saved him from a similar situation.

Ricky took a deep breath and let the gun rest in his lap—still pointed in Keith's direction, though. "First, of course I remember. And I'll always be indebted to you for that. Second, circumstantial evidence, boy! I've never been in trouble since!

"I joined the service and learned how to fix aviation electronics. I worked in Arizona for years, but we've just moved back here. I have—maybe had—a good job at an airport close to DC." He took a quick glance toward Keith. "But let me ask you an important question, bro. Who did you vote for in the presidential election?"

Keith laughed. "You're holding me at gunpoint and stealing my truck, and you ask a question like that?"

"Just borrowing it, and your answer decides where we go from here."

"Indigo, of course. It's a shame he had to volunteer to go to the separation camp. Why, who did you vote for?"

"He didn't volunteer, Keith. The vice president abducted him. And I plan to rescue him. You in?"

"You're crazy! I don't believe that for a second!"

Ricky reached into his pocket, pulled out his burner phone, and tossed it to Keith. "Here. Call my mother. She is his secretary and she'll confirm everything I say. No! Better idea. Call Eden, and she'll verify it for you. You should be able to recognize her voice."

"Eden? You mean the President's wife?" Keith picked up the phone and scrolled through the numbers. He saw Eden on there, along with Dr. Patel, and Jonathan Sharpe, who he knew was the Secretary of Homeland Security. He put the phone down on the console between them. "I know all these numbers could be fake and you could have set this whole thing up, but I feel like you're telling the truth. So tell me the whole story. And put away the gun, Ricky. I'm not going anywhere."

Ricky took the gun from his lap and placed it on the console with his phone. "If you're willing to trust me, I'm going to trust you." And then he told him everything, including all his plans for the rescue. He waited a beat, and then he asked, "You in?"

"You know, ordinarily I wouldn't go in for such a thing. I'm not that kind of guy. But I'll go to make sure that my truck comes out with as little damage as possible!" Keith laughed.

"Good enough for me! Ah, here's our turn." He pulled out from the highway and into the deserted parking lot of a closed-down box store. Keith and Ricky, plus the men who were waiting there for them, unloaded everything from the back of the truck and then loaded it up again—with the addition of a few extra items. Then Ricky climbed into the passenger seat with a backpack at his feet, Keith climbed into the driver's seat, and they were on the road once more with a large contingent of motorcycles with them.

Keith looked at him as he pulled onto the interstate on-ramp. "You know, we could both go to jail for this."

Ricky patted him on the shoulder. "Not if we succeed, buddy. Not if we succeed."

CHAPTER EIGHTY-ONE
President

The note said *Food delivery tomorrow between 10 and 2. Be there.* So I was hanging out at the back door to the mess tent and had been since five minutes before ten. It could have been a trap; it could have been an invitation to my death; or it could have been the answer to my prayers. I chose to believe the latter and hoped for the best. Hope was all I had, and I knew time was getting short. At least it wasn't raining. Bob and Vince were content to follow me around—another indication that the end was nigh.

We had gone to the Quonset hut after breakfast so I could email Eden. Since I didn't know how many days I had left on this earth, it was all gushy stuff about how much I loved her and what a good wife and mother she was—even though she kept her last name. I had to put something funny in there, so she knew it was really coming from me.

The book code I used to send the two previous messages was a complete flop. Eden never answered and never sent a message of her own. Early in our marriage, when I told her I'd be running for office, we had devised the code just in case something untoward should happen. We'd use the first Harry Potter book, and we made sure we bought the same exact edition. Then you take the page number, the paragraph number, and the word number to create your message. How disappointing that she never got the messages. Maybe they were censored out. I realized that I may never know.

After emailing Eden, which might have been my last correspondence with her, I marched the boys over to the horse barn. After doing a quick search of the place, they stayed outside. I soothed my nervousness by brushing down the two horses. But I was sure that I got back to the mess tent in plenty of time.

Every once in a while, I would strain my ears to hear if any vehicles were approaching. And when I didn't think I heard any —because it was all a guess with all the noise in the camp—I walked around in a bigger arc, always ready to return if necessary. When lunch came, I ate as fast as I could so as not to miss my chance. I didn't want to skip eating altogether, because with my big appetite, they would have suspected something.

Although I still had a knot of people following my every move, I hadn't seen the man who had given me the note. But when I came out from lunch scanning the area for signs of a delivery truck, I saw him at the edge of the crowd. He made brief eye contact and then looked away. But as he looked away, he shook his head almost imperceptibly. I felt relieved that I hadn't missed it. Whether *it* was death or freedom, I didn't miss it.

After making up multiple excuses of why I wanted to hang out by the back door of the mess tent, including, *I want to be around people* and *I'm hoping they're getting in watermelon*, I heard the truck in the distance. It sounded like a large truck, maybe an eighteen-wheeler. There were many people in the camp who needed to eat, so it would take a big truck to feed them all.

"Okay, enough," said Bob. "I need to use the facilities."

"I don't, but don't let me stop you. I need a few more minutes here."

The gates swung open for the truck, and it drove into the compound, made a wide circle, and then backed up to the mess tent. The driver got out, unlocked the back door, opened it, and let down the ramp. Then he returned to the cab of the truck while several men from the mess tent started hauling out all the food. As they carried all the food into the mess tent, I watched their every move, not knowing if I was supposed to do something or not. From where I was standing, I could smell the distinctive diesel smell coming from the still-running truck. But I didn't turn away.

Looking into the back of the truck, I saw there wasn't much left to move. Then random people who had been watching started being more vocal, and I saw a little pushing and shoving going on. Several people jumped up into the truck, handed the remaining food to people still outside on the ground, and those people took off running with it. There was one basket full of cantaloupe. A man, the one who had handed me the note, picked a cantaloupe off the top and threw it to me.

I had played enough football in my time to know what to do when someone throws me something. Catching the cantaloupe against my chest, I started running as fast as I could toward the front of the truck, not knowing what I would do when I got there. Behind me, I heard Bob and Vince say, "Hey!" and then I heard what sounded like the two men getting tackled and landing in the mud.

The passenger door of the truck opened, and a man jumped out. He was a large black man whom I immediately recognized as Ricky. I heard the ramp slide in and then a big thump in the back, like someone had closed the back gate of the truck. Ricky stepped in front of me, and using my momentum, picked me up off the ground, swung me around and delivered me inside the cab of the truck, and then jumped in beside me. I dropped the cantaloupe during the maneuver, and it splattered on the ground.

The driver stepped on the accelerator and the truck started out slowly, then picked up speed. We headed straight toward the gate that was closed.

"Oh, no! The gate! My poor truck!" the driver said, but didn't slow down.

Then the gate opened, and the truck plowed on through, going faster and faster.

"Hey, I told you I'd take care of you, bro!" said Ricky. "Oh, sorry gentlemen. President Dan Indigo, meet Keith Enright. Keith, this is President Dan Indigo."

"Nice to meet you, Mr. President."

"Nice to meet you, too, Keith, but please call me Dan. You just rescued me and very possibly saved my life."

"All right, Dan. My pleasure."

I leaned forward and looked at the side-view mirror, but couldn't see much. There were motorcycles beside us and behind us. "How did you manage this, Ricky? Won't they be coming after us?"

"Not for a while, and by then we'll be long gone. I have guys just outside the gate who closed and barred it after we went through. Ain't nobody getting out of there anytime soon. Did you see the motorcycles at the gate? They'll let us know if anything changes."

I leaned forward again to look out the windshield. All that was above us was sky. "Won't they send for reinforcements— send a helicopter after us or something?"

"I've set up a cell phone signal jammer and have cut off all communication in and out of the place. No cell phones, no internet, and in case they have a satellite phone, that's jammed, too. I take care of you, Dan!"

I had been sitting partway on Ricky's seat and mostly on the truck console. Ricky was a big guy, and I was no small fry, either. It was getting uncomfortable, but I wasn't going to complain. I was alive.

Ricky pointed out the window. "Take the next exit, Keith. We're almost at our stop." He turned toward me. "You can ride a motorcycle, can't you, Dan?"

"And who taught *you* to ride, little man?" I asked, but I already knew the answer. *I* had taught him to ride. We all laughed. It was a good feeling.

"Where are we going from here?" I asked.

"The White House, baby. We're going to take back what's ours."

"Will Marcus even be there?" It was around one o'clock, but I didn't know where we were or how long it would take to get there.

"He'll be there. I made sure of that."

"Where are we, anyway?"

"West Virginia. D.C. is only a few hours away."

Keith put on his turn signal, the truck slowed, and we pulled off the highway. The motorcycles that had accompanied us drove to the edge of the clearing to wait. Several more guys on motorcycles were already waiting at the place we stopped. Ricky opened the door and helped me move off the console. As I slipped out the door, I turned around to Keith. "Thank you, and I'll see you again."

The men on the motorcycles crowded around me and started shaking my hand. I was delighted to see my secret service agents: Eric Costa and Justin Kirkpatrick, Gavin Dennison and Derek Moran, and Jeff Egan. Clive Holmes wasn't there, though. I didn't ask why, because I probably knew—he had voted for Marcus and couldn't be trusted to rescue me.

"Mr. President, what happened to your ear?" asked Justin. "It looks gross!"

"Long story. I'll tell you when we're settled. All right, who is going to let me drive? I'm the president, and I shouldn't be a passenger, even if I do owe you all my life."

"No worries, Mr. President, sir!" said Ricky from behind me. He was walking toward me with a Harley Davidson Road King Special—a powerful touring bike. "Only the best for you, sir!" Behind Ricky, Keith was holding up a second motorcycle he had gotten out of the truck.

Ricky handed me a helmet from the backpack, and I put it on. He put on his helmet, got on his own bike, all the guys got on theirs, and we were off to retake the White House—or die trying.

CHAPTER EIGHTY-TWO

President

We entered the White House the same way we had left it when I moved to the ranch—through the underground garage. Once we got inside the East Wing, the agents gave me a bulletproof vest to wear. And we made our way toward the West Wing.

After Derek checked to see if Marcus was in his own office—which he wasn't, of course—and where Marcus's agents were, we continued. One of his agents was outside the Rose Garden door, and the other was by the door to the Presidential Study and Dining Room. The arrogant bastard had left the door by Jann's office unguarded.

We entered through the Lobby entrance and wound our way through the lobby and back around to the Press Secretary's office.

After we all entered the small office, Gavin closed the door securely and cautioned all of us to whisper.

Several people waited for us inside besides Corrie. Isa was there, and Jon Sharpe, which surprised me. I nodded to them and said, "Thank you for being here."

But the most surprising of all was my son Douglas. We hadn't spoken in months, maybe a year. Nothing like fear of imminent death to bring families back together. I was okay with that—whatever it took.

"So good to see you, Dad! I've been so worried." He hugged me and wouldn't let me go.

"But how did you know?" I asked.

"Ricky called me." He smiled at Ricky, who came over and shook his hand and then hugged him. Doug was always like a little brother to Ricky. But they hadn't seen each other since Ricky went away all those years ago.

"All right," said Gavin, "time to rock. Let's go as quiet as possible, please. We don't want him to know we're coming."

"Good luck, gentlemen. We've done our bit, so we'll stay here. We're routing for you!" Isa said. I would find out later that Isa, Corrie, and Jon were part of the team who made sure that Marcus stayed in his office until we arrived.

Gavin opened the door without making a sound, and we tiptoed through the hallway and into the Cabinet Room. There we huddled in the far corner. I could hear Dr. Stan's raised voice coming from the Oval Office.

I noticed Ricky had pulled out his burner phone and was texting someone. "Who are you texting?"

"No message, just a head's up."

In the other room, I heard Marcus say, "For the final time, Stan, get out of here! It's a done deal. In two hours bombs will fly, and there's nothing you or anybody else can do about it! Now get out of my office!"

I heard footsteps coming toward us, but I had a more important question to ask. "What's he talking about?"

"Tell you later, Dan," said Ricky. "Next!"

As Dr. Stan entered the room, my son, Doug, squeezed my shoulder and walked out.

"What's he doing?" All the comings and goings were making me dizzy. And we still had to face Marcus.

"They're trying to keep Marcus off balance before we go in. It won't take long," said Ricky.

I heard Marcus say, "What are *you* doing here?"

"Hi, Marcus. Where's my dad?"

"Your dad? Don't you listen to the news, boy? It's been all over the news!"

"Ah, Marcus, they closed down all in-person classes at the university, and I've had my hands full creating new lesson plans for online classes.

"So where's my dad? He's okay, isn't he?"

"Did you even know he had bat flu?"

"No, I didn't. So he's in the residence? I never thought to check there."

I heard Marcus's sarcastic laugh. "Yeah, that's where he is, Doug. Go see him there. I've got things to do here. Big day tomorrow."

"Bye, Marcus."

Doug walked into the room, and Gavin said, "Now," and moved us all forward. The agents—minus Ricky, who gave me the thumbs up signal—surrounded me as we walked in the door to the Oval Office.

"What? What's going on here?" Then Marcus must have glimpsed who was behind the wall of agents. "Dan? How the hell did you get out?" Without waiting for an answer, he shouted, "Men!" And his two agents came running.

"Kill them!" He shouted. "Kill them all!"

"Sir?" asked one agent, confused.

"I said, *kill them*! Don't you understand English? Kill them all, starting with him!" He pointed toward me.

"But they're not threatening you, sir," the other agent said.

"I don't pay you to talk, I pay you to follow my every instruction. Now kill them!"

I moved my body so that my head was between two of the men in front of me, so I could be seen clearly. "Stand down, everyone! Stand down!"

No one said a word until we heard footsteps outside. Everyone looked in that direction as Clive entered the room.

"Ah, Clive, my man. You're just in time. Finally, someone with some brains and some balls. Could you please kill these imposters? My two weaklings," Marcus motioned toward his two agents, "are too scared."

Clive walked up to Marcus and stood behind him. I couldn't believe what I was seeing. Neither could my agents. They pulled themselves together shoulder to shoulder to make an impenetrable shield in front of me. Clive had been at my side for years, protecting me. I couldn't believe it

Neither could Jeff, his partner. "Clive? I know you voted for the bastard, but really? You're on *his side* in this whole fiasco?"

Clive ignored him and put his hands on Marcus's shoulders. "So, who would you like me to take out first, sir? Point him out to me."

Marcus held out his arm and pointed straight at me—through the men, of course. And in one swift motion, Clive grabbed his arm, twisted it behind him, and slapped on a pair of handcuffs while pulling the other arm into position.

"That's what lying will get you, Marcus. I *never* voted for you. But I never stopped the rumor, because who I voted for is nobody's business but my own. And how convenient it is that you believe your own damn lies!" He pulled Marcus to his feet and shoved him away from the Resolute Desk.

Epilogue

It had been a few days since my amazing rescue. I had been working like mad, trying to fix everything that Marcus had messed up. Stopping the attack on China had to happen the moment they carted Marcus out of the Oval Office. While General Skora was happy that I was out of the separation camp—at least he wasn't part of the failed coup d'état—he felt disappointed that his plans had been thwarted. He wasn't so much one of Marcus's minions as he was an opportunist—taking advantage of Marcus's craving for power and glory. But I had stopped the bombing in time, and that's all that mattered.

The second most important item on the agenda was to close all the separation camps. The people were all transported home, apologies given, and compensation currently being discussed in the Senate and Congress. What could make up for that kind of treatment? Since I had experienced it myself, I felt no reward was too large. Not to mention all of them would have a large hole in their right ear to remind them of their incarceration.

Everyone who had bat flu2 was still contagious. After much study, though, scientists had determined bat flu2 was a much milder form of the virus. Not one person out of the thousands who had it, had become seriously ill, and there had not been one death attributed to it. There was, however, one benefit that bat flu2 *granted* that nobody could ever have anticipated: it cured cancer.

Zoey was the first to find out. After returning to Pennsylvania to visit her doctor and reschedule her next chemotherapy session, the doctor checked, rechecked, and did tests, and she had not one sign of breast cancer. It was completely gone.

When hearing of this, Dr Stan called for widespread research across the U.S. and thousands of patients had been found cured of cancer.

So now, anyone with a hole in their ear was likely to be stopped on the street and asked to please infect them. Many people offered them large sums of money. What a miraculous and unexpected happening!

Although the original bat flu had taken its toll on human life across the planet, bat flu2 had taken over. There were very few cases of the original left—not just in the United States, but in the world.

The third important item on my agenda was signing an executive order to create term limits for the Senate and Congress. There were many people vehemently against it, but I felt it was an opportune time to finalize my most important campaign promise. Not many would go up against a president who had been abducted, imprisoned, and had a hole punched in his ear.

Although I had wanted to continue my work on getting everything straightened out, Eden made me promise to take the day off. Yes, I had done no work while I was in the separation camp, but she convinced me it was a stressful experience, and I needed to take a break. So I'd take it easy for now until the weddings started. The White House would host two weddings today: Ricky and Keesha, and Keith Enright—the truck driver who rescued me—and his bride, Jeni.

And *I* would officiate! After learning that Barack had received a temporary officiant's license through the District of Columbia and was a signatory on the marriage certificate, I decided I could do that, too. I considered Ricky my son, and what better gift to give to the man who helped rescue me, Keith, than marrying him at the White House—in the Rose Garden, to be exact.

In addition, right before the wedding, those two men, Ricky and Keith, would each receive a Medal of Honor award. Normally, it was reserved for the military, but since there was no precedent of rescuing a president, I got special dispensation for awarding two civilians the medal. After how they risked their lives to rescue me, they deserved it.

As Bear sat at my feet, I rubbed the large hole in my ear that sometimes still throbbed. And I thought, considering everything, it had turned out all right.

If you liked this book and feel so inclined, please leave a review on Amazon. Thank you! I appreciate it!

Other books published by Ralston Store Publishing:

Short Stories by JK Lincoln writing as Lucas Archer
Presidential Crisis: Ebola
Presidential Crisis: Isis

Time Travel Sweet Romance
Cowgirls in Time Series by Erica Einhorn
A Chill Wind
Wind Beneath My Wings
Against the Wind
The Healing Wind
Ride Like the Wind
Wind of Change
The Way the Wind Blows

Suspense
Darkness in the Light by J.K. Lincoln

India
Not My Guru by Parvati Hill

Cozy Mystery
The Rutledge Historical Society Cozy Mysteries by Jerri Kay Lincoln
Message for Murder
Death over Divorce
Kousins Can't Kill
Rogues to Riches
Secrets for Sale

Caregiving
The Journey that Matters by Jodie Lightener

Women's Fiction/Reincarnation
Two Lifetimes, One Love by Thea Thaxton

Children's Books
Sparkles the Unicorn
Cooper's Smile
Why do Puppy Dogs have Cold Noses?
The Invisible Lion
The Little Unicorn Who Could
Do Bears Poop in the Woods?
Can Pigs Fly?

Yoga Books
Bathroom Yoga
Airplane Yoga
Wheelchair Yoga
Essential Yoga on Horseback
Exercises for Therapeutic Riding

www.ingramcontent.com/pod-product-compliance
Lightning Source LLC
Chambersburg PA
CBHW071306200626
46813CB00015B/378